Maggie's Journey is not your average romance, but then again, Lena Nelson Dooley is not your average author. With meticulously researched details, she brings to life the hardships of the Oregon Trail, the elegance of a Seattle mansion, the rigors of train travel, and the quiet gentility of Little Rock, all the while crafting a memorable story of the sometimes difficult relationship between a mother and daughter as the daughter embarks on a journey of self-discovery.

—AMANDA CABOT
AUTHOR OF *Tomorrow's Garden*

Engaging, inspiring, and romantic. From the first to the last page, Lena Nelson Dooley never disappoints.

—MARYLU TYNDALL
AUTHOR OF THE SURRENDER TO DESTINY SERIES

Lena Nelson Dooley's stories always satisfy, and *Maggie's Journey* is certainly no exception! She'll grab you on page one with characters and events that reflect real-life joys and heartaches that change the characters forever and won't let go until you've read "The End." Make room on your "keepers" shelf for this first title in the MeKenna's Daughters series!

—LOREE LOUGH
BEST-SELLING AUTHOR OF EIGHTY AWARD-WINNING
BOOKS, INCLUDING *From Ashes to Honor,*
BOOK 1 IN THE FIRST RESPONDERS SERIES

Lena Nelson Dooley has once again penned an impossible-to-forget novel filled with love, faith, and the real meaning of what it is to be a family. Filled with characters so real they practically leap off the page, *Maggie's Journey* is a treat that is not to be missed!

—KATHLEEN Y'BARBO-TURNER
AUTHOR OF *Beloved Counterfeit* AND
The Confidential Life of Eugenia Cooper

Maggie's Journey is the beautifully written story of a young woman on a journey to discover both her past...and her future. Lena Nelson Dooley's sensory tale will pull readers in and make them glad they've taken the time to travel alongside Maggie.

—JANICE HANNA THOMPSON
AUTHOR OF *Love Finds You in Groom, Texas*

Chapter 22

Chapter 23

McKENNA'S DAUGHTERS SERIES
BOOK 1

UNION RAILWAY | LITTLE ROCK ARKANSAS

SINGLE PASSENGER ONE WAY | ROUNDTRIP TICKET.

MAGGIE'S JOURNEY

JAN
FEB
MAR
APR
MAY
JUN
JUL
AUG
SEP
OCT
NOV
DEC

LENA NELSON DOOLEY

REALMS

Most CHARISMA HOUSE BOOK GROUP products are available at special quantity discounts for bulk purchase for sales promotions, premiums, fund-raising, and educational needs. For details, write Charisma House Book Group, 600 Rinehart Road, Lake Mary, Florida 32746, or telephone (407) 333-0600.

MAGGIE'S JOURNEY by Lena Nelson Dooley
Published by Realms
Charisma Media/Charisma House Book Group
600 Rinehart Road; Lake Mary, Florida 32746
www.charismahouse.com

All Scripture quotations are from the King James Version of the Bible.

The characters in this book are fictitious unless they are historical figures explicitly named. Otherwise, any resemblance to actual people, whether living or dead, is coincidental.

Cover design by Rachel Lopez; Design Director: Bill Johnson

Visit the author's website at http://lenanelsondooley.blogspot.com.

Library of Congress Cataloging-in-Publication Data:
Dooley, Lena Nelson.
  Maggie's journey / Lena Nelson Dooley.
    p. cm.
  ISBN 978-1-61638-358-9 (trade paper) -- ISBN 978-1-61638-580-4 (e-book) 1. Self-realization in women--Fiction. 2. Family secrets--Fiction. I. Title.
  PS3554.O5675M34 2011
  813'.54--dc23
                                              2011029053

11 12 13 14 15 — 9 8 7 6 5 4 3 2 1
Printed in the United States of America

Dedication

THANK YOU TO my agent, Joyce Hart, and Realms editor Debbie Marrie for believing in this series and bringing about this special deal. And thanks to Lori Vanden Bosch, my special editor, for your insight in making my book stronger. Every author needs an editor like you. I look forward to working with everyone at Realms on all aspects of the McKenna's Daughters series.

I praise the Lord for my wonderful family—my daughters, my sons-in-law, my grandsons, my granddaughters, and my great-grandson. Eric, I borrowed your name but used the Scandinavian spelling Erik. But most of all, for my precious husband, James, who understands the gifts God poured into my life and supports me in all the important ways—spiritual, physical, emotional, financial. I am who I am because you are who you are to me.

And every book I write is dedicated to my Lord and Savior Jesus Christ, who loved me before I really knew Him and had greater plans for me than I could ever have imagined.

But when it pleased God, who
separated me from my mother's womb,
and called me by his grace.

–Galatians 1:15

Prologue

September 1867
On the Oregon Trail

FLORENCE CAINE HUDDLED near the campfire outside their wagon, one of over thirty that were circled for the night. Winter rode the winds that had been blasting them for the last few days. Their destination couldn't come soon enough to suit her.

She brushed her skirt with the palms of both hands trying to get rid of the ever-present dirt. *Why did I ever agree to Joshua's plan?* If she'd known all the dangers they would face along the way, he would have had to make this journey without her...if he kept insisting on going. Her husband's adventurous spirit had first drawn her to him, but she would have been happy to stay in Little Rock, Arkansas, until they were old and gray. Instead, she finally yielded to his fairy-tale vision—a new start in the West. The words had sounded romantic at the time, but their brilliance had dulled in her memory.

Florence rubbed her chapped hands, trying to help the warmth to go deeper. Her bones ached with the cold. After months of traveling the plains through scorching heat and choking clouds of dust, she had welcomed the cooler temperatures when they crossed the Rocky Mountains. That respite was the only thing she liked about the treacherous route they had to take. Because of the steep trail that often disappeared among the rocks and tree roots, they had dumped many items the men thought weren't essential.

Huh. As if men understood the desires of a woman's heart and what brought her comfort. The tinkling and crashing of her precious bone china from England breaking into a million pieces as the crate tumbled down the hill still haunted her dreams.

Florence kept many of her favorite things when they traveled from Little Rock to Independence, Missouri, where the wagon trains started their journeys. She had struggled with what to sell to lighten the load before they left. The one piece of furniture she'd been allowed to keep, her grandmother's small rosewood secretary desk, had probably been used as wood to stoke some other traveler's fire out there on the prairie where trees were so widely scattered. When they had to dump the treasure, a piece of her heart went with it. She'd twisted on the wagon seat and gazed at the forlorn piece until it was just a speck on the empty horizon. Joshua had promised there would be other secretaries, but that didn't matter anymore. She squeezed her eyes tight, trying to force the pictures out of her mind. Regrets attacked her like the plague.

More than the journey sapped her strength. She doubted there would be the proverbial pot of gold at the end of their travels. No promised land for her, because what she really wanted, a child of her own, wouldn't be found in the greener pastures of the untamed wilderness.

Clutching her arms tightly across her chest, she forced her thoughts even farther back, all the way to Arkansas. Their white house with the green shutters nestled between tall trees that sheltered them from the summer heat and kept the cold winds at bay. She remembered the times the two of them had sat before the fire—she knitting or sewing while Joshua read aloud to her from one of their favorite books. Or he might be poring over one of the many newspapers he often brought home after work. Now for so many months, they hadn't heard any news except whatever they could glean at the infrequent stops along the Oregon Trail or from the few riders who passed the wagon train. Sometimes the men stopped to share a meal and spin yarns for the ones on the journey.

She had no idea how much of their information was even true. But the men hung on to their every word. Loneliness for family and the desire to know what was going on back East ate at her.

A shiver swept from the top of Florence's head and didn't miss a single part of her body on its way to her feet. Even with multiple layers of woolen hosiery, her toes felt like ice. She'd often worried that one of them would break off if she stubbed it. She yearned for the snug house where never a single cold breeze seeped inside. Would she ever feel warm again?

She glanced around the clearing, hoping Joshua would soon return to their campsite. If not, dinner would be overcooked or cold. Sick of stew that had been made from rabbits or squirrels these last two weeks, she longed for fried chicken or a good pot roast with plenty of fresh vegetables. At least the wagon master assured them they were no more than a three-day journey from Oregon City. Taking a deep breath, she decided she could last three more days. But not one minute more.

Strong arms slid around her waist. Florence jumped, then leaned back against her husband's solid chest. His warmth surrounded her, and she breathed deeply of his unique musky scent mixed with the freshness of the outdoors.

"What were you thinking about?" Joshua's breath gave her neck a delicious tickle.

"That our journey will soon be over."

She could hardly wait to be in a real house with privacy. She had never felt comfortable knowing that people in nearby wagons could hear most of what went on in theirs, and she knew more than she ever wanted to know about some of the families on the train. She moved slightly away from him but missed the warmth he exuded. Suddenly an inexplicable sense of oppression or impending disaster gave her more of a chill than the cold wind. This time the shivers shook her whole body.

He turned her in his arms, gently held her against his chest, then propped his chin on top of her head. "I know how hard this has been on you, Flory."

He didn't often use the pet name he gave her while they courted. The familiarity warmed her heart for a moment.

"You're just skin and bones, but soon we'll be in the promised land, and I'll make sure you have everything you've ever wanted."

Words spoken with such conviction that they almost melted her heart...almost, but the strange cold dread wouldn't depart.

She pulled away and stared up into his eyes, basking in the intense love shining in them. "You're all I've ever wanted." That wasn't exactly true, but she wouldn't mention their inability to conceive a child. No use bringing that hurt to his eyes. "So what did Overton have to say to the men tonight?"

"Not all the men were there. Angus McKenna wasn't. Neither was the doctor."

A stab of jealousy jolted through her as she realized this could mean only one thing. Lenora McKenna was in labor. Florence stuffed her feelings of inadequacy and envy deep inside and tried to replace them with concern for Lenora. The poor woman had ridden on a pallet in the back of the McKenna wagon for about three weeks. She was actually the reason they took the easier, but longer, Barlow Cutoff instead of crossing the Dalles. The wagon train wouldn't continue on to Fort Vancouver as originally planned. But the wagon master assured them plenty of land awaited near Oregon City. No one but Florence minded the change. At least, no one complained, and she didn't voice her feelings about prolonging her time on the hard wagon seat. No use letting anyone else know how she really felt. No one would care.

"Should I go see if I can help?" Florence really didn't want to, but she didn't want Joshua to see the ugly side of her personality. She didn't want him to think less of her.

Thunder's deep rumble in the clouds hovering low above the wagon bounced against the surrounding mountains and back. Lightning shot jagged fingers above them, raising the hairs on her arms. She had never liked storms, even from the inside of their house. Out here in the open was far worse.

Joshua hugged her close again. "I think a couple of the women who've...had children...are there with the doctor." He dropped a kiss on the top of her head. "No need for you to go. The wagon would be too crowded."

He didn't mean the words to hurt her, but her greatest shame was her inability to give him children. She had watched Joshua as he enjoyed interacting with the various youngsters on the wagon train. He really had a way with them, and they often gathered around him when they were camped, listening intently while he regaled them with wild tales.

He had told her it didn't matter to him that they didn't have children, but that inability mattered to her...more than anything else in the world. *What kind of woman am I?* Eight years of marriage should have brought several babies into their family. Every other couple they knew had several by the time they had been married as long as she and Joshua.

She slid from his arms and bent to stir the bubbling stew, hoping he wouldn't notice how his words bothered her. Without turning her head, she gritted her teeth. "Hungry?"

His melodious laughter, which always stirred her heart, bounced across the clearing, and some of their neighbors glanced toward them. "That's a foolish question, woman. When have I ever turned away from food...especially yours?" He patted his flat stomach for emphasis.

Florence went to the back of their wagon and withdrew two spoons and crockery bowls before ladling the hot soup into them. She had already cut the hot-water cornbread she baked in her cast-iron skillet over the coals, so she grabbed a couple of pieces. They sat on the split log bench they carried in their wagon and set out at each campsite.

Joshua took her hand and bowed his head. "Lord, we thank You for Your provision during this journey and especially for tonight's meal. Bless these hands that prepared this food for us." He lifted her hand and pressed a soft kiss to the back of it. "And Lord, please be with the McKennas tonight."

His words brought a picture into her mind of him caring for her while she was in labor with their child. She needed his tenderness, but that was one kind she'd never have. She swallowed the lump that formed in her throat and blinked back the tears.

Since the McKenna wagon was at the far side of the circled wagons, Florence hadn't heard many of the sounds of the labor. Occasionally, a high shrill cry rose above the cacophony that divided them, announcing Mrs. McKenna's agony. Just that faint sound made Florence's stomach muscles clench. She wouldn't relish going through that kind of pain, but the reward...oh, yes, she would welcome it to have a child.

Her stomach growled and twisted. Hunger had dogged her the last few weeks as the food dwindled. They dove into their bowls, and she savored the stew which contained the remnants of the shriveled carrots and potatoes they'd bought at Fort Hall, the last place they had stopped that sold food to the wagon train. She wasn't sure what she would cook when this pot of stew was gone, but they should have enough to eat for a couple of days, maybe three if they were careful. At least the cold air would keep it from spoiling. Hopefully by then they'd be at the settlement.

Joshua cleared his throat. "By the way, Overton mentioned that the impending birth might delay our departure tomorrow." Then he shoveled another spoonful of stew into his mouth, grinning as he closed his eyes and relished the taste, a habit he'd formed soon after they married.

Florence's food turned bitter in her mouth. She rubbed her hand across her barren belly where her empty womb mocked her. A few tears leaked from her eyes. Why had God chosen not to fulfill her desire to be a mother? And this news was most unwelcome. She might go mad with the delay.

Another flash of lightning, followed by a loud burst of thunder, opened the brooding clouds. Cold rain sprinkled down on them, then gradually grew in intensity. They scrambled to gather their belongings and thrust them into the wagon. Last she covered the stew pot and hung it at the edge of the wagon bed. Then they clambered under the protection of their canvas roof. At least the rain kept Joshua from seeing the tears, which would upset him. He tried so hard to make her happy through their arduous journey.

Long after her husband's comforting snores filled the enclosure, Florence lay awake, listening to the storm and imagining how she would feel holding her child to her breast. Lullabies filled these daydreams, and her fingers could almost feel the velvety softness of a sweet cheek and silky curls. She wondered if her babies would have blonde hair like hers or the rich brown of Joshua's.

Once again, tears leaked from the corners of her eyes. She carefully brushed them away and willed herself to fall asleep and squash the thoughts that plagued her. Just before her eyes closed, a light appeared at the opening of the wagon. Florence slid their Wedding Ring quilt up to her chin and sat up, but Joshua didn't stir.

Reverend Knowles stood in the glow of the lantern, water dripping from the brim of his floppy felt hat. "I'm sorry to bother you folks, but I'm asking everyone to pray for the McKennas. She's having a hard time, and it's difficult for him too."

"Of course we'll pray."

Florence whispered the words so she wouldn't awaken Joshua. He had been really tired lately. She could keep a prayer vigil throughout the night because she knew she wouldn't sleep with the storm raging around them. For hours she whispered petitions for Lenora McKenna, interspersed with occasional prayers for a child of her own. She knew it was selfish, but since so many people were praying to the Almighty right now, maybe He would answer her personal request as well.

"Noooooooo!"

The screaming wail that reverberated all around the clearing broke through Florence's slumber, jerking her wide awake. Nothing like the weak sounds she'd heard earlier, and the voice was too deep to be a woman's. She shook her head and glanced out the opening to the soft, predawn light. Evidently she had fallen asleep, but she didn't feel rested.

Joshua stirred beside her. "What was that?"

"I'm not sure." She sat up and clutched the quilt close to her chest. "It almost sounded like a wounded animal...but not quite."

He started pulling on his trousers. "I'm going to see what's going on." He kissed her on her nose. "Don't leave the wagon until I get back and tell you it's safe. You hear?"

She nodded.

He leaned to give her one of his heart-melting kisses. "I don't want anything to happen to you."

Florence didn't want anything to happen to him either, but he wouldn't appreciate her asking him to stay with her and let the other men take care of things. After he jumped down from the wagon, she stretched a sheet of canvas across the opening and started to dress for the day.

Joshua loved her so much. Her father had never kissed her mother in front of anyone, even the children. But Joshua showed her how much he loved her no matter who was around. Why wasn't his love enough for her? *If only that love would produce a child.*

God must be tired of hearing all her petitions for a baby. But just as Rachel in the Bible kept telling God that without a child she would die, Florence would continue begging Him for one until she had no breath.

She slid the covering from the opening and peeked out. Sunrise lit the area with a golden glow. Everything looked new and fresh after the rain washed away the dust. Even the bare branches of the trees glistened with diamondlike drops clinging to the bark.

Joshua hurried across the circle toward their wagon. He was deep in conversation with Overton Johnson. Even from here she recognized the seriousness that puckered both of their brows. She wondered what they were discussing so intently.

A few feet from the wagon, her husband glanced up and waved. She stepped down and waited for the two men. Maybe Overton would stay while she fixed breakfast. A single man, he often took turns eating with the families.

Overton approached. "Miz Caine, sorry the yell woke you. Miz McKenna died birthing three babies. Her husband took it real bad. What with the three babies and all. He shore weren't prepared for such a thing."

"Three babies?" Florence clutched her dress above her heart. Pain speared through her. She could almost feel her empty womb heave inside her.

Could anything be worse? She couldn't even have one baby, and they had three. Her breathing deepened, and she fought to hide her thoughts from the men.

But Lenora died. The words bounced around inside her brain. Chagrined, Florence kept her mouth shut. How could she be so callous and selfish?

Joshua slid one arm around her and cradled her by his side. "What's going to happen now?" He aimed his question at the wagon master.

Overton pulled off his hat and held it in front of him, turning it nervously in his hands. "We'll have a funeral service and bury 'er today."

"I could help plan a group meal." Florence had to do something to redeem herself, at least in her own eyes.

"That'd be right nice, Miz Caine." He scratched his bearded chin.

"Mr. McKenna will have his hands full caring for those triplet girls. That's for sure."

The long day rushed into eternity. A funeral and burying. A grieving husband. A somber noontime meal. Three baby girls without a mother. Everything ran together in Florence's mind while she hurried to aid whomever she could. Late in the day after nursing the child, Charlotte Holden placed one of the babies into Florence's waiting arms before she headed back to her wagon to nurse her own baby.

Having never held a newborn, Florence couldn't believe how tiny the infant was. She settled onto a stump and cuddled the crying child, trying to calm her. Emotions she'd never experienced before awakened inside her, and a mother's love flooded her heart. As Florence rocked back and forth and held the infant close, the cries diminished, and the tiny girl slept. She cradled the baby in one arm and with the other hand lightly grasped one of the tight fists until it loosened. The skin felt just as velvety as she had imagined. She tucked the baby's arm and hand inside the swaddling blanket and touched the fuzzy red curls that formed a halo for the tiny head. Everything going on around her in the crowded circle faded from her awareness. She couldn't get enough of studying everything about the baby girl.

Wonder what your father will name you. She gathered the fragile baby even closer against her and dreamed of holding her own child. Surely it wouldn't hurt for her to pretend just for a little while that this infant was hers.

Florence lost all sense of time while she enjoyed this little one. The baby rested in her arms, totally trusting that Florence would take care of her. Florence hadn't thought about what it would feel like for someone to completely depend on her. She leaned over to kiss the baby's forehead and crooned a nameless tune. *Is that what a real mother does?*

"Florence." Joshua's voice drew her back to the clearing between the circled wagons.

But her husband wasn't alone. All the clamor of the camp had masked the sound of the approaching footsteps of the two men. Mr. McKenna accompanied him with a blanket-wrapped baby in his arms. For a moment she almost hadn't recognized the man they'd known for so many months, but the sleeping baby on his shoulder was a good clue. He looked as if he hadn't slept for a month. Bags hung under his red-rimmed eyes, and the remnants of tears trailed down his cheeks. He hadn't shaved for at least a week, and his clothes hung on him as though they belonged to someone else. He resembled a man at least ten years older than she knew him to be. He clutched the baby, as if he were afraid someone would take her away from him.

Florence rose, knowing what that felt like. *He's going to take this little angel from me.* What could she say to a man who had been through what Mr. McKenna had? She had no words to offer. And after luxuriating in the feel of this child in her arms, how could Florence ever give her back to her father? The pain would be like amputating another part of her heart. How many more hits could her heart take before it completely stopped beating?

"Mrs. Caine." Angus McKenna came to an abrupt stop and cleared his throat before starting again. "I've come to ask you something that...I never dreamed I'd...ever ask anyone." His voice rasped, and he stopped to take a gulp of air, staring off into the distance.

She couldn't take her eyes from him, even when the baby in her arms squirmed. "How can we help you?"

New tears followed the trails down his cheeks and disappeared into his beard. He grabbed a bandanna from his back pocket and blew his nose with one hand.

"I've just lost the most important thing in my life." He paused and stared at the ground. "I don't know how I can go on without her." His voice cracked on the last word. Once again he paused, but much longer this time. His prominent Adam's apple bobbed several times. "I've been crying out to God, but I don't think He's listening to me right now. If He were…"

What a thing for a man to admit to them. Florence knew he must be near a breakdown. He did need help, but what could they do?

"I've decided…it would be best to find another family to raise one of my girls." He stood straighter. "I've watched you with Margaret Lenora…"

"Is that what you've named her?" Florence gazed at the sleeping baby, and her heart ached for the child. To grow up without a mother.

"Yes." He stared across the clearing with unfocused eyes. "My wife's parents couldn't agree on a name for her when she was born. Her father wanted Mary Margaret. Her mother wanted Catherine Lenora. So they gave her all four names." Mr. McKenna seemed relieved to be talking about something else besides what had happened that day. "I've named this one"—he indicated the baby on his shoulder—"Mary Lenora."

He didn't say anything about the third girl, and Florence was afraid to ask.

Angus looked straight at Joshua, and her husband gave a slow nod. "Your husband has told me…how much you've wanted a child."

For a moment, anger flared in her chest. Joshua shouldn't share her secret with anyone. She took a deep breath to keep from saying something she'd regret. Even though she didn't even look at her husband, she could feel his gaze deep inside. She was grateful he couldn't see the ugly jealousy and covetousness that resided there.

"What I'm trying to say, Mrs. Caine, is…" His Adam's apple bobbed again. "Would you consider adopting one of my daughters and raising her as your own?" He snapped his mouth shut and just stood there waiting, staring at the ground and clinging to the tiny baby in his arms.

As her own? Was this God's answer to her prayer for a baby? *It could be.* She knew she should try to encourage Mr. McKenna to keep his daughters. He might marry again and want all three of them, but she pushed those thoughts aside before they could take root. This might be the only chance she would ever have for a child, and she didn't want to lose it. Finally, she turned her attention toward Joshua.

"I'll be happy with whatever you decide, Florence." Love poured from her husband and enclosed her in its warmth.

How could she refuse? She held this precious bundle close to her heart right now, and she didn't want to ever let her go.

"I'm just asking you to keep the name I've given her." Mr. McKenna looked as if he might collapse at any moment.

"I'd be honored to have your daughter. I love her already." She kissed the fuzz atop the sleeping baby's head.

Finally, it hit her. *I'm not going to have to give Margaret Lenora back.* Florence swayed. Joshua was instantly at her side with his arm supporting her.

"I'll send some clothes and blankets for Margaret Lenora. Melody Murray will come over a little later to nurse her. She and another woman are working together to feed the babies."

Her heart broke for him as she watched Mr. McKenna turn and trudge toward his own wagon. Along the way, other people spoke to him, but he just kept going as if he didn't even notice them.

Florence didn't even think to tell him that Charlotte Holden had already fed Margaret Lenora. She clutched the baby girl close to her breast, rejoicing over his gift to her…to them. If only she didn't feel so guilty for what she'd been thinking.

Chapter 1

September 1885
Seattle, Washington Territory

MARGARET LENORA CAINE sat in the library of their mansion on Beacon Hill. Because of the view of Puget Sound, which she loved, she had the brocade draperies pulled back to let the early September sunshine bathe the room with warmth. Basking in the bright light, Maggie concentrated on the sketch pad balanced on her lap. After leaning back to get the full effect of the drawing, she reached a finger to smudge the shadows between the folds of the skirt. With a neckline that revealed the shoulders, but still maintained complete modesty, this dress was her best design so far, one she planned to have Mrs. Murdock create in that dreamy, shimmery green material that came in the last shipment from China. Maggie knew silk was usually a summer fabric, but with it woven into a heavier brocade satin, it would be just right for her eighteenth birthday party. And with a few changes to the design, she could have another dress created as well.

Once again she leaned forward and drew a furbelow around the hem, shading it carefully to show depth. The added weight of the extra fabric would help the skirt maintain its shape, providing a pleasing silhouette at any ball. She pictured herself wearing the beautiful green dress, whirling in the arms of her partner, whoever he was. Maybe someone like Charles Stanton, since she'd admired him for several years, and he was so handsome.

"Margaret, what *are* you doing?"

The harsh question broke Maggie's concentration. The charcoal in her hand slipped, slashing an ugly smear across the sketch. She glanced at her mother standing in the doorway, her arms crossed over her bosom. Maggie heaved a sigh loud enough to reach the entrance, and her mother's eyebrows arched so quickly Maggie wanted to laugh…almost, but she didn't dare add to whatever was bothering Mother now. Her stomach began to churn, a thoroughly uncomfortable sensation. Lately, everything she did put Mother in a bad mood. She searched her mind for whatever could have set her off this time. She came up with nothing, so she pasted a smile across her face.

"I'm sketching." She tried for a firm tone but wasn't sure it came across that way.

"You don't have time for that right now." Florence Caine hurried across the Persian wool carpet and stared down at her. "We have too much to do before your party."

Of course her mother was right, but Maggie thought she could take a few minutes to get the new design on paper while it was fresh in her mind. She glanced toward the mantel clock. *Oh, no.* Her few minutes had turned into over two hours. She'd lost herself in drawing designs again. No wonder Mother was exasperated.

She jumped up from the burgundy wing-back chair. "I didn't realize it was so late. I'm sorry, Mother."

Florence Caine took the sketch pad from her hand and studied the drawing with a critical eye. "That's a different design."

Maggie couldn't tell if she liked the dress or not, but it didn't matter. Designing was in Maggie's blood. Her grandmother was a dressmaker who came up with her own designs instead of using those in *Godey's Lady's Book* or *Harper's Bazar*. And, according to Mother's sister, she never even looked at a Butterick pattern. Aunt Georgia had told her often enough about all the society women who wouldn't let anyone but Agatha Carter make their clothing. They knew they wouldn't be meeting anyone else wearing the exact same thing when they attended social events in Little Rock, Arkansas. Not for the first time, Maggie wished she could talk to her grandmother at least once.

With the news about people being able to converse across long distances with something called the telephone, someday she might talk to her that way. But Maggie wanted a face-to-face meeting. Knowing another dress designer would keep her from feeling like such a misfit. Mother kept reminding her that she didn't really fit the mold of a young woman of their social standing in Seattle. At least, Daddy let her do what she wanted to. She didn't know what she'd do without him to offset Mother's insistence, which was becoming more and more harsh.

According to Aunt Georgia, the business Grandmother Carter started was still going strong, even though her grandmother had to be over sixty years old. Maggie planned to go visit her relatives in Arkansas, so she could tour the company. She hoped her journey would happen before she was too late to actually meet Agatha Carter. Her deepest desire was to follow in her grandmother's footsteps, since she had inherited her talents.

The sound of ripping tore through her thoughts. Aghast, she turned to catch her mother decimating her sketch. She lunged toward the paper, trying to save it, but Mother held the sketch just out of her reach.

"What are you doing?" Tears clogged her throat, but she struggled to hide them.

Dribbling the tiny pieces into the ornate wastepaper basket beside the mahogany desk, her mother looked up at her. "Just throwing it away. You had already ruined it anyway."

Anger sliced through Maggie's heart, leaving a jagged trail of pain. She still wanted to keep the sketch. She could use it while she created another. Her plan was to ask her father to help her surprise Mother. The design would set off her mother's tall stature and still youthful figure. She planned to ask him for a length of the special blue satin brocade that would bring out the color of Mother's eyes. The dress would make Mother the envy of most of her friends when the winter social season started in a couple of months. Now she'd have to begin the drawing all over again. So many hours of work and her dreams torn to shreds.

"Darling." That syrupy tone Mother used when she was trying to make a point grated on Maggie's nerves. "When are you going to grow up and forget about your little pictures of dresses?"

Little pictures of dresses? The words almost shredded the rest of Maggie's control. She gripped her hands into fists and twisted them inside the folds of her full skirt.

They'd had this discussion too many times already. She gritted her teeth, but it didn't help. In a few days she would be eighteen, old enough to make decisions for herself—whether her mother agreed or not.

She stood as tall as her tiny frame would allow her. "Those aren't just 'little drawings,' Mother. I *am* going to be a dress designer."

The icy disdain shooting from her mother's eyes made Maggie cringe inside, but she stood her ground.

"Margaret Lenora Caine, I am tired of these conversations. You will *not* become a working girl." Mother huffed out a very unladylike deep breath. "You don't need to. Your father has worked hard to provide a very good living for the three of us. I will not listen to any more of this nonsense."

Maggie had heard that phrase often enough, and she never liked it. Mother swept from the room as if she had the answer to everything, but she didn't. Not for Maggie. And her sketches were not nonsense.

She tried to remember the last time she pleased her mother. Had she ever really?

Her hair was too curly and hard to tame into a proper style. And the hue was too red. Maggie wouldn't stay out of the sun to prevent freckles from dotting her face. She could come up with a long list of her mother's complaints if she wanted to take the time. She wasn't that interested in what was going on among the elite in Seattle. She had more things to think about than *how to catch a husband.*

Maggie wanted to get married someday. But first she would follow her dream. Become the woman she was created to be. That meant being a dress designer, taking delight in making other women look their best. If it wasn't for Grandmother Carter, Maggie would think she had been born into the wrong family.

The enticing aroma of gingerbread called her toward the kitchen. Spending time with Mrs. Jorgensen was just what she needed right now. Since she didn't have any grandparents living close by, their cook and housekeeper substituted quite well in Maggie's mind.

She pushed open the door, wrinkling her nose and sniffing like the bunny in the back garden while she headed across the brick floor toward the cabinet where her older friend worked. "What is that heavenly smell?"

Mrs. Jorgensen turned with a warm smile. "As if you didn't already know. You've eaten enough of my gingerbread, for sure."

Pushing white tendrils from her forehead, the woman quickly sliced the spicy concoction and placed a large piece on a saucer while Maggie retrieved the butter from the ice box. Maggie slathered a thick coating on and watched it melt into the hot, brown bread.

"Here's something to drink." Mrs. Jorgensen set a glass of cold milk on the work table in the middle of the large room.

Maggie hopped up on a tall stool and took a sip, swinging her legs as she had when she was a little girl. Mother would have something else to complain about if she saw her. *That's not ladylike and is most unbecoming.* The oft-spoken words rang through Maggie's mind. But Mother hardly ever came into the kitchen. Mrs. Jorgensen met with Mother in her sitting room to plan the meals and the day's work schedule.

"This is the only place in the house where I can just be myself." Maggie took a bite and let the spices dance along her tongue, savoring the sting of spices mixed with the sweetness of molasses.

"*Ja.*" The grandmotherly woman patted Maggie's shoulder. "So tell me what's bothering you, *kära.*"

Tears sprang to Maggie's eyes. "Why doesn't Mother understand me? She doesn't even try."

She licked a drip of butter that started down her finger, then took another bite of the warm gingerbread. Heat from the cook stove made the enormous kitchen feel warm and cozy, instead of the cold formality of most of the house.

Mrs. Jorgensen folded a tea towel into a thick square, then went to the oven and removed another pan of the dessert. "What's the bee in her bonnet this time?"

Maggie loved to hear the Scandinavian woman's quaint sayings.

"She won't consider letting me continue to design dresses." Maggie sipped her milk, not even being careful not to leave a white mustache on her upper lip. "I've drawn them for our seamstress to use for the last five years. As many of them have been for Mother as for me. And she's enjoyed the way other women exclaimed over the exclusive creations she wore. I don't understand why she doesn't want me to continue to develop my artistic abilities."

"Your father is a very wealthy man, for sure." The cook's nod punctuated her statement. "Your dear mother just wants what is best for you."

"Why does she get to decide what's best for me?" Maggie felt like stomping her foot, but she refrained. That would be like a child having a tantrum. She would not stoop that far now that she was no longer a child. "Soon I'll be eighteen. Plenty old enough to make my own decisions."

"Yah, and you sure have the temper to match all that glorious red hair, *älskling*." She clicked her tongue. "Such a waste of energy."

After enjoying the love expressed in Mrs. Jorgensen's endearment, Maggie slid from the stool and gathered her plate and glass to carry them to the sink. "You're probably right. I'll just have to talk to Daddy."

The door to the hallway swung open.

"Talk to me about what?" Her tall father strode into the room, filling it with a sense of power.

"About my becoming a dress designer."

A flit of pain crossed his face before he smiled. "A dress designer?"

Maggie fisted her hands on her waist. "We've discussed this before. I want to go to Arkansas and see about learning more at The House of Agatha Carter."

Her father came over and gathered her into a loving embrace. "I said I'd *think* about letting you go. There are many details that would have to be ironed out first. But I didn't say you couldn't go."

Maggie leaned her cheek against his chest, breathing in his familiar spicy scent laced with the fragrance of pipe tobacco. "I know. But Mother won't let me. Just you wait and see."

He grasped her by the shoulders and held her away from him. "Maggie, my Maggie, you've always been so impatient. I said I'd talk to her when the time is right. You'll just have to trust me on this."

His eyes bored into hers, and his lips tipped up at the ends. She threw her arms around his waist. "Oh, I do trust you, Daddy."

"Then be patient." He kissed the top of her head, probably disturbing the style she'd work so hard on this morning.

Mrs. Jorgensen stopped slicing the gingerbread and held the knife in front of her. "I thought you weren't going to be home for lunch, Mr. Caine."

"I'm not. I've only come by to pick up my beautiful wife. We'll be dining with some friends at the Arlington House hotel downtown." He gave Maggie another hug and left, presumably to find her mother.

"Would you be wanting another piece of gingerbread, *kära*?"

Maggie shook her head. "I don't want to ruin my lunch. I have some things I need to do. Can I come back to eat a little later?" She hoped her father could prevail against Mother's stubborn stance on the question of a trip to Arkansas.

Mrs. Jorgensen waved her out the door. "You're probably not very hungry after that gingerbread."

Maggie went into the library to retrieve her sketch pad, then headed upstairs to her bedroom. She wanted to get the drawing on paper again before she forgot any of the details. She pulled her lacy panels back from the side window and scooted a chair close. With a few deft strokes, she had the main lines of the dress on the thick paper. Then she started filling it in. As each line appeared on the drawing, she felt an echoing movement in her spirit. Deep inside, she danced through the design as it took shape, much faster than the first time. She was so glad she could recall every detail.

While she drew, her thoughts returned to Grandmother Carter. Everyone said she took after her grandmother... everyone except Mother. *Why isn't she happy about my talent?*

Maggie wandered through her memories, trying to recapture how it was when she was a little girl. She remembered Mother playing with her when they lived in the smaller, but comfortable house in Oregon City. They didn't have servants then, but the three of them laughed and enjoyed life together. Then for some reason, her mother had started talking to her father every chance she got about moving to a larger place. Now that Maggie looked back on those memories, she realized that her mother seemed almost frantic to get away from where they lived, as if something were wrong with the town. Maggie never understood why.

She couldn't have been more than five years old, but some of the events stood out. The hurry to leave town. The long trip. For quite a while after that, she missed playing with her friends. And she didn't make new ones when they arrived. No other small children lived in the neighborhood. Even when she started school, she stayed to herself. She had been shy as a young girl.

After they moved to Seattle and her father bought one of the empty buildings and opened Caine Emporium, Mother changed. She became more distant, almost cold. She was no longer the laughing woman. If Maggie didn't know better, she'd think something made Mother bitter. Maybe that was one reason she wanted to design this special dress. To brighten her mother's life. Bring back the woman who sometimes flashed through her memory at odd times, making her long for the warmth she had luxuriated in as a small child.

Finally, the drawing met her approval. Just in time to eat lunch. Maybe this afternoon she could finish the other sketch with the changes to make the dress more appropriate for her mother than herself.

Once again the kitchen welcomed her, and she enjoyed eating there with Mrs. Jorgensen. If Mother had been home, they would have had the meal in the formal dining room, complete with china, crystal, and silver. Such a fuss for an ordinary day.

❖ ❖ ❖

"Margaret." Her mother's voice rose from the foyer below. "I'm home."

Looking at the names of people she'd placed on the invitation list, Maggie finished writing Charles Stanton's name and put the pen down. "Coming, Mother."

She rushed out of her room and stood at the top of the staircase. "Did you want me?"

"Yes, dear. I thought we could get some shopping done this afternoon." Her mother still wore her gloves and cape.

"Is it cold?"

Mother nodded. "It's a bit nippy, so wear something warm."

"I'll get my things." Maggie hurried back to her room and gathered a light jacket, a handbag, and her gloves.

When she arrived in the foyer, Mother stood tapping her foot impatiently. "I had hoped we could buy most of the things we'll need today."

Maggie bit her tongue to keep from reminding her that she wasn't the one who had frittered away so much of the day. If Mother wanted to go shopping, why didn't they do it earlier? She could have gone along for the lunch with Daddy. But evidently Mother preferred spending time with Daddy instead of her. She took a deep breath and followed her mother to the coach sitting in front of the house.

Mrs. Jorgensen's son, who was their driver, stood beside the open door, ready to assist them into the conveyance.

"Erik, please take us by the Emporium." Mother took hold of his hand as she stepped up into the vehicle.

Maggie followed suit. "Why are we going to the store? Are we going to shop there?"

The door snapped shut, and Erik climbed into the driver's seat.

"I forgot to get money from your father when we were at lunch." Mother settled her skirts as the coach lurched forward. "I believe your father is signing papers with young Charles Stanton this afternoon. It will be nice to see him again. Did you add him to your guest list?"

Maggie nodded, a faint blush coloring her cheeks. She hadn't seen Charles since she was about sixteen, but she still remembered the girlish secret infatuation she'd had when she was younger. He'd been so handsome, and kind too. Would he be changed since he'd graduated from university? She would soon find out.

She settled back into the carriage seat, suddenly looking forward to the afternoon's events.

Chapter 2

CHARLES STANTON STOOD in the office above the furniture store he'd recently inherited from his grandfather. With his hands shoved into the pockets of his trousers, he studied the whitecaps on the water of Puget Sound, barely visible from his position. The movement of the waves soothed him even though he wasn't close enough to hear them lapping against the shore. It was a sound that always calmed him, and that's what he needed right now.

Am I doing the right thing? He'd asked himself that question more than once during the recent negotiations.

When he turned fourteen, Grandpa started teaching him about the business, grooming him to eventually take it over. Charles never considered such a thing would happen when he was only twenty-two years old. Maybe his grandfather had somehow sensed he wasn't long for this world. Two years ago, when Charles graduated from Territorial University, Grandpa increased the depth of Charles's training. Even on his deathbed, Grandpa assured Charles he didn't have anything to worry about. Grandpa trusted him with the business he had built. Charles only wished he felt as certain.

I can do it. He repeated the phrase in his mind more than once. He stood taller and lifted his chin. After all, he was smart and well trained. And his grandfather had entrusted him with a fine furniture store. He was on top of the world, and he needed to enjoy it.

Turning from the vista, he crossed to the large cherrywood desk where his grandfather had held sway as long as he could remember. Charles spent much of his childhood playing between the desk and the bookcases that lined two walls of the expansive room. Father had been as involved in the store as Grandpa back when Seattle was a raw settlement, not the modern city it was today. Then the unthinkable happened. Charles's mother and father perished in a cholera epidemic when he was just ten years old. Those memories piled upon his more recent grief became almost too much to bear today. He blinked away the tears and drew his hands along the smooth surface of the desk as he approached the chair. Then he dropped into the seat and picked up the contract.

Buck up, man. You can do this. Actually, it was almost a done deal. This afternoon he would sign papers that would combine his furniture store with Joshua Caine's mercantile. This merger should improve business for both stores, which sat side by side on Second Avenue. He believed shoppers would like having access to such a vast array of merchandise without going outside, especially with all the inclement weather in Seattle.

He pulled out his father's pocket watch and glanced at the polished face. *Time to get going.* Charles stuffed the contract into a large envelope. His lawyer, Harvey Jones, would bring the other copy when they met at Joshua Caine's office. He shrugged into the jacket of his suit, then folded an overcoat over his arm. The winds blowing from the Sound could reach all the way to the bones this time of year, especially later in the afternoon, and he wasn't sure just how long the meeting with Joshua and Mr. Jones would take. He added a beaver hat and descended the staircase that went down the outside of the building.

Mr. Caine's office also occupied the upper floor of his store. After completing the merger, they would connect the two offices, and Charles wouldn't have to go outside to talk to his partner. On rainy days, that would be especially welcome.

His soon-to-be partner quickly answered his firm knock. Although Charles was tall, Joshua Caine equaled his height. His kind eyes were almost brown, to match the suit he wore, but tinges of green shone through. Threads of silver along the sides of his brown hair made him look distinguished, but not too old. Charles guessed he was nearing the half-century mark.

"Come right in, young man." Joshua pulled the door open wide.

"Your solicitor is already here, and I've been going over the completed document." He rounded his desk and sat in a fine leather chair.

Taking a more utilitarian chair beside Harvey Jones, Charles leaned forward in the hard wooden seat. "Does the contract meet with your expectations?" he asked the lawyer. He didn't want to seem too eager, but he had to know.

Before Jones could answer, a soft knock sounded at the door. Charles wondered who would be so bold as to disturb their important meeting.

"Who's there?" Joshua Caine turned his attention toward the door that crept open a bit.

"I'm sorry to bother you, sir." The assistant manager of the store poked his head inside. "But Mrs. Caine and your daughter want to speak to you a moment."

A slight frown flitted across his Joshua's face before he broke out with a wide smile. "Gentlemen, I've made it a practice to always welcome my wife when she comes by. Please excuse me."

Interesting. Charles had never considered making a decision like that. But he wasn't married yet. Maybe that was something all married businessmen did. He was sure Grandpa never would have turned Grandma away either. He filed that information away in his mind for his own future. Who knows, maybe he'd soon have a wife of his own.

"That's quite all right." Charles stood and walked over to the windows, staring out toward the Sound.

The hinges squeaked slightly when the manager opened the door all the way.

"Joshua, I'm sorry to interrupt."

Out of the corner of his eye, Charles could see Mrs. Caine approach her husband, who smiled down at her.

"Charles, I didn't know you would be here."

He'd recognize that voice anywhere. Turning, he stared into

the incredible green of Maggie Caine's eyes. For just a moment, he wondered if she still went by that nickname. She had really changed since the last time he saw her. No pigtails to pull now, and where were those lovely copper dots across her nose and cheeks he'd loved to tease her about?

"Maggie." He kept his voice quiet so it wouldn't intrude on the Caines' conversation. "So good to see you. How have you been?"

"Just fine. I don't believe I've seen you since you finished university, and that was over two years ago, wasn't it? Are you going to another church?" Maggie smiled up at him with a hint of concern in her eyes.

Evidently, her caring personality hadn't changed, even though she had.

"I must admit I've been remiss in not attending services." That admission cost him a lot. Why hadn't he started back to the church? The last time he'd been inside one was for Grandpa's funeral. "But I do still study the Bible and pray."

"I'm glad to hear that." One red brow rose in a quirk, just as it always had. "I'd hate to think that you had walked away from your faith. You were so strong when we were younger."

Her words brought a veritable kaleidoscope of memories racing through his head. Even though he was four years older than Maggie, as children, they were often involved in the same activities and events. He had picked on her when she wore pigtails and teased her when she was more of a tomboy, but he'd always enjoyed being around the pretty girl. Now she was so different. He would have to get used to seeing her this way.

"I'm sorry I wasn't at your grandfather's funeral." Tenderness filled her gaze. "Mother and I had traveled to Portland to visit with her sister. We didn't find out about his passing until after we arrived back home."

He lowered his gaze to the shiny hardwood floor. "After he died,

I didn't want to go to church services and have everyone sympathize with me."

Her dainty hand landed as soft as a butterfly on his arm. "You're all right now, aren't you? But I'm sure you still miss him."

"Every day." He wouldn't have said that to anyone except Maggie. She was like the little sister he never had.

She took a deep breath. "And now you own a thriving furniture business."

"Yes, Grandpa trained me well before he was gone. I want to make him proud of me."

"I'm sure he would be, and I hope the Lord lets him know about your success."

"Margaret, come along." Mrs. Caine turned her smile toward them. "We have a lot to accomplish today."

Charles reached for Maggie's hand. "I'm glad we got to see each other again."

"I am too." With those quick words, she flitted out the door behind her mother.

Just before she was out of sight, she gave him one last glance. A glance that warmed him somehow. Her concern for him touched him deeply.

Mr. Caine returned to his chair. "Now where were we? Oh, yes. Harvey, prepare to serve as witness." Mr. Caine dipped his pen in the ink pot and signed his copy with a flourish. "Now let me see your document. I'll sign it, then you can sign both."

Charles pulled out the contract and handed it to him. His heart swelled as he watched his new partner make it official.

"I believe the ink is dry now, Charles. Why don't you sit here while you sign?" Mr. Caine rose, walked to the front window, and stared out toward the Sound. "It's a mighty fine day when two businessmen can make a deal that will profit both of them." He clasped his hands behind his back and rocked up on the balls of his feet. "A mighty fine day."

Charles agreed completely. He turned to the task of finishing the deal. He hoped he wouldn't make an ink smudge on either document. He carefully dipped the nib into the ink and signed his name. *Get a hold of yourself, man.* He didn't want to seem like a fumbling idiot in front of these men.

After affixing his signature to the second document, he moved from behind the desk, a feeling of accomplishment thrilling him. "Your turn, Harvey."

The lawyer settled into the chair and took even less time to sign both documents. "All finished, gentlemen."

Striding across the thick carpet, Mr. Caine held out his hand. "I'd like a handshake to seal the deal."

When Charles thrust his hand toward the man, his new partner applied a strong grip and pumped his arm several times. Charles welcomed the strength, knowing it was indicative of the man's character and ideals. *An honest man, just like Grandpa would have chosen.*

Mr. Caine smiled. "I've always wanted a son, but never had one. If anything were to happen to me, I believe I could trust you to make sure my wife and daughter are taken care of."

"Thank you, sir." Charles couldn't help letting a smile split his face. For the first time he really felt like a responsible adult sitting here with two other businessmen.

The three men parted ways, and Charles headed toward the cemetery. He knew his grandfather was in heaven, but he felt close to the beloved man at his grave site. Today, Charles needed to talk to him.

The cold wind stinging his cheeks brought understanding why some men grew sideburns in autumn, but he didn't mind the cold. And he never had wanted facial hair. He walked between the headstones, trying to gather his thoughts. First he stopped beside his parents' graves. Standing with his head down, he paraded memories of them through his mind.

"I miss you both." He glanced at the clouds hovering low. "Please, God, let them know I love them and that they raised a good son."

A few feet over, the twin headstones of his grandparents stood sentinel beside their graves, the stark whiteness of Grandpa's stone beside the gently weathered one that marked the resting place of his wife.

Charles smoothed his gloved fingers across the engraved lettering. "Grandma, you've been gone a long time, and I still miss you."

At least she'd lived a few years after his parents were gone. He'd needed her compassion while he fought against his loss. Without her calming influence and love, he might be an angry man today. Grandpa wouldn't have entrusted the business to him if he were.

Then he stepped closer to his grandfather's grave. "Grandpa, I hope you know how much you meant to me. Now that you're gone, I still want to make you proud." He stopped and stuffed his hands deep into the pockets of his overcoat. "Before I make any decision, I ask myself what I think you would do about the matter. Then I make my choice based on that assessment. That's why I agreed to this merger with Mr. Caine. I believe he is an honest man and that the merger will benefit both of us, helping the store grow and prosper." He rested one gloved hand on the frigid stone. "I wish you could really tell me what you think about the way I'm taking care of the business you entrusted to me."

He put his hand back in the warmth of his pocket and bowed his head. After standing there for a few minutes, peace poured through his heart and soul like a soothing warm bath, cleansing him from all his doubts.

With a light heart, he made his way back to the mansion he'd inherited, the only home he remembered living in. He whistled

Grandma's favorite song all during the brisk walk, and memories of the wonderful woman surrounded him with warmth.

He had just proven that he was man enough to make sensible decisions. Satisfaction filled his heart, giving a jaunty new swagger to his walk. *Life is good and is going to get better. I can feel it.*

Chapter 3

AFTER LUNCH WITH his wife, then the meeting with Charles Stanton, Joshua Caine worked on several projects. Finally, he swiveled in his chair and peered out his window toward Puget Sound. A train loaded with long logs chugged its slow way across the Columbia and Puget Sound railroad bridge, a sign of progress and the growing economy in Seattle. Joshua welcomed the changes that would benefit him and his new partner. People migrated to Seattle in record numbers, and the construction of houses signaled the growth. New inhabitants would need clothing, accessories, and the furniture that the soon-to-be-expanded store would offer under one roof. A very progressive prospect.

He turned toward his desk and looked at the neat stacks of papers. He knew what was in each stack, and he realized which ones needed immediate attention. Since nothing really was pressing today, he mulled over the new partnership. After moving to a worktable against one wall of his personal office, he pulled a large piece of paper from the shelf under the table and started drawing with swift strokes. Before long, he had re-created on the paper the exact layout of the store below and the one on the other side of the connecting wall.

With an eye for detail, he erased and redrew several lines on the drawing, being careful to brush off any residue that might mark the sketch. Then he studied the changes from three angles, making a few more adjustments. When the floor plan was finished, he grinned like a schoolboy with a new toy.

He didn't know how much planning that Stanton boy had done, but this schematic was the best way to make the improvements in both stores and probably the most cost-effective way to connect them. He could hardly wait to show the drawing to Charles. He felt sure the young man would agree with his assessment.

Always glad to get home to his two favorite women, Joshua left the store earlier than usual. At the house, he thrust the door open and called out, "I'm home."

A movement on the stairs caught his attention, and he watched Florence descend like a graceful swan. She didn't look a day older than she had when he married her. Ever since that rough time on the wagon train, he'd wanted to make her completely happy. Sometimes he felt he'd been successful. Sometimes he didn't.

Today, she gave him a brilliant smile and leaned up to plant a quick kiss on his cheek.

"Was your shopping trip successful?" His words brought a slight cloud to her expression.

"Not exactly." She headed into the parlor and he followed, settling beside her on the divan. "We started a bit late and didn't find much we liked."

Mrs. Jorgensen stopped in the doorway. "Erik told me you were home, Mr. Caine. If you'd like, I can have dinner on the table in two shakes of a lamb's tail, for sure."

Joshua grinned at her humorous sayings. They always amused him, but Florence didn't like them much.

His wife stood. "That would be fine, Mrs. Jorgensen. We'll dine as soon as you have it ready."

Just then Maggie descended the stairs. His daughter had turned into a beautiful young woman. God had blessed him in so many ways.

Maggie came to the open doorway. "Did I hear Mrs. Jorgensen say we are going to eat soon?"

Her mother looked at Maggie and smiled. "Yes." She moved toward their daughter. "I was just telling your father that we didn't find much today. I thought we should go shopping again tomorrow."

He noticed Maggie's expression sink a little before she answered. "Could you go without me, Mother? I'm still working on writing out the invitation list and other plans for the party. I could stay home and finish them."

Florence just stared at her a minute. "I guess I could go shopping without you."

Once again, he sensed tension between the two most important people in his life. How he wished he could understand women better. If only there were something he could do to smooth over the troubled waters.

The next morning Maggie's mind was on her grandmother's legacy. Her mother left soon after they shared breakfast, but without much conversation. Evidently Mother was still miffed that Maggie didn't want to spend another day shopping. She had other things she wanted to do today. Not the least of these was to finish the dress design. She wished she could consult her grandmother and get her ideas.

Just then Maggie remembered Aunt Georgia telling her that Mother brought on the wagon train some of the dresses Grandmother designed for her. Would she have kept them? If so, Maggie wanted to find them to study the lines of the garments. Perhaps they were stored in the attic. She knew the third floor of their home was unheated, so she went to her room and pulled on a heavy jacket before heading up the attic stairs.

Even though the maids sometimes cleaned up there, dust motes danced in the sunlight streaming through the dormer windows. One end of the room that spread across the whole mansion was filled with cast-off furniture. Maggie studied the pieces. Most of them were beautiful. Evidently Mother had tired of them or found something she liked better.

A rosewood writing desk sat pushed up under the eaves, with a matching chair beside it. Maggie went over and slid her fingers along the grain of the wood, disturbing the layer of dust. She would ask Erik to help her take it downstairs to her room when she was finished up here. It would fit neatly underneath her window that faced Puget Sound. She would enjoy drawing designs while sitting at the desk. But right now, she needed to find the dresses.

Numerous chests were stacked haphazardly on the other end of the room, and some clothes hung across a rope clothesline. Old sheets protected them.

Maggie removed the first sheet and looked through the garments. A green satin dress caught her eye. As she studied how it was made, she found her grandmother's name embroidered on the facing at the back of the neck. She held the dress up to her and moved over in front of the wardrobe that had a mirror on the door. Although the dress was far too long, it would fit her otherwise. Maybe she could get Mrs. Murdock to shorten it. She would like to wear something her grandmother had made. This could be her new dress for the holiday season. She could keep her own new design just for her mother. *Should I ask Mother, or should I just do it?*

She draped the dress across the railing above the staircase. She'd take it downstairs when she went. Maybe Mother wouldn't even notice. How often did she come into the attic anyway?

Going back to the clothing hanging on the line, Maggie moved the outfits aside to study the next design. The lines of these dresses awakened all kinds of designs in her mind. Her fingers itched to get them on paper, but this time she'd be sure her mother wouldn't find the drawings before she finished them.

As the wind blew through the trees with some limbs scraping against the windows, streams of sunlight crept across the attic, almost like a lantern revealing more items. In the back corner on the end farthest from the stairs, a cluster of trunks and wooden crates made a large intriguing pile. Maybe some of them contained more clothing. Maggie's curiosity drove her to investigate.

The first trunk held flower-sprigged, cotton dresses, something Mother would never wear. Differing designs in the sometimes faded dresses opened more memories in her mind. Mother had worn some of these. She could see her in the kitchen of the house back in Oregon, preparing meals for the three of them. How long had it been since her mother cooked for the family? Maggie couldn't remember her ever using the large stove in the kitchen far below. They didn't have a cook in Oregon, but Mrs. Jorgensen was in all her memories of this house in Seattle.

After poking around in several trunks, she opened one containing handmade quilts. Had her mother made these or were they gifts from someone else? Did the women on the wagon train her parents had traveled west on make these covers? She'd never seen them on the beds on the second floor of the mansion. She picked up four or five of the quilts and set them aside. Faded clothing with tattered sleeves and worn places on the hems were folded neatly beneath them.

Maggie lifted out the men's and women's clothing that smelled old and musty. Why did Mother keep all this? Without a doubt, she would never put on anything like this ever again.

Just as Maggie was going to start putting the items back into the trunk, a stream of sunlight bounced off the corner of something white and hard. She pulled back the plaid flannel shirt covering it and revealed a small white chest.

What's this? She lifted it out and set it on the floor. Made from painted wood, the lid had a carved floral design, and pale remnants of pink paint shadowed the blossoms. Faded now, this chest had to have been a thing of beauty when it was new. She wondered who made it. She'd never known her father to do any woodcarving, but he could have when he was younger. Maybe he created this beauty.

She lifted the lid. The hinges squealed as if they hadn't been used for a long time. A soft knitted blanket, yellowed by time, spread across the top of whatever was in the chest.

Maggie stared at the blanket. The thin yarn and tiny loops of the knitting made it appear to be for a baby, so it must have been hers. But Mother didn't knit. Neither did Aunt Georgia. *So who knitted this?* Her fingertips gently explored the texture, and a strange feeling tugged at her heart.

She picked up the soft fabric and clasped it to her chest. Underneath was a tiny white dimity dress covered with pink embroidered roses. Mother occasionally worked on needlepoint, but not embroidery. Maybe her grandmother made the dress. Other dresses and gowns were packed together with a tiny sweater, cap, and booties. Maggie fingered each piece before she set it on the floor beside her. They looked almost new, as if they hadn't been worn much. Maybe Mother kept them for special occasions, but if so, what did she wear the rest of the time?

At the very bottom of the trunk, she found a miniature portrait in an oval silver frame. Tarnish dimmed the glow of the metal but didn't obscure the intricate design of interwoven hearts all around the frame. With one hand, she dusted off the curved glass and turned the picture toward the sunlight.

Maggie gasped. Staring back at her was a faded portrait of…herself. *But that's impossible.* The woman's face was the same heart shape as Maggie's. The woman's eyes held the intense expression that often stared back at Maggie from her own mirror. The same large eyes, the same pert nose, the same bowed mouth, and the same curls escaped from the woman's hairstyle, too. *Who can this be?* Why had Maggie never heard of someone in the family who looked just like her? A feeling of unease crept up her spine, making the hair on the back of her neck prickle.

She peered deep into the small chest and noticed a sheet of yellowed paper with writing on it lying flat on the bottom. She picked it up and turned it toward the weak sunlight.

September 19, 1867

I, Angus McKenna, do hereby give my daughter, Margaret Lenora, to Joshua and Florence Caine to adopt and raise as their own child. I promise not to ever try to contact Margaret Lenora.

Signed,

Angus McKenna

Joshua Caine

Florence Caine

Witnessed,

John Overton

Matthias Horton, MD

The words leapt from the page and stabbed her bewildered heart like thin shards of broken crystal. Maggie stared at the note until everything ran together. Then the paper fluttered to the floor beside her, and shock leaked from her eyes, making hot trails down her cheeks.

Maggie wasn't sure how long she sat on the dusty floor weeping. Her body ached, her eyes felt gritty, and she was sure her face was swollen and blotchy. When she glanced up, the shaft of weak sunlight had made its way across the attic, leaving her in shadows. *What if Mother finds me here?*

With the scrap of paper clutched in her fingers, she scrambled to her feet. They were tingling because she had sat on them so long they had almost gone completely to sleep. After she tapped them on the floor several times, the numbness began to recede, leaving pinpricks of pain behind. *What should I do now?*

The small white chest beside where she had been sitting caught her eyes. Quickly she replaced all the items inside, trying to remember what went where. Did it really matter? Finally, out of anger, she just shoved in what was left and closed the latch. She wasn't going to put the chest back in its hiding place, so it wouldn't matter.

A thought pushed its way into her shock-numbed mind. *What am I going to do about what I found out?* The idea of talking to Mother about the picture and adoption paper made her stomach turn. They weren't really mother and daughter. Not by blood anyway. No wonder Maggie couldn't please her.

Maybe that was why Mother kept the secret from her. Maybe she was sorry she ever adopted her. What was it about her that kept the women in her life from loving her? First her real mother, whoever she was, then Florence. Both had rejected her in different ways. The pain from that admission radiated from her heart, burning a trail to her churning stomach.

But if that was true, why was Mother always trying to change her, make her into the perfect daughter? Were her real parents terrible people? Was Mother afraid Maggie would turn out like them? Her head started to throb with all the thoughts bumping into each other. She couldn't make heads or tails of any of them. More tears slid down her cheeks.

And why hadn't Daddy told her anything about the adoption? What did he have to hide? Scenarios whirled inside her brain as if they were alive. Maggie would have to learn to accept all of this on some level before she was ready to hear the absolute truth from the people who raised her as their own. Who was Angus McKenna, and why did he give her up for adoption? From what little she knew about her parents' trip west on the wagon train, the adoption had to have happened close to the time they arrived in Oregon. Was it actually on the trip, or had it happened soon after? And where was her natural mother in all this?

Quickly, to return the attic the way it was before Mother came up there, Maggie rearranged the clothing and boxes. All except for the white chest and the green dress.

She carried those downstairs to her room and hid them in her wardrobe. Thank goodness Mother never bothered with Maggie's clothing anymore. Today was Ingrid's day off. When her maid returned tomorrow, she wouldn't ask any questions about the things Maggie had added to her personal storage space. Because they had become friends, Ingrid understood the importance of maintaining complete trust between them.

When Maggie closed the wardrobe door, she noticed her reflection in the mirrored center panel. She stared at her face, so like the one in the faded photograph, yet so different. Maggie's eyes were red and swollen, and much of her hair hung out of the carefully created style. *Such a mess.* Florence was always trying to get Maggie to keep her hair tamed into a neat hairstyle. Now she knew why that had been such a problem to her.

She went to her washstand and poured water into the bowl, then dipped a cloth in and wrung it out. She dropped onto her chaise lounge and pressed the damp cloth over her eyes. *Just who am I really?* If her last name were McKenna, no wonder she had red hair. Did the woman in the photo have it too? She almost had to be her mother, didn't she?

Why did my real mother and father give me away? And why didn't my mother sign the adoption paper?

Somehow, she had to find answers to these questions.

Chapter 4

MARGARET, COME SEE what I found." Mother's voice carried up the staircase to Maggie's room.

The strident tone grated on Maggie more today than it ever had before. The one thing she didn't want to do was look at whatever it was Mother bought today. She didn't even want a birthday party, but if she mentioned that, her mother would want to know why. She wasn't prepared to answer that question yet.

Smoothing the last of the curls into her upswept hairdo, Maggie glanced into the mirror. The cold compresses had done their work. No one need know that she had been so upset. She straightened her shoulders and headed down to the parlor.

Mother stood beside the piled packages and boxes on the divan of the parlor suite. "I bought so many wonderful things." She picked up a package wrapped in brown paper and tied with twine, then sat on the divan. "Just look at what I found at Pinkham's Variety Store."

Mother carefully untied the twine. Pulling back the edges of the brown paper, she revealed a large amount of burgundy-colored moire taffeta. "We can have Mrs. Murdock make the tablecloths for your birthday party from this. Isn't it the most luscious color? We can put the lace ones we already have over them."

Maggie stared at the mass of maroon fabric. It almost made her sick to her stomach. How many times had she told her mother that she didn't really like that shade? More times than she could remember, but Mother didn't listen to what she said. Before, she really hadn't noticed just how many times her mother ignored her wishes. Now the fact grated on her. Anger began to simmer deep inside.

Maybe that was what Mother had been doing. Trying to smooth out everything that made Maggie an individual, unique. Maybe trying to erase anything that reminded her of Maggie's real mother. A bitter taste filled her mouth. She clasped her hands together until her knuckles ached. *I want to be me, not someone you're creating.* It took all her willpower to keep from shouting the words. She didn't even want to call the woman Mother, because she really wasn't her mother. *You'll be only Florence to me now.*

"This is such a royal color, don't you think?" Finally, Florence turned her attention toward Maggie. "Are you all right? You're kind of quiet."

"I have a bit of a headache." Maggie's words sounded clipped, but she didn't care.

She really hadn't told a lie. The stress of the afternoon, coupled with Florence's complete disregard for her wishes, combined behind her eyes and began a slow, steady throb. At least it wasn't a full-blown headache.

"I hope it's not hurting you too much. I have so much more to show you."

With those words, Florence began opening each package and displaying the merchandise.

Maggie didn't see a single thing she liked, but she endured the woman's raving about all the things she'd purchased.

Maggie took the twine from the packages and folded each piece of brown paper. She needed something to keep her hands busy. She answered the questions with noncommittal sounds when needed, all the while trying to decide what bothered her the most. That she'd been lied to all her life, or that no one wanted to know what she really felt about anything. Even Daddy either spoiled her or took sides against her on occasion. But he didn't even know her. Maybe no one wanted to really know her. No one except Mrs. Jorgensen. What would she have done without that wonderful woman?

"I'll take these things up to the sewing room for you." Maggie gathered as much as she could carry and started up the stairs without glancing back.

When Daddy arrived home, they dined together, but no one had much to say. Maggie was glad. The last thing she wanted to do today was keep up a meaningless conversation when so many more things were going on in her head and heart.

After dinner, her father retired to his study, and Florence went upstairs, evidently to make more of her own plans for the party. The event would be more for her than for Maggie anyway. Maggie was probably wasting her time writing plans that would be ignored. But she didn't want to be alone with her thoughts. She went to her room and picked up the list she had been working on. After reading a few words, she slammed it down, then paced across the bedroom a couple of times.

Maybe reading a book would take her mind off things. She pulled one from her bookcase, not even bothering to read the title. Her eyes scanned the first page at least three times before Maggie realized she didn't know a single word she'd read. She tossed the book onto her bed. Her own tumultuous emotions had broken through her concentration, annihilating it.

The events from earlier today in the attic overwhelmed her. Her problems wouldn't let go of her. What could she do about the information she'd uncovered? All the items had been cleverly hidden below mounds of useless castoffs from the past. She was sure neither her father nor Florence wanted her to see them.

With both parents busy with their own pursuits, now would be a good time to question the housekeeper. And much safer than bringing things up to her moth…Florence.

Maggie went down to the kitchen and poured herself a cup of hot tea. She sat in a chair at the table, warming her icy fingers around the mug.

She watched Mrs. Jorgensen washing dishes for a moment, then glanced back down at the hot brew. "Remind me how long you've known Mother and Father." She lifted the cup for a sip, holding her breath waiting for the answer. She didn't glance at the woman's face, afraid to betray her agitation.

"Ja, and I've told you this before, for sure." The older woman went to work, vigorously drying a bowl.

"I know." Because her hands shook, Maggie set her drink down. She wiped her sweaty palms against her skirt.

"Well, your parents moved into the house beside the one where my dear departed husband and I had lived here in Seattle. When they first came to town, that is."

When she stilled, Maggie finally looked at her face. With seriousness pinching her eyes, the woman studied Maggie intently.

"I was glad to have such nice neighbors, being a new widow and all. And why would you be wanting to be told all that again?"

Maggie glanced across the immaculate room toward the windows, then studied the clouds scudding across the gray sky. "Just because. So where did they move from? Do you know?"

The water swished in the dishpan. Maggie turned her attention toward the cook.

"They had been in Oregon City since they came there on the wagon train." Mrs. Jorgensen stopped and stared into space. "I remember your dear mother told me that when they first moved in, but she never wanted to talk about her life in Oregon or on that wagon train."

"I wonder why?" Maggie hoped her question would prompt other memories from the housekeeper.

Mrs. Jorgensen set a bowl on the table. "I wondered the same thing. Did some event cause them to leave and come to Seattle? The way she reacted when I asked that one time, I knew better than to ask again."

Even though the woman's voice had a note of finality to it, Maggie couldn't let the subject alone. "And I was about five or six years old then?" Maggie puckered her brow. That seemed so long ago, almost a lifetime.

"Ja, I remember your sixth birthday party. Your mother had big plans, inviting every child for blocks around…and their parents. A lot of people for such a small house. She always had a knack for entertaining." The housekeeper opened the cupboard door and placed the bowl in its usual position.

Maggie wasn't interested in Florence's parties. She stood and turned toward the housekeeper. "Where did we live?"

Mrs. Jorgensen's eyes probed Maggie until she was afraid the woman could see the secrets in her heart. "Not in such a grand neighborhood like this one. Closer to the wharves."

Maggie knew the area. The houses looked like hovels when compared to the mansion they lived in on Beacon Hill. She couldn't imagine Florence ever surviving in those conditions. Even though Maggie could tell the housekeeper wanted to ask her something, she turned back to the dishpan and started washing a plate instead.

Maggie didn't want to inquire about so much that she would open herself to deeper questions, but she had to ask this one more. "Did she ever mention an Angus McKenna?"

"Dear me, I don't think so. The name doesn't ring a bell with me, for sure." The older woman folded her arms across her chest. "What's going on, Margaret?"

When Mrs. Jorgensen used that tone, Maggie knew she had gone too far. And she wasn't ready to reveal anything more. "Nothing." She quickly finished the tea and set the cup beside the sink. "The name just came to me, and I thought maybe I'd heard it somewhere." She knew the words didn't make any sense the second they crossed her lips, but she wasn't going to elaborate.

She hastily exited the room. Knowing she'd told an outright lie should have made her feel terrible, but why should she care? Everyone else had been lying to her for years.

A long-forgotten feeling from childhood swept over her like a tidal wave breaking against the wharves on the Sound. Part of her was missing, but she didn't know what part it was. She'd felt it more often as a young girl, and now the emotions involved were more intense. They sucked the life right out of her. She wanted to crumple to the floor and weep. But she wouldn't give anyone the satisfaction of watching her lose control. Taking a deep breath, she squared her shoulders, holding her spine as stiff as the trunk of a tall pine tree.

So she didn't really know who her parents were. That shouldn't give her this kind of emotional upheaval. The first time she experienced the feeling, she hadn't known that the people she lived with weren't her real parents. This thing that upset her balance didn't really have anything to do with the others. Something deep inside her was missing, a piece of her heart, maybe a piece of her soul. But what was it, and where had it gone? And could she ever find it again? Maybe if she could, she'd feel whole, a complete human being. Accepted for who she really was, with no one trying to change her into something else.

She climbed the back stairs and went to her room, closing the door quietly behind her. She leaned against the flocked wallpaper. Maggie wanted to be herself, not someone Florence had molded her into, but who was she anyway? Her stomach tightened and a lump settled in her chest, almost cutting off her breath. Tears streamed down her cheeks, and she swiped at them with both hands. Why didn't she carry a handkerchief the way other girls did? Too bad a *lady* never used her sleeve to wipe her face. Dropping her face into her hands, she tried to stifle the sob that escaped.

Florence walked down the stairs contemplating the new developments in her husband's business. Charles was a nice young man, but she remembered that even as a boy, he had a stubborn streak. So did Joshua. They would make good partners, but who would come out on top if they ever disagreed? She'd like to be hiding in the corner when that happened. It ought to be quite a show.

She went to the kitchen, hoping to find her daughter, but the room was empty. Then she went to Joshua's study, where she knew she'd find her husband.

"Everything is under control, but I can't find Margaret." She settled into one of the chairs beside the fireplace.

Joshua came from behind his desk and sat in the chair beside hers. "I'm a bit worried about Maggie. She didn't seem like herself this evening."

"I noticed that." Florence studied her husband's face. How could he read their daughter so well, and yet so often have no idea what Florence was feeling? "We have a lot to do to get ready for Margaret's birthday party." She straightened the edging of the antimacassar on the arm of her chair. "We haven't sent the invitations around yet. I wish Margaret would finish writing her guest list."

Not looking at her, Joshua fiddled with the lace doily on the lamp table beside his chair. "You know she will, in good time."

What did he find so fascinating with that bit of lace? He'd seen it thousands of times. Why wouldn't he look at her?

"I didn't say she wouldn't. She's just dragging her feet about everything I'm trying to accomplish." She huffed out a breath. He always took the girl's side about everything. Just once, why didn't he see things from her perspective? "I'll try to find her and talk to her about it." She started to rise.

He stopped her with a gentle hand on her arm. "Just sit with me a bit. We do need to talk about our daughter."

She slumped back into the chair and stared at him. *This must really be serious.* "Why? What has she done?"

Leaning forward, he clasped his hands between his knees and studied the design in the Persian carpet as if he had never seen it before. "She hasn't done anything wrong, if that's what you mean. But we've got to make a decision about the journey she wants to take."

The words felt like heavy blows to her chest. She had hoped everyone would forget Margaret's whim about going to Arkansas. Even with the railroad, the trip would be long and hard. And Florence didn't look forward to going. She didn't want to be away from home for several weeks. That last trip she and Margaret took to visit her sister, Georgia, in Portland had seemed endless. She didn't like being away from her own domain, and she had to admit she had missed dear Joshua as well, in spite of all his faults.

"I think maybe this is what's bothering her, Florence. She wants to visit with your mother, and we should let her go." His words held a firmness he seldom used with her.

"Let *her* go. Do you mean you'd let her go without us?" Florence straightened her back like a ramrod. "You don't want us to go with her? She surely can't go alone."

"Maybe if we let her go without us, when she comes back, things will be better between the two of you." His eyes pleaded with her to understand, but she didn't.

Does he blame me for what's happening? She hoped not. Their girl could be so exasperating. She'd tried hard to be a good mother, but Margaret never understood that. She always bucked like a wild horse against anything Florence suggested.

Before she could voice her objections, he continued, "Your sister will be here for the party. She could stay and go along with Maggie. I'm even thinking of asking Charles to accompany them. Be their protector. We can make our plans for the business before they leave, and I can oversee the work while he's gone. If I need to communicate with him, I can always send a telegram. Communication is easier than it was when we came west on the wagon train."

Florence let those words sink in without a comment. *What can I say?* If she didn't agree, the misunderstandings between her and Margaret would escalate. Perhaps Joshua was right. Her refusal would even affect her relationship with her husband. And heaven knows she didn't need any more trouble between them.

"I'll think about it." That was the most she could give him at this time. "Really think about it."

Chapter 5

MAGGIE HAD LOOKED forward to her eighteenth birthday party for almost a year. But now that the time had arrived, she had a hard time working up enthusiasm for the festivities. Too many things pushed them to the back of her mind, not the least being her discovery in the attic several days ago.

A soft knock sounded at the door. She opened it for Ingrid, her personal maid, who also was Mrs. Jorgensen's granddaughter.

"Miss Maggie, Grandma sent up tea and finger sandwiches. She said you should eat something before I help you dress. You hardly touched your lunch." Ingrid set the tray on the table beside the window. "Should I pour you a cup?"

Maggie wasn't hungry, but she didn't want Mrs. Jorgensen to keep worrying about her. "Yes. You know how I like it."

The girl picked up the china teapot and poured the fragrant beverage into the matching cup. After stirring in one teaspoon of sugar until it dissolved, she added a teaspoon of milk. "Here you are. Do you want me to get out that pretty green dress you had Mrs. Murdock hem?"

Maggie took a sip of the tea, the warmth only slightly settling the cold dread in her belly. "Yes."

She probably should fortify herself for Florence's reaction to her wearing the dress. Without a doubt, her adopted mother wouldn't like the fact that she'd countermanded her own directions to Mrs. Murdock.

While Ingrid retrieved the gown from the wardrobe, she kept talking. "And how will you be wanting your hair styled? Should I put most of it up and form a few long curls to drape over your shoulder in front? If I wind the matching ribbon through your style and accent it with some beads, you'll look like a princess."

A princess? Wouldn't it be interesting if she really were a princess? She shook her head. Not much chance of that. *No one would give away a princess.* Maybe she was the daughter of a pauper. Was that why Angus McKenna gave away his daughter? He was too poor to take care of her.

"That sounds like a good idea." Maggie picked up a sandwich and took a bite while Ingrid collected her silk undergarments.

The first taste teased Maggie's appetite, so she finished the piece and picked up another.

"Grandma will be pleased you decided to eat, for sure." Ingrid arranged the hair ornaments on the dressing table beside the silver brush, comb, and mirror.

"I didn't realize how hungry I really was until I took the first bite. Be sure to thank her for providing just what I needed...once again." Maggie dropped into the chair beside the table so she could eat the rest of the delicious food. She hoped it would fortify her for the evening and all it would bring.

Why didn't Florence notice what she needed? Maggie wasn't really selfish or vain, was she? But shouldn't a parent want what was best for their child, no matter how they acquired the infant? Had she only been a plaything that Florence tired of before she grew up? Her thoughts over the last days had proven torturous. But she saw no way to find out without actually asking her parents. And she wasn't ready to do that.

Before Ingrid finished arranging Maggie's hair, a quick knock on the door interrupted them. "Margaret, can I come in?" Her mother's younger sister called through the door.

"Of course you can." Maggie twisted on the dressing stool and watched Aunt Georgia enter and close the door. She loved her aunt. Having her in the house would serve as a buffer between Maggie and Florence. "When did you arrive?"

"Not very long ago." Georgia wrapped her arms around Maggie and kissed her cheek. "I told Florence to let me surprise you after I cleaned up from traveling. The train was late leaving Portland, and I was afraid I'd miss your party altogether."

"I'm so glad you're here." Maggie clung to her for another long moment before letting go, relishing the hug and the love it represented. But would Georgia feel differently when the truth came out?

Georgia moved to the side, so Ingrid could continue with her ministrations. "Are you all right, dear?"

Maggie stared at her aunt, noticing her sleek dark hair pulled into a figure-eight bun on her nape, so different from Maggie's own wild, almost-untamable curls. "We've just been very busy getting ready for the party." That wasn't exactly a lie. They had been busy, but her words didn't answer the question. Maybe Aunt Georgia wouldn't notice.

Her aunt gave a quick nod, then sat on the edge of the bed. "So where did you get that dress? It's not one you designed, is it?"

Should Maggie tell her? The truth couldn't hurt. "I found it in the attic. I remembered you saying Mother had brought along some of the dresses your mother designed when she came west." At least that was part of the truth. "When I saw the label, I knew it was one of them." And one of the reasons she wanted to wear it to the party.

Aunt Georgia gazed up and down Maggie's figure. "I'm surprised it fit you so well. I thought Florence was taller than you when she wore that."

So more information had to come out. "I had Mrs. Murdock, our seamstress, hem it for me, but the rest of the dress fit just fine."

"My sister was very thin when she was younger, which made her as small as you are, just taller." Georgia watched Ingrid's fingers as they fairly flew while she created the elaborate hairstyle. "My goodness, you are really good at that."

Ingrid blushed at the compliment. "Thank you, ma'am." She didn't slow down a bit, continuing to weave the ribbon and green beads through the curls and anchoring them with hairpins.

When she finally laid the three long curls beside Maggie's slim neck, she stepped back to admire her own handiwork. "Does it look all right, Miss Maggie?"

After turning her head this way and that, so she could see every part of the style, Maggie smiled. "I believe this is the best you've ever done. Thank you, Ingrid."

"You'd be the belle of the ball even if you weren't the birthday girl." Aunt Georgia came to stand behind her. "You're very beautiful indeed."

"But I don't look a bit like you or Mother." The soft words slipped out before Maggie could corral them.

She stared in the mirror at her aunt's startled reflection. Maggie wondered if Florence would share that same startled expression when she walked down the stairs in the dress. *Of course, she will. Maybe worse.* Maggie's lips pulled into a slight smile at that thought.

Florence stood in the foyer of their home beside her husband, content with the knowledge that everything looked perfect, just the way she had intended for it to be. It wasn't every day that a family could celebrate their daughter's coming-of-age party.

"So glad you could join us." She extended her gloved hand to Mayor Yesler and his wife, Sarah. She loved welcoming people into their home, especially important people. This was a far cry from their first home at the end of the long wagon trip west.

Oregon City was very provincial, but just for a moment the memory of happy times there flitted through her mind. Even so, they couldn't stay there where everyone knew her shame. That was why she talked Joshua into moving to Seattle. And even though they lost some of the more fun aspects of their life with the move, just look at the contacts they had made. They held an important place in the society of this lovely city.

"Thank you." The mayor moved on to Joshua, and the men's

deep voices blended into the general hubbub. Probably talking about business, which was the way of most men.

Light laughter and murmuring rippled through her parlor, where the furniture had been moved aside to make room for the string quartet and dancing. As Florence turned toward the next people coming through the front door a scuffing sound drew her attention toward the top of the stairs. Georgia started down the steps. Her sister looked lovely in that particular shade of blue, and the cut of the dress really showed off her svelte figure. And then Margaret came to the top of the stairs.

Florence's heart almost stopped beating. That wasn't the dress she told Mrs. Murdock to make for Margaret. Instead, her daughter wore one of the dresses her mother had designed for Florence when she was younger. An off-the-shoulder style in a brilliant, emerald green silk. The brocade shimmered as Margaret descended the stairs, outlining every move her daughter made. She glanced around, and the eyes of every man in the room followed Margaret.

Florence remembered wearing the dress and never really feeling comfortable in it. Of course, it hadn't looked as good on her as it did now on her daughter. *What has been going on in my own home without my knowledge?* After the party, she'd get to the bottom of this. However, no need to create a scene in front of all the people attending. She pasted a stiff smile on her face and accepted the hand of the next guest.

Charles Stanton loved parties and had been looking forward to Maggie's birthday celebration. Now his attention was immediately drawn to Maggie as she started down the curving staircase in the foyer. He'd always thought of her as pretty, but tonight she was more than that. The green dress showcased her womanly figure to perfection, and the color brought out her eyes. Even though he was standing a few feet away he could see every detail. The golden flecks in her eyes glittered in the light from the gilded, crystal chandelier.

He hoped to catch her eye, but her attention was fastened on someone close to the door. He shifted, and through the crowd, he spied Mrs. Caine. The women acted as if no one else was in the room. For a moment, some unspoken communication passed between Margaret and her mother. Mrs. Caine's lips thinned and her jaw clenched before a tight smile masked her reaction. Maggie slowed momentarily and swayed slightly, concern puckering her brow.

If only he knew what was going on with them. For the first time in his life, he actually wished he could read minds. Florence Caine had been nothing but kind to him. So had Maggie. What caused this evident animosity between them?

Quickly he made his way through the throng until he stood near the archway that led into the large parlor. He propped his shoulder against the wall and crossed his arms. His gaze followed Maggie as she greeted people in the crowd, always polite and friendly. Soon another woman, who looked like a younger, softer version of Florence, joined Maggie. They greeted each other with wide smiles. No animosity there.

What a beauty! Her golden hair was swept to the top of her head with tendrils caressing her cheeks. The blue silk dress emphasized her femininity and intensified the hue of her eyes. She looked like one of the china dolls for sale in the store, but she was very much alive. Now there was a woman he could be interested in. She had to be some relative, maybe Mrs. Caine's younger sister. She couldn't be more than a year or two older than he was. He hoped he'd get a chance to meet her. *Wonder if she lives in Seattle.* If so, why had he not met her? He might have if he had gone to church more. He promised himself he'd remedy that this coming weekend.

The two women went to the refreshment table and put a few items on each of their plates. He couldn't take his gaze from the new woman. Then he noticed something odd about Maggie. While she continued to visit with others at the party, she never took a single bite of the food on her plate. Her fork just nudged the morsels around.

Quickly he crossed the room. When he arrived near Maggie, the other fascinating woman stood beside her.

"Are you going to introduce me to you friend?" Even though Charles was talking to Maggie, he couldn't take his eyes off the blonde beside her.

"You mean my aunt Georgia? But she *is* my friend as well." Maggie's words snatched his attention.

"Your aunt?" He had guessed right.

"Yes. Aunt Georgia, this is Charles Stanton. We've been friends for a long time."

"Since you were in pigtails." When he laughed, Maggie didn't join him. He wondered why. She used to like to be teased.

"You would bring that up." The frown in her tone matched the one on her face. "Actually, sometimes Charles got me into trouble, but I have to admit that often he also got me out of trouble."

The aunt lifted her hand. "I'm Georgia Long."

He glanced at her ring finger. It was adorned by a dinner ring with lots of pearls, but no wedding band. *Good.* He lifted her hand and pressed his lips against the back. For a moment her eyes widened, and she looked flustered before she withdrew it. At that moment, he decided to claim a dance from her later in the evening.

Before long, the musicians began playing and people drifted into conversation groups. Then one of the other young men asked Maggie to dance. She gave her plate to one of the maids circulating through the room with trays.

Charles kept watching her as one after another of the young, and sometimes older, men claimed her. When they danced, she held herself away from them, although she danced smoothly with each one. They chatted, but she wasn't as animated as he'd remembered her. She looked aloof and disconnected.

When no one asked Georgia to dance, Charles made his way through the throng and stopped in front of the chair where she sat beside her sister.

Florence was the first one to flash a smile up at him. She turned toward the lovely Georgia. "Have you met Joshua's new partner?"

Finally, the object of his attention turned toward him. "Yes, Maggie introduced us." He couldn't decipher the flash in her eyes, almost as if she were planning mischief. "Are you enjoying the party, Mr. Stanton?"

"I'd enjoy it more if you'd give me the pleasure of this dance." When he extended his hand toward her, he almost expected her to decline.

After staring at him for a moment, she rose gracefully and placed her long, slender fingers in his. Without hesitating, he whirled her onto the dance floor, where they moved perfectly in concert with each other. Step matched step as Georgia swept her full skirt across the floor in a swaying waltz. Enjoying the feel of her in his arms, Charles almost forgot to engage her in conversation.

"Well, Aunt Georgia, why have I never seen you before? I've known the Caines for a long time." Smoothly, he guided her through the twirling dancers.

She smiled up at him. "It could be because I live in Portland."

Charles remembered Maggie saying something about her and her mother visiting an aunt in Portland at the time of his grandfather's death. That must have been Georgia Long.

"How long will you be here in Seattle?" He clasped her fingers more tightly in his.

"I'm not sure." She wiggled her fingers and he released some of the pressure.

"I hope we'll see each other again. Maybe get better acquainted."

She didn't answer. Instead, her gaze roamed around the room, never coming to rest on his face. *What is that all about?* He wondered if he'd offended her.

He gave another whirl and realized that Georgia was watching Maggie with some intensity. And he could see why. This was Maggie's party, so she should be having a good time. But evidently, she wasn't.

The music stopped and he led his partner back to the chair where she had been sitting. After she slid onto the cushioned seat, he bowed and thanked her for the dance.

Charles made his way back to the spot where he could watch Maggie. Something was going on with her. She didn't smile and laugh as she always had before. Pain and uncertainty bruised the depths of her eyes. She seemed to be hiding a secret from everyone else. One that was painful.

His protectiveness rose up inside him. He wanted to shield her from whatever caused this situation. He wondered who or what had brought this sadness to Maggie. The atmosphere in the Caines' house had been welcoming and comfortable. Some outside force had to be at work here.

Finally Charles saw his chance. Her dancing partner had left for another girl, and Maggie stood by herself.

"May I have this dance, young lady?" He smiled at his old friend.

"Charles." Her eyes lit up while her lips tilted. "I haven't noticed you dancing."

"I've been watching everyone else, except when I danced with your aunt."

"Then why ask me?" She dipped her head slightly and studied him from under her long eyelashes.

She probably didn't realize how provocative that looked, not a good thing if she looked at other men that way. He didn't want any man to take liberties with his good friend.

"I thought you might like to sit out one number. You've been dancing a lot and would welcome a respite. We could get some food and find a quiet corner for a visit."

"What a good idea." She tucked her arm through his. "I know just where we can go so it'll be quiet enough to enjoy conversation."

After they chose their food, she led the way to the library. With the door wide open, they were still part of the festivities, but they could hear each other without having to raise their voices over the general hubbub.

Maggie sat in one plush wing-back chair and placed her plate on the table that sat to one side. She turned up the wick on the lamp beside her plate. "My feet will welcome the rest." She took a bite of chicken and slowly chewed.

Charles chose the chair on the other side of the small table. "Quite a nice party, isn't it?"

"Yes. It's wonderful." Although she showed interest in talking to him, shadows still haunted her eyes. "How is the new merger working out?"

"Just fine. I think of it as a blessing from God. I believe God was looking out for me in my loss." He bit into the sandwich he'd made with his bread and roast beef.

"Do you think He always looks out for us?"

Her question held a note of urgency he didn't understand. He wondered just what could be bothering her. "Of course I do. Don't you?"

She stared into the fireplace where logs blazed, spreading a comforting warmth throughout the room. "Sometimes things happen that might not be for the best."

He shrugged. "We don't always understand why something happens, but the Bible tells us God's plans for us are good."

She quickly turned her attention toward him. He felt her probing gaze. "Are they always? Can't some things happen to mess up those plans?"

He shook his head. "Since God gave us a free will, we can make choices that aren't according to His best plan for us. But there is a verse in the Bible that says God can make all things work together for our good if we love Him. And He does, even if we make wrong choices from time to time." He knew that had been true in his own life.

Once again she seemed to find the fire fascinating. "I hope that's really true." She shook her pretty curls as if trying to shake troubling thoughts from her head and glanced back toward him.

More interested in finding out what was wrong with Maggie than eating, he set his plate down. "I'm sure it is. Why would you think it wasn't?"

"I do have eyes and ears, and I know that things go on in the world that aren't good." Her earnest expression emphasized her quandary.

"Very pretty eyes and ears." He tried to lighten the mood. She was far too intense right now.

Maggie reached both hands toward the sides of her head.

"Please don't hide them."

Becoming color crept into her cheeks. "Mr. Stanton, you are being impertinent."

"I didn't mean to, Margaret. Will you forgive me?" This repartee felt as though they were children again.

She lifted her chin. "I will if you'll go back to calling me Maggie."

"And you must go back to calling me Charles. I'll think you're displeased with me if you call me Mr. Stanton."

When she laughed, he joined her. However, the laughter didn't reach the depths of her eyes.

He sobered. If she could change the subject, so could he. "What's the one thing you want most out of life?"

She took the time to mull over the question before answering. "I want to be a wife and mother someday. Doesn't every young girl?

But I want my life to be more than that. I have a gift for dress designing."

"Did you design that one? It's very becoming."

The blush moved down her throat. "Thank you. No, my grandmother is a well-known dress designer in Little Rock, Arkansas. She owns a design company, and she made this one."

"She knew just what to do to enhance your beauty."

"Mr.…Charles, you're embarrassing me with your flattery. Actually, I've never met my grandmother. She made this dress for my mother when she was younger."

Interesting. Charles had to clamp his lips tight to keep from telling her that it looked better on her than it ever would have on her mother.

"I want to go to Arkansas and meet my grandmother. I'm trying to convince my father to let me go, but my mother is against it. She doesn't want me to become what she calls a *working woman.*" One of her feet beat a staccato against the Persian carpet.

He cringed at the change in her tone when she mentioned Mrs. Caine. So there really was something going on between them. He hadn't just imagined it.

"Don't you think a person should utilize the gifts God gave them?"

At her pointed question, he glanced up at her. "I don't think He gives us talents without a definite reason."

His heart warmed as he read the emotions flitting across her face—surprise, hope, then satisfaction.

"Margaret Lenora Caine!"

The sharp words shattered the comfortable conversation. He whipped around to see Mrs. Caine standing in the open doorway.

"What are you doing hiding in here? Shouldn't you be mingling with your guests?" She glared at her daughter.

Maggie visibly wilted, and the hope in her eyes flickered out. "I'm sorry, Mother." She started to rise.

He jumped to his feet and stepped between Maggie and her mother. "Blame me, Mrs. Caine. I watched your daughter dance so long that it made me tired. I thought she would enjoy a respite for a few minutes."

"Thank you for your kindness, Charles." Maggie pushed past him and walked around her mother, heading for the center of the crowd.

Her mother grimly stared at her back.

Charles didn't know what was going on, but he decided in that instant to be available for Maggie whenever she needed him. He wouldn't make a very good knight in shining armor, but he could be her friend. And it might allow him to get to know her lovely Aunt Georgia, a woman who greatly intrigued him.

Chapter 6

THE REST OF the party stretched on for an eternity. Maggie continued to mingle until they cut the birthday cake. While everyone was enjoying the special dessert, maids entered with their arms filled with parcels. Soon the table in front of the sofa held a multicolored jumble of wrapped presents. Maggie hadn't expected so many. Everyone must have brought something.

Unwrapping all the packages took quite a while, because after she saw what each one contained, she made eye contact with the person who brought it and expressed her thanks verbally. What an array of gifts—colognes, decorative combs, scarves, gloves, trinkets, jewelry, and a box of chocolate, along with books, a sketch pad, charcoal, and paints.

Soon people began to leave, each stopping by where she sat on the couch and wishing her a happy birthday. When only Charles was left in the room, her eyes were drawn to him. She wanted to get to know him better, but what would he think if he knew she wasn't really the daughter of a wealthy family? For years she'd hidden a secret desire to fall in love with this handsome man. But what did he think of her, other than as an old school friend?

"Maggie, I've really enjoyed your birthday party." He lifted her hand and brushed his soft lips against the back of her fingers. "I believe my coach has arrived to take me home."

Maggie stood. "I'm so glad you came. I enjoyed every minute we spent together."

She watched him exit the room and claim his coat from the maid beside the front door. The place where his lips had touched her hand tingled.

Finally, the door shut behind him, and Maggie started packing her presents into boxes for transport to her bedchamber. Even though she didn't look up, she sensed the exact moment Florence came into the room. The air vibrated with her presence. She knew she would have to face the music sometime, and now was as good a time as any. She turned around. Thankfully, Daddy was with Florence.

"Margaret, that's not the dress I told Mrs. Murdock to make for you. Where did you get it?" Florence crossed her arms and stiffened her spine. Her chin rose a couple of inches.

"I didn't see any reason to spend the money on another dress when I really liked this one." She tried to keep the tremble out of her voice, but the evening had tired her out.

"I believe that dress really belongs to me, right?" No softening in Florence's tone or stance.

So that was what bothered her the most. Maggie nodded. "I guess so. I found it in the attic, and I didn't think you'd really mind."

"So without even asking, you took it and did what? Did you hem it to fit you?" Florence stared at the bottom of the skirt.

"No." Maggie clasped her hands at her waist. "I had Mrs. Murdock do that."

Florence paced across the floor, returning to stand squarely in front of Maggie. "Whatever made you sneak into the attic?" The words carried a bite with them.

"Florence!" Concern laced Daddy's words. "Maggie can go to the attic if she wants to. This is her home too."

Florence's glare silenced him. "But she didn't have the right to take something that doesn't belong to her and have it altered." Icicles could have hung from the words.

"A long time ago, Aunt Georgia had told me you brought some of the dresses your mother designed for you when you came west. I just wanted to see something she'd designed." Maggie's voice faded to a whisper by the end of the sentence.

Florence tapped her foot, whether in impatience or anger, Maggie couldn't tell.

"When I saw this one, I knew it would look really good on me.

I'd never seen it, so you haven't worn it for a very long time. I wanted it to be a surprise." That time her voice broke on the last syllable.

Daddy stepped between them. "Florence, I don't think Maggie meant any harm. Maybe we could forgive her. You would never wear that dress again, would you?"

Florence gave her head a tiny shake. "But that's beside the point."

"Maggie, are you sorry you upset your mother?" Daddy's eyes pleaded with her to agree.

"I guess I didn't realize how much it would upset her." Maggie turned toward the woman who had raised her. "Can you forgive me? I had Mrs. Murdock hem it without cutting any of the fabric off. It can be restored to the former length."

"You can keep it." Florence took hold of Daddy's arm with both hands. "Joshua is right. I'll never wear it again. Green really isn't a good color on me."

After her parents left the room, Maggie collapsed on the couch. She'd wanted to startle and surprise Florence, but she hadn't realized that all of this would cause so much of a commotion. She'd probably destroyed any chance she might have had to ever visit Arkansas.

Joshua Caine stood in front of the armoire in the bedroom he shared with his wife. As he unbuttoned his shirt, his thoughts drifted to those early years when he and Florence wanted the same things out of life. Their shared dreams, hopes, and plans. Even when things didn't go the way they wanted them to, they'd clung to each other and forged ahead. When had that changed?

Somehow along the way to the present, their ideas took very divergent paths. He'd wanted to make a good living for Flory and their future family. Then when children didn't come, God had provided a daughter in a most unconventional way. Joshua had been sure that receiving Maggie as a special gift from Angus McKenna would fulfill all his wife's desires for a child. It did his. And Florence had been happy those first few years. He remembered all the wonderful times when the three of them had enjoyed every moment they could spend together.

But as time wore on, Florence changed. Withdrew from his embraces more often than she welcomed them. He missed her loving hugs that warmed the day for him. The occasional peck on the cheek was a poor substitute for the passionate kisses they'd once shared. Just remembering them sent a gentle wind across the banked embers of passion still surviving deep inside him.

Maybe he had been too busy making the money to give her the kind of life she wanted. Or was that his dream rather than hers? Had his emphasis on providing her material things robbed them of their close relationship?

Whatever changed her from the loving, laughing wife and mother, he decided to do everything he needed to get that woman back before it was too late. Perhaps if they returned to their deep emotions for each other, Florence would be better able to accept Maggie the way she was instead of always trying to change her.

Their daughter did have a unique personality. So what if she was vastly different from them? He wasn't exactly sure what mold Florence was trying to force her into, but it wasn't working for any of them. Tomorrow he would try his best to initiate a change for the better.

The door behind him squeaked open. Joshua turned and stared into his wife's beautiful face. His heartbeat quickened. Her blue eyes could warm like the summer sun or turn dark and stormy with the least provocation. And something had provoked her all right.

"I don't know whatever possessed Margaret to defy me the way she did tonight." Florence pressed her fingers across her forehead, moving them back and forth as if trying to rub out the memory of what happened. Such graceful hands. He'd always loved watching them, but not lately when they were clenched into a fist more often than not.

He hurried toward her, deciding he'd not put off until tomorrow what he could begin restoring tonight. "Are you all right? Do you have a headache?" Slipping his arms around her, he cradled her against his chest.

At first she stiffened, but then she relaxed against him. "Yes, my head does hurt." Pain wove itself into the tone of her voice.

He wanted to take every bit of the pain upon himself and release her from its clutches. "Do you want me to get you some tea? Or a warm glass of milk to help you sleep?"

He inhaled the fragrance of citrus and flowers that always resided in her hair. Memories of nights in a covered wagon out in the middle of nowhere with him burying his face in their unbound waves assailed him, almost buckling his knees. Did she remember those times too? He had to restore those memories to her. But he needed to be strong for her right now. He kept a tight rein on his overwhelming desires.

Florence pulled back out of his embrace and dropped onto the stool at her dressing table. "I think I'll be all right if I get ready to retire."

He hunkered beside her and took her hands in his. "We need to talk. There's something I want to do, and I'd like your agreement before I set it in motion."

She shook her head as if to loosen something and then squinted at him. "What are you talking about?"

"I think it's time for us to let Maggie go visit your mother."

She tried to tug her hands from his, but he didn't release them, wanting to make her understand what he was talking about. "It would be good for her *and* good for us."

"I don't think I could stand for her to be gone that long." She stared at the striped wallpaper across the room, her grip tightening.

"I've always been afraid to have her too far from me. Never wanting her out of my sight for more than a few minutes."

He stood and lifted her with him. "She's an adult now, Flory. Nothing will happen to her."

"You can't know that." Panic filled her tone. "Look at what happened to Lenora McKenna." She hadn't spoken that name in years.

Joshua let go of one of her hands and used his fingertips to tilt her face toward him. He studied her beautiful blue eyes, only now seeing the fear hiding deep in them. "That was an entirely different situation. Travel is much safer now, and she's not married and expecting a child. She'll be safe, Flory."

All the starch went out of her, and she grasped the front of his open shirt with one hand. Once more he pulled her close.

"While she's gone, maybe she can discover whatever she wants to know about Agatha...and herself. In the meantime, you and I can reconnect in a deeper way. I want us to spend more time alone together, like we used to early in our marriage."

With a sigh, she collapsed against his chest again, clutching his shirt with both hands. Her tears soaked all the way through to his heart.

"I'd like that."

He hardly heard the whispered words, they were so soft. Pulling her even closer, he held her gently until she relaxed and slipped her arms around him. He leaned down to drop a kiss on the top of her head. *Lord, please let it come to pass.*

Chapter 7

ARRIVING AT THE top of the stairs on the Caine side of the offices on the morning after the party, Charles knocked on the door.

"Come in, come in." Joshua's booming voice carried easily through the barrier. More and more over the last few days, Charles realized the advantages of his partnership with Joshua Caine. The man was brilliant, and his ideas dovetailed with the things Charles wanted to accomplish. His partner's drafting ability transferred to paper just what Charles had envisioned. In addition, Joshua knew skilled craftsmen who could accomplish the remodeling project with the quality they both desired.

Charles opened the door and found his partner's smiling eyes trained on the opening. "Have a seat, young man." Joshua rose and followed him to two leather chairs near the windows.

"I enjoyed the party last night, sir. I'm a bit surprised to find you here so early after all the festivities."

Joshua laughed. "My wife and daughter did all the work. I only had to show up—and pay for it." He paused, then leaned forward. "Have you had a chance to look over the blueprints and construction quotes I had prepared?"

"Yes, sir. From what I've seen, it looks as if we're ready to start construction." Trying to appear nonchalant, Charles crossed his legs and settled back.

Joshua thumped the chair arm, excitement gleaming in his eyes. "I think we should open up the two offices first before we start the work downstairs. That way, we won't have to go outside when we need to talk to each another."

Charles nodded. The man didn't miss a single detail. "You're right."

Joshua whooshed out a breath. "Now I want to talk to you about something else. Something on a more personal note." Joshua paused and stared out toward Puget Sound. "I'll just come right out and tell you. My daughter wants to go to Arkansas to visit her grandmother."

That was no surprise to Charles, but what did it have to do with him?

"Her aunt Georgia has agreed to accompany her."

Disappointment settled on Charles. He'd been hoping he could find a way to get to know Georgia better. If she left in the near future, his pursuit could flounder.

Joshua rose and stood by the window, staring at nothing in particular. Then he turned his attention toward Charles and clasped his hands behind his back before rocking up on his toes and back down again. This must be important. Charles had seen him do this whenever he was thinking through a problem.

"I don't feel right sending two women halfway across the continent without a protector, especially young, attractive women. Too many bad things could happen to them."

Does this mean we can't start construction until he gets back? The disappointment intensified. Once he'd seen the blueprints, he was eager to launch the project.

"I have a very special request for you." Joshua dropped back into the chair. "My wife is reluctant to undertake such a journey, and of course, I would rather not leave either her or the business behind. So, Charles, I wondered if you would agree to accompany them. My daughter is the most important person in my life besides my wife, and I wouldn't entrust her care to just anyone. I know you are dependable."

The way he stared at Charles seemed to call for an answer. "Thank you. But what about the construction project? A journey like that would take quite awhile."

"Yes, it will. Even with the speed of train travel, you'd have to be gone over four weeks, maybe five." Joshua's gaze pierced Charles. "When I was a young man, before I married and settled down, I went from Arkansas to the East Coast. I visited many of the places I'd only read about. What an adventure! Every young man needs the opportunity to travel and broaden his horizons. I'm offering you that, at my expense, of course."

The idea opened all kinds of possibilities in Charles's mind. "And the remodeling?"

"We both agreed we've hired the best men for the job, but it doesn't take two of us here to oversee the project. Besides, there will be a lot of mess until they're finished, so you might be glad to escape the chaos. If I have to contact you for any reason, there's always the telegraph."

"That's a lot to think about." Charles stood and thrust both hands into his front pockets.

"I'm going downstairs to unpack a shipment of men's suits due to arrive this morning. Give you privacy for your pondering." Joshua headed toward the door and pulled it open.

Charles cocked his head to the right. "Just how soon would this journey take place?"

With one hand still on the doorknob, Joshua turned back. "As soon as it can be arranged and the women can get packed. We'd like to fit in the journey before winter arrives."

When the door shut behind his partner, Charles dropped back into the chair. He hadn't ever considered taking a long trip before, but it did sound exciting. The short train rides he'd been on wouldn't compare to one of this magnitude. And he'd be with two women. He'd enjoy being around his childhood friend, but just thinking about spending such a long time in the company of a woman as alluring as Georgia Long awakened a multitude of ideas.

Charles welcomed the opportunity to explore a possible relationship with her. What better way than with a chaperone like Maggie along? And he felt sure she would understand when he gave her aunt more attention. He paced across the office to expend the excitement that continued to build in him. He couldn't wait for Joshua to come back to the office, so he started toward the stairs to the back room of the store below.

Joshua glanced up when he entered the room. He stood beside a large wooden crate with a crowbar. He smiled. "Have you made your decision already?" Surprise tinged his tone.

"I'd be delighted to accompany the women on their journey." Charles hoped he didn't sound as excited as he felt.

With a squeak of iron against wood, the edge of the lid lifted, and Joshua finished pulling it off before turning toward him and clapping him on the shoulder. "You've relieved my mind. Why don't you come to dinner this evening? We can discuss all the details with the women."

"I'd like that."

Charles headed out the door and up the stairs to his own office, thoughts of the journey raising his anticipation. He couldn't get Georgia out of his mind. The dance with her replayed in his thoughts. Every nuance. Each graceful movement. Their conversation. He looked forward to more time with this fascinating and sophisticated woman.

And maybe he could spend a little more time with Maggie. She seemed comfortable around him—relaxed. He wanted to see her and try to find out what was wrong. Perhaps he could help her in some way as he used to when they were younger. He hoped so.

Eighteen. *I'm an adult now.* Maggie knew this was supposed to be true, but she didn't feel one iota different from what she felt yesterday…and the day before that.

She wasn't ready to face Mother again after the fiasco when the guests were all gone last night. At least she had a good reason to stay in her own bedchamber. *My sanctuary.* Although she awoke early, she pretended to be sleeping so she wouldn't be disturbed.

When Ingrid came to her door at 10:00 a.m., Maggie asked her to bring up a light breakfast for both of them. Then the maid could help her decide where each gift should be placed, and Maggie could start writing the thank-you notes. This would keep her busy for the day.

A light tap sounded on the door, and Maggie opened it to Aunt Georgia. "Flo and I are going shopping." Florence's sister sounded chipper this morning. Maggie was thankful she hadn't observed the event after the end of the party. "Do you want to come with us?"

Maggie welcomed the news that she could spend most of the day without seeing Florence. She told her aunt her own plans for the day, and Georgia swept out of the room after dropping a kiss on Maggie's cheek. By the time her blonde maid arrived with their food, the presents were spread across Maggie's bed. With minimal interruptions, the two young women accomplished a lot during the day.

When the older women arrived back at the house, Aunt Georgia came to Maggie's room and settled on the edge of her now-empty bed. "Flo and I had lunch at the Brunswick Hotel. I wish you could have been with us."

Maggie laid down the Waterman fountain pen her father had given for her birthday. Writing with it took much less time than writing with a pen dipped into an inkwell, so she was almost finished with her task. "I would have enjoyed it, I'm sure, but Ingrid helped me get so much accomplished today. Because everyone was generous with gifts at my party, I wanted to thank them promptly. Maybe I'll come next time."

"I hope so." Georgia got up. "Oh, by the way, Flo wanted me to tell you that we're going to have a guest for dinner this evening."

Maggie heaved a sigh. She wasn't ready to entertain anyone yet. "Do you know who it is?"

"Of course I do." Georgia opened the door and started to leave before peeking back around the edge. "But it'll just have to be a surprise to you." She quickly exited and pulled the door shut behind her.

Just what kind of secret was Georgia keeping from Maggie? Her aunt was thirteen years older than her and thirteen years younger than Florence, but sometimes she seemed closer to Maggie's age. Perhaps one of the young men at the party had caught Georgia's eye. Maybe that was who was coming.

Maggie often laughed at her aunt's antics, and today was no exception. Her mood brightened as she glanced through her wardrobe, trying to decide what to wear to dinner. If she knew who was coming, it might make a difference in what she chose. But whatever she wore, it wouldn't be the green dress she'd loved so much yesterday morning. Now it hung as a dismal reminder of the huge mistake she'd made. And she didn't know if she would ever don it again.

Pushing her bleak thoughts aside, Maggie dressed quickly, choosing a navy dress with a froth of ecru lace on the bodice. Minutes later, as she descended the stairs, someone knocked. Maybe it was the mystery dinner guest.

Maggie opened the front door and stared into Charles Stanton's deep brown eyes. The intensity with which he returned her gaze made her heart flutter. She placed one hand on her throat, trying to calm down.

"Come in, Charles." She pulled the door wider and stepped back. "I knew we were expecting a guest tonight, but I had no idea it was you."

He stopped beside her. "You look lovely, Maggie." He glanced over her shoulder. "And where is your aunt Georgia?"

"She'll be down soon." She surveyed him, analyzing the cut of his jacket, the tilt of his perfectly groomed head. Charles had changed since he went to university. He had a flair about him that she wasn't sure she liked. He wasn't as down-to-earth as she remembered, nor was he the obliging older boy who had looked out for her.

Daddy came down the stairs to greet Charles. He shook his hand and clapped him on the shoulder at the same time. "Good to see you, partner. Let's go into my study."

Maggie watched the two men walk away, relieved her father would distract Charles. She wasn't sure how to talk to this newly self-assured young man. She went into the parlor and picked up the *Harper's Bazar* magazine Florence had left on the table. As she turned the pages, she glanced at the few pictures, but not a word of the text stuck in her mind.

"So this is where you're hiding." Georgia came in and took a seat on the couch beside her. "Is that the latest edition?"

Maggie glanced at the cover. "Yes. Do you want to look at it?" She held out the periodical.

"Only if you're finished with it."

"I was just killing time until dinner is served." Maggie thrust the magazine into her aunt's hands.

"Let's see what other women are wearing right now." Georgia eagerly turned the pages, then stopped. "Look at this spiderweb lace with the flowers."

Maggie bent over the drawing and studied it. Some of its features could work in a design that had been dancing through her thoughts for several days. "I'm going to get my sketchbook. I'll be right back."

When she returned, Georgia looked up. "So what are you going to sketch now?"

Maggie used charcoal first. With a few quick strokes, she had the general shape of the dress. Georgia looked over her shoulder. For some reason, Maggie didn't mind her aunt watching her draw, but she would have been a bundle of nerves if Florence were that close to her while she worked on a dress design.

A memory from long ago flashed through her head. Holding a lead pencil, a much-younger Maggie drew a picture on a tablet. Mother hovered over her, praising every mark she made. *Why doesn't she encourage me like that today?* Maggie wasn't sure she was ready to hear the answer to that question.

Maybe she really didn't want to know at all.

"I thought I'd find you here."

Maggie glanced up from her nearly finished drawing. Her mother stood in the archway between the parlor and the foyer. Something had changed since last night. Florence smiled at both of them. Maybe she was no longer angry with Maggie.

"Go ahead to the dining room. I'll get the men." Florence headed down the hallway.

Maggie closed her sketch pad and picked up her drawing tools. "I'll run these up to my room."

"And I'll go on into the dining room. Mrs. Jorgensen might need a little help."

Maggie doubted that. With her granddaughter Ingrid's help, their housekeeper probably already had everything under control.

When Maggie arrived at the table, the two men stood behind their chairs. Florence was already seated at the opposite end from Daddy, and Georgia sat near her. The only empty seat was next to Daddy and across from Charles. Maggie would enjoy facing him during the meal. Maybe she could find traces of her old friend while she watched him. She headed toward that chair.

Charles beat her to it. "Let me help you."

She dropped carefully into the chair while he smoothly pushed it just the right distance from the table. He returned to his side of the table, and both men sat down. She thanked him quietly.

Ingrid and her grandmother came in with soup bowls filled with food that filled the room with a delicious aroma. Following Florence's lead, everyone covered their laps with the white linen napkins.

Daddy waited until everyone was situated. "Let's return thanks for this wonderful food." His heartfelt prayer was soon over, and everyone could begin eating.

Conversation flowed smoothly through four wonderful courses— soup, a broiled fish dish, beef Wellington with green peas and mashed potatoes, and a honey applesauce cake. Maggie was hungrier than she had been in a long time, so she enjoyed every morsel.

When Daddy finished, he placed his fork quietly on his crystal dessert plate. "I asked Charles to join us for dinner because we have come up with another brilliant plan."

Maggie glanced at the man across from her, and his lips tilted into a crooked smile. *So he's kept a secret from me too.*

Daddy took hold of her hand that rested on the table beside her plate. "Maggie, your mother and I decided last night that it's time for you to visit your grandmother. And since it's been awhile since Georgia has been home, she's going to accompany you."

"Really?" Maggie felt like jumping up and hugging her father. She knew the trip was his idea. How had he ever convinced Florence it was a good thing?

"Yes, really." Daddy tilted his head down to gaze at her.

"And you're going, Aunt Georgia? That's wonderful." She wanted to laugh out loud and shout it from the rooftops. Finally she would get to do the thing she'd wanted to do for ever so long.

Georgia smiled at her. "I've been wanting to visit Mother, so when Joshua and Flo asked me, I jumped at the chance. It's not really a good thing for a woman to travel alone that far, by train or any other means."

"It's hard to believe that I'm going to Arkansas." Maggie stared out the window at the sky just as a bird soared by. Soon she would be as free as that bird.

Daddy gave her hand a squeeze, drawing her attention back to him. "And I've arranged for Charles to go with the two of you as an escort. I'd hate to send women who are precious to me on such a long trip without a man to look out for them. Not everyone in this country is honest. And there are scoundrels who would take advantage of unescorted women. You will be traveling through some parts of the country that aren't as civilized as it is here in Seattle."

Maggie shot a glance at Charles then pulled her hand away and clasped both of hers in her lap. "I don't know what to say. Just how soon will this journey take place?"

Florence cleared her throat. "I told your father we'd be able to get both of you ready in a week, so he's going to purchase tickets for that Monday. That is, if it's all right with you."

For a moment, Maggie couldn't even think straight. She'd be going to Arkansas in about a week. She let that fact soak in. Then she jumped up and gave her father a hug followed by a hug for her mother. The quick embrace lingered when Florence clasped her close and didn't let go. She couldn't remember the last time her mother had hugged her like that. She decided to enjoy it while she could. Sometime soon, she would have to ask her parents about the adoption paper she found. But that could wait until after she returned from Arkansas.

And Charles would be going with them. She glanced at him. Maybe they could get to know each other on a deeper level on the trip, since they were both more grown up than they were when they spent so much time together during their school years.

But Charles was watching Georgia, a small smile curving his lips. Maggie felt her heart sink just a little. The handsome Charles evidently had eyes only for her aunt.

Chapter 8

A WEEK LATER MAGGIE stood on the platform of the Columbia and Puget Sound railroad depot with her parents and Aunt Georgia. A brisk gust blew her skirt against her legs and almost lifted her hat from her head. She grasped it with one hand and held it down.

Her father had purchased their tickets ahead of time, so when they got to the station, all he had to do was make sure their luggage was loaded. In addition to their carpetbags, which they would keep with them, Maggie and Georgia each had a trunk. These held not only their clothing and essentials but also gifts for Maggie's grandmother.

Her family had arrived at the depot early, and Maggie wondered if Charles was going to miss the train. Finally, his driver brought him in his open landau. He climbed from the buggy, and his driver handed him a carpetbag and a leather portmanteau.

Maggie gazed across the tracks toward Puget Sound. The weather was just right for traveling. No rain today. Just warm autumn sunshine and a welcome wind blowing across the Sound keeping the air from feeling oppressive. She wondered how long the warm weather would linger. She hoped they would return before winter had an icy grip on Seattle and on the mountains they'd have to cross in the train.

"Are you excited our day of departure is finally here?" Charles stood much closer behind her than she had been aware.

If she turned too quickly, she might bump right into him. She took a deep breath, stepped away, then pivoted. "Yes. Are you?"

One of his sculptured eyebrows lifted. "Certainly, I'm glad to be going." His gaze slid to her aunt, and he broke away to greet her.

Maggie watched them talk, saw her aunt laugh in response to some comment he made, saw him smile. *Does that man know how devastating his smile is?* She certainly hoped he didn't. He could be a danger to every unattached woman in sight. She pulled her gaze from Charles and stared across the water.

In the distance, a mournful whistle broke the silence around them. Soon the clackety-clacks of the huge engine pulling the railcars joined with the wail. The train came into sight around a bend as it exited the forest surrounding Seattle, and Maggie's sense of expectancy grew. Within literal minutes they'd be heading south. The railroad would take them into Oregon before they headed east. And if she remembered correctly, it would take them all the way across the state of Missouri, where they'd change trains and head southwest into Arkansas.

She had heard stories, though not from her parents, about the months it took to come from Independence, Missouri, to Oregon. Those travelers probably marveled that people could now make that journey in less than two weeks. Modern travel was a wonder.

Maggie had never been on the platform when a train came in. As the iron monster approached, the wooden structure vibrated, and she widened her stance to help maintain her balance. Up close, the engine was enormous. Almost scary. What if it jumped the tracks? She stepped back as she watched it pull into the station, accompanied by metal screeching against metal and hissing puffs of steam.

As soon as the train came to a complete stop, the conductor hopped down from the steps on the middle passenger car. "You folks takin' this train?" He removed his uniform hat and tucked it under his arm.

Father stepped forward. "My daughter, my sister-in-law, and my business partner are." He indicated each one when he mentioned them. "I'd appreciate it if you'd take good care of them."

"Sure thing." The conductor slapped his hat back on his head. "This here's one of them Pullman cars. They'll be comfortable in it."

Father nodded, then he and Charles accompanied the conductor to the end of the train where freight cars were hooked up right in front of the caboose. The three men loaded the two trunks and portmanteau onto one of the baggage cars.

Mother clasped Maggie into a tight embrace. "I'll miss you, Margaret. I've seen you every single day since you were born. You be careful while you're gone."

Tears trickled down Maggie's cheeks. How could her mother have seen her since the day she was born? Did she and her father get her the actual day of her birth? So many questions without answers, but Maggie wasn't going to ask them until she got back from Arkansas. Maybe by then she'd have the courage to tell them what she had found in the white box nestled in the very bottom of her trunk. Maybe then she could ask all the questions rattling around in her brain.

Still clinging to her, Mother pressed a soft kiss to one of Maggie's cheeks. How long had it been since she'd felt this connected to her mother?

"Good-bye, Mother."

Daddy and Charles returned. Daddy wrapped his arms around Maggie and cradled her against his chest. Tears pooled in her eyes, making everything she could see melt together. Then they made their way down her cheeks.

"I love you, Maggie girl." His voice hitched on the endearing name he'd called her most of her life. "I'll miss you. Even when I didn't come home from work until after you were asleep, I came into your room and kissed you goodnight. I can't do that while you're gone." The last words came out as a husky whisper.

When he released her, he pulled a pristine white handkerchief from his back pocket and wiped the streaks from her face. "I hope you find what you need while you're with Agatha. I think she'll be good for you."

A sob escaped from Maggie's throat, and Daddy pressed the large cotton square into her hands. "You need this more than I do."

She dabbed her eyes, trying to erase the evidence of her weeping.

She looked toward the railroad car. Charles stood at the bottom step near the conductor.

Daddy walked with her to where the conductor stood and handed the man the tickets.

Charles offered his hand to help Georgia onto the train. When she stood on the small platform outside the door of the car, he reached toward Maggie. She slipped her hand into his and allowed him to lift her aboard. Soon all three were clustered on the small platform with their punched tickets in their hands.

"Aaalll aboooard!" The conductor's voice rang out before he swung himself up onto the platform too.

More screeching of metal and hissing of steam accompanied the slow, jerky movement as the magnificent machine chugged forward. Maggie clung to the railing trying to maintain her balance. The train moved faster and faster, accompanied by the incessant clacking as the engine pulled them away from the station, away from her family, and away from her home.

The conductor opened the door and ushered them inside. Maggie walked down the length of the car, keeping pace with her parents as they walked alongside the train as far as they could on the platform. All three waved the whole time. When Maggie could no longer see her parents, she dropped her hand. Why had she insisted on leaving them? Already she missed their comforting presence.

"We can sit here." Charles stood beside her, indicating two bench seats upholstered in worn red velvet and facing each other.

Georgia moved out of the aisle, then turned back. "Do you want to sit by the window, Maggie, or would you prefer the aisle seat?"

Maggie didn't remember the trip from Oregon City; all she had seen was Seattle and that one trip to Portland. Now they were going halfway across the vast continent. She didn't want to miss a single thing on the journey.

"I'd like to sit by the window." Maggie eased onto the bench with the thin padding. This would probably become uncomfortable before long.

Charles sat across from her. "This is a sleeping car. For the night, this area will be changed into upper and lower sleeping berths."

He must have known what she was thinking. Then his words sunk in. She glanced around the car. Although it wasn't full, by any means, there were several people sharing the space. A family with two young children. A scruffy old man and two other men who appeared to be traveling salesmen. Another couple huddled close together, ignoring everyone else. *Quite a motley crew.*

"We're supposed to sleep with these strangers?" Maggie hoped none of them heard her.

Georgia laughed. "These berths have privacy curtains. You and I can probably share a berth, and Charles can take the other one."

That's a relief. "But where will we change clothes?"

Georgia leaned close and whispered. "There are necessary rooms at the ends of the cars. You can go there to change, or we can just don our bedclothes inside the berth. On previous trips I've done it both ways."

As the train traveled inland, Maggie enjoyed seeing the various landscapes that slid past the windows. Lush grasslands, high mountain peaks, streams, forests, wildlife. Soon the car became stuffy as the sun rose higher in the sky.

"Can we open these windows?" Maggie fanned herself with her hand.

"I'll do it if you're sure you want me to." Charles stood and reached for the latch. "The only thing is, when the windows are open, soot often comes into the car. See the film it's forming on the outside of the glass?"

Georgia fingered her buttons. "Maybe we could just remove our jackets. We'd be more comfortable that way."

Maggie was willing to try anything to get some relief. She slipped her arms out of her fitted spencer. The space felt cooler with just her long-sleeve dimity blouse tucked into her suit skirt.

Georgia pulled the picnic basket from under their seat. "Is anyone besides me hungry?"

Charles dropped back onto his bench. "I could do with some food about now. What do we have?"

"Knowing Mrs. Jorgensen, probably enough to feed an army." Maggie lifted the hinged lid and enticing aromas of roast beef and something spicy permeated the air around them.

She looked up and noticed that the people sitting near them glanced longingly toward the food. She lowered her voice. "We can't eat in front of these people. I wouldn't feel right about it."

Georgia made a quick scan of the car. "There are less than a dozen people, counting us. Maybe some of them have been on the train for quite a while. Do you think we have enough to share?"

Maggie nodded. "But what will we do for food after it's all gone?"

Charles raked his long fingers through his hair. "The train will have to stop to take on fuel and water. Usually we can buy food where it stops. Besides, some of this will spoil before we can eat all of it."

"Then let's divide what we have." Maggie lifted the tea towel covering the food.

A large mound of sandwiches lay beneath, along with apples and cookies. Plenty to share with everyone, even the conductor if he came through their car. She put the tea towel on the seat beside Georgia and unloaded enough food for the three of them.

"Charles, will you help me distribute this?"

He grinned at her. "At your service, ma'am." He gave a low bow from the waist.

"Don't go getting all highfalutin on me." Maggie moved into the aisle and walked to the end of the car.

Charles followed her, carrying the basket. As they moved back down the aisle, she asked each passenger if he or she would like something to eat. All but one of them accepted the food. Each time she handed a sandwich, an apple, and a cookie to someone, her heart expanded a tiny bit more.

Some of the people appeared to have been traveling a long time. A few wore clothing that was ragged and worn. Maggie treated each person with the same deference, and they thanked her profusely.

Florence had been active in helping the poor in Seattle, but she never let Maggie go with her. This was a completely new experience, one Maggie would never forget. For the first time, she shared what she had and accepted the blessings spoken to her in return.

After they finished their meal, Georgia packed away the remaining food and tucked the tea towel around it.

During the afternoon, Maggie got tired and fell asleep with her head leaning against the window. When she awoke from her nap, her neck had a crick in it, and Georgia gently snored with her chin resting on her chest. She would probably also have a sore neck when she woke up.

Maggie tried to rub the pain out of her neck and shoulder, but it didn't work. Charles leaned toward her and told her to shift over to sit beside him, so they wouldn't awaken Georgia. He had her turn with her back to him, and he rubbed until her pain left her. No one had ever done anything like that for her. She turned around to thank him and found his face very close to hers.

He stared into her eyes, and she couldn't look away. Some unseen force connected them in a way she didn't understand. Her stomach tightened and her heart fluttered, but still she couldn't break the visual contact. Finally, he blew out a deep breath and turned his attention out the window. She sat with her hands clasped until Georgia gave a soft snort that woke her up.

Maggie moved back beside her, and they started a conversation.

After several minutes, Georgia lifted her gaze toward Maggie's curls. "You know, a funny thing happened before I left Portland."

"Really? What?" Maggie clasped her hands around her crossed knee.

"I thought I saw you." Georgia gave a short laugh. "I even followed the man and young woman until they went inside a store. Her hair looked just like yours. Same color, same curls. She wore it pulled back with a ribbon like you used to when you were younger. But she looked to be the same age as you. She walked the same way you do. I thought maybe you and Flo had come to Portland to surprise me."

This was really interesting. Even Charles had turned from the window to listen.

"So how did you find out it wasn't me?"

Georgia stared down the aisle toward where the conductor had entered the car. "She stopped to feel a silk scarf on the counter. Her skin looked a lot like yours only with a bit of a tan, like she had been out in the sun a lot. And her nose was covered with freckles."

Maggie giggled. "Mine would be too if I didn't protect it."

"I've heard that sometimes people meet someone who has an uncanny resemblance to themselves." Charles stared at Maggie. "Maybe this person is your double. Perhaps we could find her if we went to Portland."

"She might have come from anywhere. Right, Aunt Georgia?" Maggie would like to meet the woman, but that wasn't very likely. *My double?* That would really be something, wouldn't it?

Chapter 9

Y THE TIME the beautiful sunset spread across the sky behind the train and faded into twilight, Maggie was thoroughly exhausted. The thin padding of the train seat had all but disappeared, and her backside felt as if she were riding on a slab of rock. She stood and stretched to get the kinks out of her shoulders, then donned the spencer once again. Since the sun took the warmth with it, the railway car was now getting rather cool.

"We still have a little food left in the basket." Georgia pulled it from under the seat. "Perhaps we should finish eating all of it before anything spoils."

Maggie dropped back onto the bench, then wished she had one of the thick pillows from her bed back home to sit on. But more than that, she wished she had some inkling of what they'd find in Arkansas and if she could learn anything about her past from her grandmother. Was she on a futile journey? She hoped not.

Georgia parceled out the remaining three sandwiches. Maggie sank her teeth into the roast beef between thick slices of buttered, hearty wheat bread. Charles reached into the basket for the three Mason jars half-full of water and handed one to each of the women before screwing the lid off his. The liquid was lukewarm from sitting on the hot train all day, but Maggie's throat welcomed the fluid as an accompaniment to her sandwich.

"This stuff tastes good, doesn't it?" Georgia slowly chewed her first bite. "I'm going to savor it while I can. We probably won't get good cooking like Mrs. Jorgensen's every place we stop."

Soon Maggie had eaten all her sandwich. She picked up one of the last three apples. "I'm going to eat this and save the cookie for breakfast in case we don't have anything else. Since they're oatmeal raisin, it will almost be like eating the cooked cereal."

"It'll probably taste better." The face Charles made indicated to Maggie that he might not like hot oatmeal.

Charles finished off his apple and held out his hand for Georgia's and Maggie's cores. He headed to the end of the car and went out on the little platform. When he came back in, the cores were gone. How easy it was to toss things away. Had her mother tossed her away like an unwanted apple core? The thought hurt more than she'd anticipated. She didn't want to be just someone's unwanted garbage.

The conductor worked his way down the car, lighting the small lamps attached to the walls. Even though the light gave only a feeble yellow glow, Maggie welcomed the respite from total darkness. When the man finished that job, he started at one end of the railcar and folded out the berths where people were sitting. Several rows were empty, even the benches across the aisle from where Maggie, Georgia, and Charles sat.

"You want to use one of the berths on this side too?" The conductor reached toward the latch holding the wooden contraption in place. "That way you won't be so crowded."

They all agreed that would be best. One of Maggie's worries taken care of. She'd been dreading sharing a berth with Georgia. She loved her aunt dearly, but Maggie was used to sleeping by herself. She had already decided she might not get much sleep on the train because of sharing such a narrow bed. Now the problem had disappeared. She wished her other problems would disappear just as easily.

Georgia lifted her carpetbag up on the bench across from where they sat. "I'm going to just dress for bed while inside the berth."

"Me too." Maggie didn't even want to pull her nightdress out of her bag with all the prying eyes around them. She'd just wait until she was inside her sleeping area.

Charles had been walking from one end of the car to the other, stretching his legs. After several passes by them, he stopped. "You two should take the bottom berths. It'll be easier for me to climb into the upper one."

Georgia smiled up at him. "You're just full of good suggestions, Charles. Thanks for helping us so much."

"Just paying for my keep." He gave one if his signature bows, and the two women shared a laugh. "Always glad to help a pretty lady."

His gaze drifted toward Georgia when he said that. Was the silly man flirting with her aunt? *Surely not.*

"Oh, go on with you." Georgia waved him away. "At least you're keeping our journey from becoming too boring."

Maggie wasn't so sure she agreed with her aunt. The trip had lost its luster before the middle of the afternoon, and there were so many more days to go. But she did agree that Charles kept everything lively for them.

"Do you know why we are going south before we can head east?" Charles rested one ankle on his other knee and leaned back.

"Not really." She wondered where he was going with this conversation.

"Because the tracks lead us there." He laughed.

"That is so obvious." She rolled her eyes. "I thought you were going to tell us something important." She glanced at Georgia who covered her smile with her fingertips.

"I'm sure that someday, trains will crisscross this country in many directions." Charles lowered his eyelids as if he were thinking hard. "But right now, there are only a few places where the rails have been laid across the mountains. And that's where we have to go. The rails will lead us into Denver. Isn't that right, Georgia?"

Maggie noticed that his voice softened somehow when he said her aunt's name. *What is wrong with Charles?* Didn't he realize that Georgia was much too old for him? He needed to set his sights on someone closer to his own age. *Like me.*

But Charles wouldn't ever look at her as anything but the younger sister he never had. He hadn't even noticed she'd grown up.

"Yes, we always spent a night in a hotel in Denver on the trips back home."

"And who traveled with you, pretty lady?" Charles dropped his foot back to the floor and leaned both forearms on his thighs.

Pink seeped into Georgia's cheeks. "My husband."

Maggie had never seen such a look of consternation on Charles's face in all the time she had known him.

"I...I didn't know you were married." He had never stuttered before either.

Georgia gazed at him for a moment before answering. "I'm not. I'm a widow."

He gulped, then smiled. "A very lovely widow at that."

Maggie wondered if she was going to have to put up with his flirting on the whole trip. What had come over her level-headed friend? Some chaperone he would be.

He stared out the window as the train chugged across a tall bridge over a stream below. "I read something interesting the other day."

"And what was that?" She would welcome anything to take his mind off of flirting shamelessly with her aunt.

"You know how all the rivers run toward the West Coast." He pointed to the water flowing under them. "It's not like that all over the United States. The Rocky Mountain Range has an area called the Continental Divide. All the rivers on the other side of that ridge run toward the east, while all those on this side run toward the west."

"Did you know that, Aunt Georgia?" Maggie glanced at her aunt, who had been sitting silently for a while.

"Actually, I did, but I had forgotten about it."

Maggie stared out the window. She hadn't forgotten how she felt when Charles had helped rid her of the crick in her neck. When his fingers first touched her shoulders, tingles traveled up and down her spine. She welcomed the warmth of his hands and felt bereft when he removed them. Because he was such a gentleman, he didn't let them linger overlong.

She shook herself. She shouldn't read anything more into his touch. Since he didn't treat her any differently than he had before, she must be the only one who experienced something extra from the encounter. Clearly, she wasn't the object of his interest. And she didn't care. She really didn't. At least, not much.

After bidding her companions goodnight, Maggie set her carpetbag at the end of her berth away from the lumpy pillow, then sat on the bed, pulling her feet up and closing the curtains. The mattress was thicker than the padding on the seats, but not a lot. She tugged off her shoes and set them beside the bag. She gathered her nightdress, robe, and slippers from the luggage. As she had imagined, undressing and putting on her nightclothes wasn't easy in the confined space. Dressing in a berth at the same time as her aunt would have been virtually impossible.

After bumping her head more than once and bouncing around a little when the train went around a curve, Maggie finally had her clothes changed. She slid under the covers—a rough sheet and a scratchy blanket—far different from the luxurious covers on her bed at home. Deciding to make the best of it, she wadded the thin pillow under her head and tried to relax. During the daytime, she'd become accustomed to the unusual noises and movement of the train, but in her completely dark, solitary space, everything seemed magnified. She shifted around, trying to get comfortable, then clenched her eyes closed as tight as she could.

Sleep didn't come. An out-of-tune symphony of snoring sounds, both soft and loud, fought for supremacy with the annoying clacking and creaking of the train. In the daytime she'd been able to push thoughts of her secret to the back of her mind. But now, in the dark of night, they haunted her. Like specters from the past, they arose and surrounded her, taunted her.

Both her mother and father had made her cry before she boarded the train, not out of cruelty, but with kindness and tenderness. Yet why would they have kept the truth of her birth from her? Didn't they understand how cruel that was?

Other questions bombarded her. Even though Mother treated her much nicer since Daddy announced she could go on this trip, too many memories of her being critical flooded Maggie's mind. What was wrong with her that she could never please her mother?

And most important of all, why did her real mother and father give her away? Tears leaked from her eyes, wetting much of the pillow long before she finally drifted into fitful slumber.

Chapter 10

DRESSING FOR BED had been hard, but Maggie found that putting on her clothes before she left the protection of the berth was more of a nightmare. And she didn't have either a mirror or a maid to help fix her hair. Because she only pulled out the hairpins but didn't brush her hair and braid it last night, her curls were more tangled than a rat's nest. No matter how she tried to gently brush the knots out, she only succeeded in pulling her hair, bringing fresh tears to her eyes. The tears caused by her tender scalp were soon joined by those left over from last night. *What am I doing on this train heading toward a woman who really isn't my grandmother?* She must be crazy. But she had to meet Agatha Carter. Maybe when she talked with the famous dress designer, she'd finally get advice about her own dreams of being a designer.

Although railroad tracks looked to be smooth, the ride belied that fact. The passenger car jerked and swayed, making her task of fixing her hair even more impossible. Maybe she should just give up, climb back between the sheets, pull the covers over her head, and stay there all day.

Maggie used the brush to smooth the top of her hair, then pulled it back and tied it with a ribbon. That would have to do for today. She was tired of fighting with the mess. Why couldn't she have sleek dark hair like Aunt Georgia? Because she really wasn't blood kin. *That's why.* A few more tears streamed down her cheeks. What a mess she was this morning.

Before Maggie was ready to climb out of the berth, the conductor walked the length of the car. Along the way, he called out, "Train's gonna stop in 'bout an hour. We'll be in the station fer a while. You'll be able to get off and stretch your legs. Get somethin' to eat."

Maggie pulled her curtains back and slid her feet toward the floor. With the opportunity to get off the train for a while, maybe today wouldn't be so bad.

❖ ❖ ❖

When the engineer started applying the noisy brakes as they approached the town, Charles glanced out the window, hoping for a variety of eating places to choose from. Unfortunately, this was only a whistle stop, a small cluster of ramshackle buildings around the depot and water tank.

Georgia glanced up. "Wonder where we are."

"In the state of Oregon." The conductor said as he hurried past them on the way to the front of the car.

Maggie frowned. "Oregon? I thought we'd be farther than that by now." She sounded so disappointed. Since she exited her berth, Maggie had been noticeably quieter. Every time Charles had glanced at her, she'd turned her face away, but he noticed the red splotches crying had left on her face. What was wrong with her—homesickness? They'd only just started. How would she survive the rest of the trip?

The train shuddered to a complete stop, and he stood. "Ladies, I'd like to escort you off the train. We can get some exercise, and I'll purchase food for us." He held out his arm to Georgia.

After she slipped her hand around one elbow, they started toward the door at the end of the car, but Maggie didn't follow them. When Georgia glanced back at her and cleared her throat, Maggie looked up.

"All right. I'm coming." She arose and followed their lead.

"Let us be off." Charles helped Georgia down from the car, then turned to Maggie. "May I assist you, too, Miss Caine?"

His comment brought a tiny curl to her lips. "Of course, Mr. Stanton." She kept her face averted from him. "I'm a real mess this morning."

He leaned closer and whispered for her ears alone. "You could never be a mess, Maggie. Why, just look at them there curls waving in the breeze."

The absurdity of his words teased a full-blown smile to her face.

After they exited the car, bright morning sunlight bathed them with warmth as well as brilliance. Maggie squinted until her eyes adjusted to the difference. "Where's the town?"

"This is it." Charles waved his arm to encompass the few buildings. They made their way over to a building labeled Hardy's Hotel. Enticing aromas of smoked meat and biscuits met them at the swinging doors to the establishment. "Something smells good enough to eat, doesn't it?"

With no printed menu in sight, a woman served them plates filled with ham, scrambled eggs, and hot biscuits dripping with butter. The only breakfast available for the day. Without wasting too much time with conversation, they all three enjoyed the delicious food.

After their plates were clean, Charles signaled the waitress to come to their table. "Ma'am, that was some fine cooking. Be sure to tell the cook we said so."

"Name's Maud, chief cook and bottle washer too." A smile wreathed her face, and a jolly laugh shook her whole body as if she had been the first person to ever say that timeworn phrase.

"Then my compliments for your skills." Charles tried to encourage people whenever he could.

"Well, don't that beat all." Maud stood a little taller. "Ain't nobody tole me that before. Them's mighty fancy words."

"And sincerely spoken." Charles winked, and both Georgia and Maggie smiled at their bantering.

Several of the other diners stopped eating and leaned forward to listen. Charles felt as if they were the floor show, and their stage was a rustic dining room with handmade tables worn smooth by who knew how many diners.

"Kin I get you and your women anything else?" Maud's voice cut into his thoughts.

At those words, Maggie's eyebrows rose and her mouth puckered into an O. Georgia laughed. Charles loved hearing her. She was a very young widow, but since she didn't wear her wedding ring, her husband probably had been gone awhile. She needed attention from a man like himself. One who could appreciate her beauty and help her move on. A man with a promising future.

Charles stood and offered his hand to Maud. "I'm Charles Stanton, a businessman from Seattle, and I'm accompanying Miss Margaret Caine and her aunt, Mrs. Georgia Long, to Little Rock, Arkansas."

The woman gave his hand a quick shake, then turned toward Maggie and Georgia. "Sorry I got that wrong. Welcome to Hardy. Ole Will Hardy named this little town after hisself, since he was the one what built the first building here along the tracks."

"We were delighted to see a place to get good food." Georgia wiped her mouth then laid her napkin beside her empty plate.

"Actually, Maud." Charles smiled at the friendly woman. "I wondered if we could purchase provisions to take on the train. I'm not sure when we'll stop again."

Maud led him toward a door that opened into the tiny lobby of the hotel. "Where'd you say you was headed?"

"Arkansas." He glanced around the room with only a desk to check in at the hotel and a couple of wooden chairs beside the window.

"You probably won't find much to eat until sometime tomorrow." Maud pulled from her apron pocket a large metal ring with several keys clinking together. She unlocked another door at the back of the lobby. "We keep extra supplies on hand, and I can sell you some."

They entered a large storeroom practically crammed to the ceiling with an abundance of fresh produce, canned goods, utensils, sacks of supplies hidden from view, and even tools. Charles scanned the shelves and stacks on the floor. "Would you mind if I get our basket off the train? Maybe we can fill it."

"Sure. I'll wait fer you." Maud waved him away.

When he returned, she helped him gather fresh apples, canned peaches, canned meat, canned vegetables, cheese, and crackers. These would keep if they didn't eat them all before they stopped for food again.

"I can also wrap up the extra biscuits and ham, if you'd like." She headed out the door, then turned back. "You need a can opener?"

"Yes."

"They's some on that there shelf." She made sure he found them before leaving.

Charles liked this friendly woman. She quickly met their needs, and the price she charged was reasonable.

Maggie felt much better when she and Georgia climbed onto the train. The bright sunlight and good food, and watching the way Charles treated people, had cheered her. But they had done nothing to make the seat more comfortable. She sat down and tried to find a position where her backside didn't hurt. The smashed-down stuffing felt nonexistent.

Georgia slipped onto the bench beside Maggie. "Want me to help you with your hair?" she whispered.

Maggie held back a gasp. She'd hoped no one would notice what a mess it was. Of course, Georgia knew how meticulous she usually was about her appearance. "Do you think you can do anything with it?"

"We probably have several minutes before the train loads and pulls out. Get me your brush, and I'll try to finish before anyone else comes into this car."

Maggie pulled the brush from her carpetbag and handed it to her. Georgia untied the ribbon and started working on the knots from the tips of her hair and moving toward her scalp as she got more and more of it untangled.

In only a few minutes, Maggie could run her fingers through her curls. She relished the feeling. Before she had felt so unkempt, but now she'd look more civilized. "That's marvelous. How did you learn to do that?"

Georgia handed her the brush. "Actually, our mother has very curly hair. When we were girls, we often brushed it. That was one of my favorite things to do."

Maggie had never had anyone who enjoyed taking care of her hair, except Ingrid, and that was only the last couple of years. "Do you think I should try to put my hair up during the daytime?" Maggie pushed the brush back into her luggage.

"Not necessarily. On the train, it would be easier to just pull it back during the daytime and maybe go ahead and braid it at night." Georgia helped her tie the tresses and make a pretty bow with the ribbon.

"Aaalll aboooard!" The conductor's familiar call rang out just before Charles came through the door, carrying their picnic basket and a burlap bag.

"Well, ladies, we're all set for the next few days." He sat down opposite the women and began to display the bounty he'd acquired. "After we filled the basket, Maud wanted to give me this 'tow sack' for the rest of the items."

The way he mimicked the woman in the hotel made Maggie laugh.

"My goodness, that's quite a spread." Georgia clapped her hands.

"Our friendly 'chief cook and bottle washer,' as she called herself, sold all this to me. I think she took a liking to us." A huge smile spread across his face.

Maggie thought he sounded a little too pleased with himself, but then she decided he deserved a little praise for the way he provided for them. "Thank you, Charles. I appreciate all you've been doing for us."

His eyes lit up when she said that. She hadn't stopped to think that he was making a real sacrifice, leaving his business in her father's hands and traveling so far with them. Even though her father was very capable of taking care of things, Charles's thoughts must often return to what he left behind. Maybe she should pay more attention to letting him know how much they needed him.

The train started moving, accompanied by its usual squealing and hissing, and in an odd sort of way, the sounds were comforting. Maggie looked toward the front of the car. No one sat between them and the doorway. Their seats were about a third of the way back. She twisted on the bench and glanced the other direction. Only three people sat in all the area behind them.

"Where is everyone?" she asked Charles.

"A couple of people got off at Hardy. And the family moved to the next passenger car where there are other children. I overheard them saying the children could help amuse each other." He stopped and gazed at her until she felt like squirming. "Are you afraid of spending time with me without many people around?"

The quirk of his lip revealed he was only teasing. She smiled back. Maggie liked this side of Charles. He was more like the Charles she remembered from when they were younger.

The puffing train became Maggie's whole world, Charles and Georgia her only friends and family. For several days, they traveled through the states of Oregon, a bit of California, Nevada, and then Utah territory. Most of the stops were similar to Hardy, with a few buildings and only one or two places to get something to eat.

Sometimes their meals were bountiful, as they had been in Hardy. Others served stingy or tasteless food, but she was glad to find sustenance. Having food became more important than the way it was prepared.

Then they reached the Rocky Mountains.

Chapter 11

CHARLES WATCHED THE majestic Rocky Mountains come closer and closer. "Georgia, how many times have you made this trip by train?"

"Only two times, besides when we moved west." Her gaze roved the approaching foothills. "I never get tired of looking at these wonderful mountains."

"Would you like to sit by the window?" He scooted toward the aisle and opened a place for her on the bench seat beside him.

Georgia glanced at Maggie, who slept with her head against the window. "She isn't really sleeping that well on the train. I know she's tired." She carefully moved to the space he'd made for her so she wouldn't disturb Maggie. "I would hate to awaken her."

Charles slid a little closer to the fascinating woman with eyes the color of the sky outside the window. "What do you like best about the mountains?" Georgia hadn't seemed to mind his presence closer beside her. Things were working out for him.

"Just look at those jagged peaks thrust toward the sky in a variety of formations." She kept her focus on the heights that were rapidly approaching. "Some look like fingers pointing to God. At other places, they look almost like stair steps to heaven."

The woman had the heart of a poet to go with her beauty. The sun streaming through the window provided a soft halo around her upswept golden hair. She reminded him of an angel. He wondered if her smooth cheek felt as soft as velvet. Maybe sometime he would be able to find out.

She turned and caught him staring at her. A becoming blush crept into her cheeks as his gaze traced her jawline, getting lost in the tangle of the hair that had wriggled from her style. He'd never known a woman so sophisticated, yet with that touch of purity that allowed her to blush. The young women who had tried to catch his eye at every soiree he attended paled in comparison.

Because he didn't want to make her uncomfortable, he turned

toward the vista before them but maintained awareness of her with peeks from the corner of his eyes. "I wonder how many men have tried to climb the mountains up ahead."

She took a breath and slowly released it. "I know that often men try to conquer the giants in their paths. Someone had to go up there and find the place to lay the tracks. The journey must have been arduous and dangerous."

As the train seemed to inch higher and higher, Charles stared at the approaching terrain. Just how did one climb such peaks? Surely the men didn't ride horses. Perhaps they had pack mules.

Georgia never took her eyes from the scenery. "So Charles, have you ever wanted to do anything as daring as climbing these mountains?"

How should he answer her? As a boy, when he'd first read about the Rocky Mountains, he had dreamed of being one of the explorers who was the first to set eyes on those peaks. But did he still desire such a thing? His life had become more mundane with things like maintaining and then adding to the business his father and grandfather had built.

"I'm sure most boys dream those kinds of dreams, but I don't aspire to such a thing now. I have other things on my mind." *Not the least of which is obtaining a wife.* He glanced at her and found her eyes trained on his face. For a moment, he couldn't tear his gaze away. "And what of your dreams, Georgia?"

"My life has taken many twists and turns." She cleared her throat and turned away. What should he do now? How could he find out if she had any interest in him as a man?

❖ ❖ ❖

As Maggie awoke, she became aware that Georgia and Charles were deep in conversation on the opposite bench. They didn't even notice that she'd opened her eyes.

121

What was Charles trying to do? Was he pursuing Georgia? Did he have any idea how old she was?

Yes, her aunt looked almost as young as Maggie, but surely he could tell that she wasn't. Maggie's parents wouldn't have allowed someone her own age to be her traveling companion, even if Charles was accompanying them.

She glanced out the window as the train serpentined around one of the many mountains. Seeing the peaks bathed in sunlight brought out the various colors of the rainbow, but in muted tones. And she'd never seen some varieties of the trees before. Wild flowers and flaming foliage looked as if the Creator had thrown multicolored paint across the hillsides. Maggie wished she'd thought to keep her sketch pad out of her trunk. On the return journey, she'd be sure she had the pad, charcoal, and colored pencils in her carpetbag so she could capture the scenes around her. Their beauty was the only redeeming quality of an otherwise arduous journey. That and the company she traveled with, but it was becoming tiresome to watch Charles flirting shamelessly with Georgia. Sketching what she saw might take her mind off all the discomfort.

The conductor came down the aisle, stopping occasionally to speak with one of the passengers. Finally he reached them.

"How are you folks doing?" From his smile, Maggie could see how much the man enjoyed talking to the different people on the train.

"We're just fine." Charles quickly answered the man. "I'm taking care of the ladies."

Maggie just rolled her eyes and shook her head, but neither Georgia nor Charles noticed. That man was just too cocky. *He* was taking care of the *ladies*. Smugness dripped from his tone. Before they left Seattle, Maggie had toyed with the idea that Charles might be a good man for her, but after this first part of their journey, she could see that he would never look at her as anything but a younger friend. He had his sights set on someone older, hopefully wiser, and definitely more sophisticated.

But what was Georgia doing flirting back? Was she bored, or did she really find him fascinating? Maggie was sure Charles believed the latter. She watched the conductor move on down the aisle toward the back of the car.

"So, Charles, why did you think it was a good idea to go into partnership with Joshua?" Georgia's question pulled Maggie's attention back to her traveling companions. "What will you gain from the merger?"

Maggie wanted to hear what he would say about that. Although she knew her father wouldn't enter into a deal unless he knew it was a good one, was Charles mature enough to look at it that way too?

Charles stretched his long legs until his feet were under the other end of the seat Maggie sat on. He stared at the roof of the railroad car as if something interesting was written there. "I believe my grandfather would have made the same deal. In this modern time, we need to be innovative. Stepping bravely into the future, making a difference."

What is he going on about? He sounded as if he were making some kind of political speech. In addition to being brash, he was wordy. Why didn't he just say what he meant?

"I read the *New York Times* when it reaches Seattle. All kinds of innovations are taking place on the eastern side of our country."

More drivel. *Where is the young man I remember?* He sounded like a stuffed shirt.

"They have new stores that are a combination of an emporium, like the one Joshua owns, and stores that sell other merchandise. Some are called department stores, because they have several different areas that showcase specific items."

He propped one ankle across the other one and laid his arm along the back of the seat only a hair's breadth from Georgia's shoulders. Maggie wondered why her aunt didn't move farther away from him.

"That's not exactly what we are doing. Since both the Caine Emporium and Stanton Fine Furniture carry only top-quality items, and because we share the same building, Joshua and I felt that by combining the two stores, we'd have a lot to offer the discerning customer."

He flashed his smile at Georgia, and she seemed to be hanging on to his every word. At least Maggie could hold her derisive laughter inside. She wondered if he had any idea just how pompous he sounded. This was going to be a long journey.

The door at the end of the car opened, and the conductor headed back toward them. "We'll be stopping in Denver overnight."

He stopped beside their seats, and Charles straightened and turned his attention toward the man. "That's something to look forward to. Is there a hotel where we can spend the night?"

"You might like the Windsor. A mighty fine place." He nodded. "Haven't been inside myself, but it's a recent construction. People say it's a good place to stay."

Charles rose to his feet. "Do you think we'll have any trouble getting a room there?"

"I'm on this run most of the time, and none of our passengers have had a problem."

The train jerked from side to side even more than before, and he grabbed hold of the back of the seat. So did Charles.

The conductor peered out through the window. "We're approaching the Continental Divide. You folks might find it fascinating."

He gave them a salute and headed on down the aisle.

When Charles had told them about this phenomenon, it had been hard to picture. Anything Maggie could have imagined would have never matched the enormity of the peaks with so much rocky area above the timberline. For a while the train seemed to have trouble puffing up the rails that wound toward the top. And for some reason, Maggie had a hard time catching her breath.

Not too long after they finally crossed the mountain and headed down the other side, they arrived in Denver. When the train pulled into the station, Charles made arrangements for their transportation to the Windsor Hotel, a luxurious place with soft feather beds and beautiful, lushly carpeted rooms. Electric lights made the place bright and welcoming.

And the food in Denver was especially delicious. Maggie enjoyed the fine cuisine instead of the home cooking they'd had along the way.

After she finished eating, Maggie arose. "Please excuse me. I'm really tired, and I want to get all the rest I can while we have real beds."

She hoped Georgia would accompany her back to the room.

Charles stood. "I've made all the arrangements for anything you might need. And I think I'll stay here and have some of that pie the waitress told us about. Georgia, would you like to join me?"

When her aunt agreed, Maggie had to grit her teeth to keep from rolling her eyes. What were the two of them thinking? Shouldn't they also try to get extra rest? She imagined even more of the flirting that would take place in this dining room. At least she didn't have to watch it.

Perhaps the best part of staying in the hotel was the large brass bathtub that Charles ordered brought to the room she and Georgia shared. Soaking in the warm water and washing her hair made Maggie feel like a new woman.

The next morning she didn't want to get back on the train, even though it was taking her closer to her grandmother, and they had come too far to turn back. They left Denver and headed east away from the mountains. During the rest of Colorado and Kansas, the landscape was fairly level, with gently rolling hills. The scenery was also more monotonous after the wild beauty they'd enjoyed.

On this side of the Continental Divide, the railroad stations were situated in larger towns and had more modern restaurants where they stopped. Maggie felt as if they had returned to civilization.

They got off the train in St. Louis. They had to change trains, and theirs wouldn't leave until the next day. Charles took them by trolley to the Hotel Barnum, where they once again bathed and went to the dining room for a good meal.

After they had ordered their food, Charles turned toward Georgia. "Have you stayed here on any of your trips back home?"

"No." She glanced around the room with electric lights on the walls and lovely wallpaper above the wainscoting. "It's a lovely place."

"I'm glad I'm the first man to bring you here." He murmured the words softly.

But Maggie heard every one. She felt like an intruder in this group of three, and she was getting tired of it.

Georgia glanced at Maggie. "How do you like this hotel?"

She turned her attention toward her aunt and gave a wan smile. "It's lovely, but I'm really looking forward to sleeping in a real bed once more. As soon as I finish eating, I'm going up to the room."

"So soon?" Her aunt sounded concerned. "But it will be so early."

"Georgia, we could stay and visit for a while longer." Charles had eyes only for her aunt. "Or we could take a stroll. The weather is really nice outside."

"I'd like a walk after being on the train so long."

While they ate, the conversation bounced around the table, but mostly between Charles and Georgia. Maggie didn't contribute much to the discussion. And she didn't want to spend more time with them tonight. She hurried up to the room on the third floor and quickly got ready for bed. If they wanted to carry on such a blatant flirtation, let them. She would get a really good night's sleep.

After breakfast, they took the trolley to the station to board the train bound for Little Rock. They had been riding the other train east. This one took them southwest from St. Louis. After they'd ridden through a large section of Arkansas, they could see the Ozark Mountains in the distance. These mountains weren't as tall as the Rockies, but they had their own unique qualities. The train had crossed the Ozarks in Missouri before they reached St. Louis. The same mountains spilled from Missouri into Arkansas.

Maggie could hardly believe the train had almost reached their destination. She'd known the trip would be long, but this one had seemed endless. She couldn't imagine how those thousands of people who crossed half the continent on a wagon train kept from going crazy. Riding the train was monotonous, but being confined to a wagon behind slowly plodding oxen had to be far worse. Maybe after they returned home, she'd ask Daddy and Mother about their journey. Now she had something with which to compare it.

Florence sat on her dressing stool, fascinated as she watched Ingrid dress her hair in an elaborate style. When she gave the girl to Margaret as her personal maid, she'd had no idea she was so talented. Thinking about her daughter made her wonder where Margaret and Georgia were right now. Had they reached Little Rock? Were they all right?

Even though she worried about them on their journey, she felt more settled than she had in a long time. Could it be because Margaret wasn't in the house? If that was the truth, why did her being gone make a difference?

She wouldn't let her thoughts return to the night of her daughter's birthday party. Too many painful memories would assail her, and she wasn't ready to delve into the reasons Margaret had been like a stranger to her that night. If she ignored the situation, maybe the pain would eventually subside, and when her daughter returned home, they could discuss it dispassionately. High emotions had contributed to their impasse.

"How do you like it now?" Ingrid stood behind her awaiting her approval.

"It's really beautiful, Ingrid. You may go now."

The girl curtsied. "Thank you, ma'am." She turned and left the room.

Florence leaned closer to the mirror and tried to smooth the crow's feet beside her eyes and the grooves on either side of her lips. She remembered the smooth face that had smiled back at her for so many years. Her youthful beauty has slipped away without her noticing. Had Joshua taken note of its disappearance?

The last week and a half with him had been wonderful. Of course, he worked every day, but he hadn't gotten home late a single time. And often, he came home early.

He'd planned several special times for them. He took her to Squire's Opera House on Commercial Street to hear a young singer from Norway who was touring the United States, billed as *The New Jenny Lind*. Too bad the poor girl had that name tied to her performances. The phrase was all the people remembered. Right now Florence couldn't even remember her name. Something like Mara, or Maya, or Maria, or something like that. *Magda. That's it.*

At least the girl could really sing. She sang several arias and even a couple of duets with one of the local male singers. A thoroughly enjoyable evening.

They had dined out with friends on three occasions, and she and Joshua had spent pleasant evenings at home. When they were here, he didn't bury himself in work in his study as he had for years. Instead, they really talked to each other. He always brought up memories of times gone by when they were so happy, making them live again in her mind. And when they retired for the evening, she welcomed being cradled in his arms, receiving his love in a way that they had almost lost over the years.

Tonight they were going to a ball at the Arlington House hotel. She went to stand before her cheval mirror. This blue taffeta evening gown set off her figure to perfection. She loved the sound of the swish when she moved. *And Margaret designed it.* The thought crept into her mind. Why did she resent her daughter's abilities? Hadn't she enjoyed the fruits of her labor many times?

Florence hoped Margaret was enjoying her trip, and she wasn't going to let her thoughts linger on the problems with her daughter. If she did, they would inevitably take her to that long-ago night and her own selfish desires. A blight upon her soul.

Tonight she planned to enjoy her husband's company and push everything else from her mind.

Chapter 12

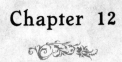

MAGGIE DIDN'T HAVE any idea what to expect when they arrived in Little Rock, but excitement throbbed through her veins. As the train pulled into the station, she noticed the hustle and bustle of a busy town instead of a country village. Several clusters of people waited on the platform. Perhaps they were meeting arriving passengers or were there to start their own travels. A smile spread across her face. All this boded well for the time they'd be here. They wouldn't be stuck in some backwoods place without modern conveniences.

When the train stopped, Charles helped the women gather their belongings. He went down the steps and set his luggage beside him on the platform, then reached for Maggie's carpetbag as well. She slipped her hand into his proffered one and let him help her. Even though she had been annoyed by the way he pursued Georgia on the trip, she still enjoyed the feeling of connection when their hands met. Too bad he didn't experience the same thing. She pulled hers away, sure he hadn't noticed her quickened heart rate, because Charles turned his attention toward Georgia, even grasping her fingers much longer than needed.

Turning around, Maggie let her gaze rove over the area. She especially noticed the people. Many of the ladies were dressed in the height of fashion that she had seen in *Harper's Bazar*, while others looked as if they'd just come in town off a farm. The diversity mirrored what she saw in Seattle every day.

Her aunt, who was taller than she, stood on her tiptoes and searched the crowd. "There he is." Georgia hurried toward a tall man dressed in livery, his hat tucked under his arm.

Maggie grabbed her bag and followed as fast as she could. She didn't want to lose sight of her aunt, who easily wove through the crowd without displacing anyone. Charles followed behind Maggie.

"There you are, Miss Geor…Miz Long." The black man with grizzled hair pumped Georgia's hand enthusiastically, while his wide smile revealed a gold tooth nestled in front. "So good to have you home again."

Not exactly the way servants in the Caine household would act. Maggie knew Florence would not allow such a thing. Since she had a more relaxed relationship with the Jorgensens when Florence wasn't around, she wondered if things would be different when they were around her grandmother too.

"Thank you, Tucker." Georgia turned back just as Maggie caught up. "He's been Mother's driver since before I left home. I don't think your mother ever met him though."

Charles thrust out his hand. "Glad to meet you. I'm Charles Stanton."

After staring at it for a protracted moment, Tucker slapped his hat on his head and gave Charles a hearty handshake. "And this must be Miz Agatha's granddaughter." The man's eyes twinkled when he turned his smile toward her. "She real excited you come for a visit."

Knowing that her grandmother had been talking about her sent pleasure streaking through Maggie. For the first time in a while, she felt wanted, and maybe even loved. And the woman hadn't even met her yet.

He turned toward Georgia. "Tell me how much luggage y'all have."

Charles handed over two of the carpetbags. "These belong to the women. But that's not all. We have more in the baggage car. I'll help you retrieve them."

"Coach be sittin' over yonder. I'll just take these and stow 'em in the boot and come back t' get the other things." The driver whistled as he ambled across the street, swinging his arms as if the bags were very light, and Maggie knew hers wasn't.

Georgia held out her hand for Charles's bag. "I can take this to the coach. Maggie and I will wait there." She glanced toward the train. "They're unloading things right now. You can make sure they don't miss any of ours."

Charles let her take the carpetbag, then walked swiftly toward the train.

Maggie crossed the street with Georgia, and they made their way between other waiting conveyances—farm wagons, plain buggies, other coaches. The warm musky smell of horses wafted through the autumn wind. "The name Little Rock sounds like a village, but it's not."

"No. It's the state capital and the largest city in Arkansas." Georgia handed the last bag to Tucker, who quickly stowed it under the canvas at the back of the coach, then headed across the street to join Charles.

"The town is pretty, but what a funny name." Maggie caught an errant curl and twisted the hair around her finger before she pushed it toward the bun it had escaped. "Why use such an unusual name? Does it have any special meaning?"

"The town originally started from a settlement on the Arkansas River. An outcropping of white rock on the bank was used by the Indians, then early travelers, as a landmark. The French called it *La Petite Roche*, which means 'the little rock,'" Georgia explained. "Maybe while you're here, we can go down to the river so you can see the landmark."

"I'd like that. I want to see everything I can while we're here."

Maggie realized this might be her only visit to this area, and she didn't want to return to Seattle and regret missing something interesting. Since her life felt completely unsettled right now, she wanted good memories in case something drastic happened when she got home and talked to her parents. She dreaded that conversation, so she pushed it to the back of her mind. She didn't want to let it spoil her day.

Because they had been sitting for such a long time, Maggie didn't want to climb into the coach until the men arrived with the other luggage. She walked back and forth, enjoying stretching her legs by moving at a fast clip. She tried to take in everything around them. "The train depot in Seattle is by the wharf. It's not as pretty there as it is here by this train station. I love all the trees and fall flowers. This is almost like a park."

Georgia waited beside the door to the coach. "I guess I just take it all for granted, because I've been here so often. But they have planted more than I remember from the last time I was home."

Maggie stopped short in front of her aunt. "How long were you married before Uncle Scott passed away?" She covered her mouth with her fingertips for a moment. "I'm sorry. That was too personal of a question. I shouldn't have asked."

Georgia patted her arm. "It's all right. We had seven wonderful years together before his accident. It's been long enough now that it doesn't hurt to talk about him or his passing. Although I miss him terribly. He was the love of my life."

For a moment, she just stared at her aunt. This was the woman who'd just spent over a week bantering with Charles. Did she even realize the man was smitten with her?

Maggie was glad her words hadn't brought hurtful memories to her aunt's attention. But they brought a deep longing to her own heart. Would she ever have a love-of-her-life experience? She was frightened to even consider letting anyone that close. Too many secrets were buried inside her. Maybe someday, after she found out who she really was. "How long has it been since you were here?" Maggie hoped changing the subject would help her relax.

"I was only eighteen when Scott and I married and moved to Portland. I missed my mother...a lot." Georgia stared into the distance with a wistful smile on her face. "Scott understood, and he made sure I saw my mother every few years. But I haven't been home in the few years since he's been gone. In addition to grieving for him, I've been trying to figure out what I want to do with the rest of my life."

Before she could ask another question, Maggie noticed her trunk bobbing above the heads of the people on the platform as it moved toward the street. The crowd parted in front of Charles as he approached. She knew he was strong, but her trunk was extremely heavy. He had it hoisted on one shoulder, and he carried his portmanteau with his other hand, making the feat look effortless. Tucker followed him, carrying Georgia's trunk on his shoulder.

"Didn't they have a hand truck you could use to get the trunks over here?" Georgia frowned as each man lowered his burden to the street.

"We didn't want to wait our turn to use it." Charles dusted his hands together, exhibiting no ill effects from such a great effort. "So we did it the old-fashioned way. Muscle power."

While Tucker loaded the larger pieces of luggage into the boot, Charles assisted Georgia into the coach, then he turned to Maggie. He clasped her fingers, and once again her heartbeat accelerated. She quickly raised her foot to the step. His nearness set her mind and balance in a whirl.

Charles followed her into the conveyance and closed the door. When he dropped onto the seat across from where she and Georgia sat, he faced the back of the coach.

"Don't you want to see where we're going?" She couldn't keep the breathless quality from her voice.

His smile widened. "I trust our driver. I'd rather look at two beautiful ladies."

"As if you haven't been looking at us for almost two weeks." The vehicle started moving, and Maggie glanced out the window, then back at him. "Besides that, you've seen us at our worst."

He leaned forward with his forearms resting on his thighs.

"I've not seen anything but two lovely women making the most of circumstances."

She couldn't help noticing his muscular thighs, and his words sounded like a caress. A caress she couldn't receive...and probably didn't deserve. And perhaps he was aiming the smooth words at Georgia anyway.

Maggie took a deep breath and pushed both shoulders against the deeply cushioned seat. Despite her resolve not to get entangled in caring for Charles, his presence kept her in knots. Wasn't her life complicated enough without all this turmoil from a man? She sighed and turned her focus to the window.

What she saw delighted her. Most of the stores were built of brick, both red and buff colored, and had arched windows. Attractive displays of goods filled the windows—clothing, furniture, incidentals, even a store that sold only leather goods.

"There are a lot more stores here than in Seattle." She turned toward Georgia. "They might have more modern conveniences too."

"Little Rock was here long before Seattle was established." Georgia sounded as if she were stating the obvious, which she was.

Tucker drove the coach into a residential neighborhood and soon stopped in front of a stately home. Maggie's eyes lit up.

"Is this where my grandmother lives?" Maggie leaned close to the window and her gaze roved over the house and expansive grounds.

"Oh, my goodness, no. This is The House of Agatha Carter—her business."

The coach halted, and they climbed out. Maggie followed her aunt across the thick lawn toward a discreet sign affixed to one of the white columns spanning the front of the house.

Maggie traced the raised letters with her fingertips, enjoying the sensation. Was it possible that someday she might run just such an establishment? Wonder what she could call hers? "I never dreamed her business was this large."

Georgia advanced up the steps and through the front door with Maggie and Charles tagging along.

"When I was young, she conducted her dressmaking business from the parlor of our tiny house. That's all Florence remembers. Mother moved the business here about eighteen years ago." Georgia stood on the polished hardwood floor in the foyer and waited expectantly. For an extended moment, the only sound was the wind blowing through the open windows and a muted murmur from the second floor.

Soon a young woman descended the stairs and stopped beside them. "May I help you?"

"You're new since I was here last. I'm Georgia Long."

"Welcome home!" Her gaze shifted to Maggie. "You must be Margaret Caine." The girl couldn't be much older than Maggie. "Mrs. Carter will be so glad you've arrived." She rushed back up the stairs, leaving them standing where they were.

Maggie had a hard time believing this was a place of business. The rooms—tastefully decorated in shades of royal blue, rose, and hunter green with floral accents—looked like a regular home. She would enjoy living in a place so lovely.

"Does Grandmother live here too?" She trailed her fingers along a rosewood table set against the wall. A tall china vase with fresh flowers welcomed them from the center of the table's lace runner.

"No. But her home is just as lovely."

"Finally!" A woman's voice from the top of the stairs interrupted the conversation.

Maggie watched the tall slender woman, with a mass of brown curls piled haphazardly on the top of her head, hurry down the curved staircase. Only a few white strands laced through her hair. She looked much too young to be Maggie's grandmother.

"I'm getting to see my only granddaughter." As soon as the words were out of her mouth, she enveloped Maggie in a tight hug.

Relishing the enthusiasm her grandmother expressed, Maggie

wound her arms around the woman. Warmth and comfort flowed over her soul. This welcome was just what she needed.

When Agatha finally released her and took a step back, she gently touched Maggie's hair. "We haven't had a redhead in the family that I know of, but look, Georgia, she inherited my curls."

The words sent ice through Maggie's veins, and she shivered. She didn't inherit anything from Agatha Carter. Not her ability to design dresses, not even the curls. If her grandmother thought so, she couldn't know the truth either. Why hadn't Florence told her own mother about the adoption?

For a moment, Maggie felt light-headed, and she had a hard time taking a breath. This visit might prove to be more difficult than she'd ever imagined. Maybe coming here was a huge mistake.

Her grandmother didn't seem to notice her discomfort. But she did notice Charles hovering behind them. "And just who is this young man?"

Maggie glanced at him, but his attention was trained on Agatha, instead of her. "This is Charles Stanton. He and Daddy are combining their stores right now, so they are partners."

"You don't say. That's interesting." Agatha thrust her hand toward him. "Welcome to The House of Agatha Carter. I assume you are also my daughter and granddaughter's traveling companion."

Charles gently took her hand, but Agatha gave his a vigorous shake, much like any businessman might. "That's been my pleasure. I've heard a lot about you, and I'm glad to finally meet you, Mrs. Carter."

She studied him a long moment. "I can see that Joshua made a good choice for a partner and for a man to travel with our daughters. Welcome to Little Rock."

Her grandmother turned from him and linked arms with Maggie. "Let's go home. I can show you around here another day. Tucker's wife, Shirley, has a banquet prepared in your honor. I hope all of you are hungry."

Maggie let herself be ushered out the front door, along with Charles and Georgia. Tucker stood beside the coach awaiting their arrival.

On the ride to the house, Agatha and Georgia carried on a lively conversation. Maggie listened to the two women with half an ear, all the while wondering what it would feel like to actually be a part of this family. She hated living a lie. *A lie not of my own choosing.*

"There's the house." Maggie glanced in the direction Georgia indicated.

Although the structure wasn't as large as the Caine mansion on Beacon Hill in Seattle, neither was it just a bungalow. The two-story white clapboard had windows along both the first floor and the upstairs. Dormer windows in the roof indicated an attic as well. Each window was flanked by dark blue shutters, and the rocking chairs scattered across the front porch matched. With curtains fluttering behind the open windows, the whole thing looked homey and welcoming to Maggie.

Tucker drove the coach up the white gravel driveway and stopped beside the front of the house, at the end of a brick walkway. After everyone exited, he drove on toward the back of the building. Evidently there was a coach house and maybe a stable back there. Perhaps tomorrow she could check them out. Florence never let her go around the horses in the stable back home. But she wasn't here to monitor Maggie's every move. She could do anything she really wanted to without censure.

"Well, come on in my house, girls." Agatha herded them across the walkway, then turned around. "And I should have said for you to come too, Mr. Stanton."

Charles was already right behind them. "Just call me Charles, Mrs. Carter."

"And I'm Agatha." She gave a quick nod. When she smiled, tiny lines crinkled beside her eyes, revealing she wasn't as young as she looked.

Maggie couldn't help liking this hospitable woman. How she wished Agatha really was her grandmother. Then the thought cut through her. *Maybe I have grandparents somewhere who don't even know about me.* She stopped short, overwhelmed by the idea.

Charles grabbed her shoulders to keep from running into her. "You should let people know when you're going to stop like that, Maggie," he whispered into her hair near her ear.

His breath felt warm against her skin, and those errant curls that had made their way out of her bun tickled when they moved. She wanted to reach up and push them back where they belonged, but she didn't want to chance encountering his face. After the way he'd acted on the train, she didn't want to experience such a personal touch.

"I'll try to remember to give some kind of signal next time." Heat rose up her neck and settled in her cheeks. She was sure they flamed red. No telling what he'd think about that.

She hurried to catch up with Agatha and Georgia on the porch. Charles kept pace with her.

A dark woman, dressed in black with a white apron and a white ruffled cap on her head, opened the door right before they reached it. "Miz Agatha, this your grandchile?"

Agatha put her arm around Maggie's shoulders. "She sure is."

"Ain't she a pretty little thing?" The woman held the door wide open for them to enter. "And who is this strappin' lad? Her gentleman friend?"

Maggie didn't think her cheeks could blush any more than she already had, but even more heat flushed her face all the way to her hairline. She hoped she wouldn't start sweating. She was mortified, knowing all that red skin would clash with the flaming hair. She dropped her head, hoping no one would notice.

Charles took charge of the situation. He held out his hand to the older woman. "I'm Charles Stanton, Mr. Caine's business partner."

"That's right nice of you." She stared at his hand for a moment but didn't take it. "I'll have dinner on in a jiffy."

Maggie knew that Florence wouldn't have let any of her servants speak so casually with guests in their home, but Shirley and Tucker seemed to be just as much a part of the family here as the Jorgensens were at home.

In Seattle, more Indians and Chinese worked as servants than black people. Maggie couldn't remember seeing a single one in the homes of their friends. Of course, Mother refused to use any of these people in her house. She had to have Europeans.

Maggie never understood why that made a difference to her mother. But then she often had a hard time understanding her at all. And it wasn't any wonder, since they came from different backgrounds. If only Maggie knew what hers was. With a name like McKenna and with her red hair, evidently she was Scottish. She had studied about them coming to the United States over two hundred years ago, with many of them settling in the mountains in the eastern part of the country. She wondered what caused Angus McKenna to come west. Would she ever know?

Chapter 13

MAGGIE THOUGHT SHE would probably sleep late as her grandmother urged her to after their long evening. However, the aroma of coffee mixed with bacon and biscuits enticed her from slumber early the next morning. She quickly donned a navy skirt and a shirtwaist with tiny navy stripes on a white background. After brushing out her sleeping braids, she pulled her hair back and tied it with a white ribbon. As usual, many curls sprang forward, framing her face. At least they didn't fall in her eyes. For just a moment, she wished she had Ingrid with her to dress her hair.

When she reached the bottom of the stairs, she headed toward the kitchen, bypassing the empty dining room. Charles sat at the kitchen table, his elbows propped on the top and his chin resting on his clasped hands, visiting with Georgia. For a moment, she stopped and enjoyed the view. Relaxed like that, he appeared younger than she knew him to be, and totally at home in the kitchen. She wondered if he spent time in the kitchen of his own mansion. Maybe he had, since his grandparents reared him after his parents were gone.

"So everyone is up early. Right?" Maggie hated to disturb them, but she wondered where her grandmother was.

Shirley set a filled plate in front of Georgia. "Miz Agatha done left to go to work before any of you got up."

"Something smells wonderful." Maggie snatched a tiny piece of crispy bacon from Georgia's plate. Her aunt slapped at her hand.

"Don't you worry none. I fix you a plate right now." The black woman bustled toward the stove and commenced filling a plate with way too much food for one person.

"I won't be able to eat that much after what we had last night." Maggie slid into the chair between Charles and Georgia at the small square table.

"Don't you worry none about that. We feed the dog what you

144

don't eat." Shirley set the plate of steaming food in front of her. Scrambled eggs, biscuits, and bacon, just as her nose had alerted her.

Maggie picked up the biscuit and split it, dipping half-melted butter to slather on. Then she glanced at the array of other spreads—honey, apple jelly, strawberry jam, and sorghum molasses. The molasses shone such a dark brown color that it was almost black, and threads of it dripped from her spoon when she tried to put some on the biscuit.

Georgia glanced from Maggie to Charles and back. "Maggie, do you want to go to The House of Agatha Carter today or later?"

"Today would be good for me." Maggie really wanted to see what happened on the upper floor of her grandmother's business.

"Then I shall accompany you ladies." Charles gave one of his bows, and Shirley laughed.

"What time do you want to leave?"

"Tucker ain't got back from runnin' errands for me." Shirley started picking up the empty plates from the table. "He be back anytime now."

Maggie arose from her chair. "How about we all get ready so we can leave as soon as he is free?"

After Georgia and Charles agreed, Maggie followed them as they climbed the stairs. She wondered if they had been flirting at the table before she came down. Maybe Georgia wouldn't carry on in front of Shirley. At least Maggie hoped not.

Maggie memorized the route to the business while Tucker drove them in an open surrey. While the horses high-stepped it up Main Street to Fifth, then across to Pulaski, Maggie took note of the stores she wanted to visit before they went home. Many interesting things caught her eye, especially one called *Les Chapeaux* with a window filled with various styles of hats for women. After they turned on

Pulaski, they passed more residences than stores until they reached The House of Agatha Carter.

Tucker stopped the carriage and turned toward the passengers. "You sure, sir, you want to spend most of the day with the ladies? Lots of fabric and fripperies in that house."

Charles chuckled. "You're probably right, Tucker. What did you have in mind for me?"

"Well, I could show you around some places that won't be interesting to the ladies." He gave them a gentle nod. "If you ladies don' mind."

"Now, Tucker, don't go taking Charles anywhere that he'll get into trouble." Georgia arched a teasing eyebrow at Charles.

Tucker gave a laugh that sounded almost like a snort. "You know me better than that, Miz Long. I'm a God-fearing man myself. Won' fine me in none o' those places."

"Me either, or I would tremble at the consequences." Charles sent a glance Georgia's way, implying he would more enjoy the consequences than tremble at them, but Georgia was looking away. Maggie caught the look and frowned.

Grow up! she telegraphed toward him.

The smile slid from his face, and suddenly he was all business.

"Let me escort the ladies to the door, and I'll come back. We can go wherever you want to take me." Charles assisted Maggie to descend, then Georgia. He pulled Georgia's hand through the crook of his elbow and swept up the sidewalk.

As soon as they reached the front door, Georgia quickly entered, but Charles stayed on the front porch. Maggie didn't even glance at him as she followed her aunt into the house. *Thank goodness he's not staying here all day.* With him gone, maybe she could keep her mind on what she wanted to learn from her grandmother.

As they entered, Agatha walked regally down the stairs, the

queen of this realm. "Oh, good, you're here. Let's take a tour of the downstairs first."

Maggie eagerly tried to take in everything as her grandmother led them through the sitting room. "Here's where I often meet with clients for the first time. And when husbands come to see the dresses we're making for their wives, I have newspapers and magazines available for them while the women are dressing. I really don't let any of them come upstairs. It would cause too much of a commotion and disturb the women working."

That intrigued Maggie, even as she imagined men sitting in the matching wing-back chairs, reading the paper while they waited. Or lounging on the sofa upholstered in a coordinating floral pattern. No lace or tassels on the pillows thrown carelessly along its length. "Just how many women do you have working for you?"

Agatha stopped walking. "It depends on the season and whether we have many orders. I do almost all the designing, but I'm training two young women in the art of crafting patterns. They might take over some of the design work eventually."

Georgia gave an unladylike huff. "Mother, you know that day will never come."

Agatha gave a decisive nod. "It might. You never know what will happen. Now let's go through here. The dining room is used when we have a lot of orders to be filled quickly. I have Shirley come here to cook for the women. That way we don't waste any extra time."

The solid oak table was long with ten Windsor chairs around it. A tablecloth that coordinated with the rest of the decor in the downstairs draped the table, and dishes and silverware were set at each place as if awaiting the diners.

Maggie imagined having a business where she would need a large dining room and a cook to feed the workers when they had a lot of work. Too bad Mrs. Jorgensen worked for Florence. She'd be a wonderful asset to her company...if she ever had one.

"So do you have ten women working here now?" Maggie knew that if Agatha could afford to hire that many workers, she must be making a comfortable living.

Agatha stood beside Maggie. "See that portrait?" She indicated a painting on the wall of the dining room. A woman stood with her hand on the back of one of the wing-back chairs in the parlor. Her federal blue gown had a jabot with a frothing of lace. Her hair was smoothed back, its length gathered in a snood attached to a jeweled comb at the top of her head. "That's Lizzie Quaile Berry, wife of the former governor, in a dress I designed for her. She had me create most of her wardrobe. She was good for my business. I had more than ten women working for me that year, because a number of other women in Little Rock wanted dresses designed by me after they saw what I made for her. But we usually only have around eight or ten working at any given time. The new governor isn't married, so I don't have to contend with so many political requests."

Maggie took a deep breath. How wonderful it must be to design clothing for someone as important as the governor's wife. Would Maggie ever get the opportunity to be as successful as her grandmother is? The money involved wasn't what interested her as much as the opportunity to use her talents to make clothing that would help women feel beautiful. She wondered if that would ever happen. *Not if Florence has her way.*

After they went through the kitchen, Agatha led them to a room on the opposite side of the downstairs. "This was a bedroom, but I use it as a dressing room when a husband wants his wife to model the clothing for him. We also use it when I have some dresses already made up for women to choose from. That's not always the case, but when we don't have pressing orders, we do make a selection. Some women like to come in and try on various styles to see what suits them best."

Next her grandmother led them toward the front of the house.

"The room on this side of the foyer is what I consider my office, but it looks more like a library."

Maggie had to agree with her assessment. Books lined two walls of the large room. Light from outside filtered through the many panes of the expansive window on the front of the house. She could imagine herself sinking into the plush upholstered chair and curling up with a good book. Before she left Little Rock, she planned on checking out Agatha's bookshelves to see what her grandmother liked to read. She wondered if their tastes were similar. Of course, she doubted that Agatha would ever pick up a dime novel, and Maggie had been known to read a few of those. She loved the strong heroines, hoping someday to be like them.

"Now let's go upstairs." Agatha led the way. "I had the second floor extensively remodeled to meet my needs. There were several bedrooms up here, and I connected the three across the back into one large workroom."

When they went through the doorway, Maggie noticed Georgia was already there talking to one of the women sitting at a treadle sewing machine. When the seamstress saw Agatha, she leaned over her machine and started running fabric under the needle. Even though she kept her eyes on what she was doing, she continued to carry on the conversation. Maggie doubted she could do those two things at the same time. But if she learned to run one of the machines, perhaps she could, too.

"As you can see, the cutting table is on this side." Agatha gestured toward the right where a heavy table, its top covered with heavy canvas, took up a large area. "I designed the kind of table I wanted and had a carpenter build it for me. He had to actually cut the lengths of lumber and build it in this area. It's too large and heavy to move up the stairs. I guess when I'm gone they'll have to dismantle it to get it out of the house."

"Maybe someone will want to purchase your business and keep it there." Maggie wished she could be that person.

Two women had fabric spread across the table and were arranging pattern pieces on top, weighting them down with ornate pieces of silverware, more table knives than anything else. Maggie hadn't ever wondered how they kept the pattern pieces from shifting when they cut out the garments. Now she knew how her grandmother did it.

"How's everything going?" Agatha went over and checked on the progress of the women's work.

Maggie watched the way they interacted with her grandmother. They showed respect, but also exhibited a sense of equality with her. If Maggie ever opened a business of her own in Seattle, that's the kind of relationship she would want with her workers, mutual respect. Perhaps that's one of the things she had always craved. *Respect.*

Agatha walked toward the other half of the room. "As you can see, I have six of these Singer treadle sewing machines. We don't always need to use all of them, but usually at least four are utilized at any given time."

As she said, four women of a variety of ages worked at the machines, each one using a different type of fabric.

"These are my regular workers." Agatha stopped by one of the machines. "Loraine has been with me for a long time."

The woman smiled up at Agatha, but didn't stop running the fabric through the machine. Her legs rocked the treadle at a fast rhythm. She must feel as though she were running. Using one of these saved a lot of time, but probably wore the women out by quitting time.

Maggie tucked each morsel of information into her brain. After she got home tonight, she planned to write down all they had seen, discussed, and done. If she were ever going to start a business like this, she wanted to know as much as she could about what it would take.

Agatha led the way through another door that opened into a large room toward the front of the house. Two women sat in rocking chairs doing handwork. Other padded rocking chairs were scattered around the area.

"The machines aren't able to take care of the finer details like buttons, buttonholes, hems, and adding anything decorative, so I have women who are excellent with hand sewing. These two are my regulars." Agatha picked up a folded blouse with rows of ruffles edged in lace down the front. "You did a good job on this, Etta."

The woman she had complimented smiled, but continued to make tiny stitches on the hem of a skirt. Maggie leaned close so she could see just how tiny her stitches were. She lifted the edge where Etta had already finished the hem. From the outside of the garment, the stitches were invisible.

"Such beautiful work." Maggie knew Mrs. Murdock, although a very good seamstress, couldn't produce this quality. For a moment she wished her mother could see this place. Then Maggie's heart lurched. She'd never be able to share her joy in designing with the woman who reared her. Therein lay many of her problems.

Agatha led the way out on the landing at the top of the staircase. Two doors were on the other side of the landing. She went to the one closest to the workroom and opened the door to a fairly large room without a single window. "This is the storeroom."

Maggie gasped. She'd never seen so much fabric or lace or thread, even in a store. "Where do you get such a variety?"

"Since I use so much material, I often order from the manufacturers. Seldom will a store carry the complete selection of what I use." Her grandmother stepped into the small space left in the room. If more than two people had been there, they wouldn't have fit inside. "I've even gone to New Orleans to meet some of the ships that come into port. I've bought fabric at the dock before. And I've been known to draw a design and send it to a manufacturer to have the fabric made just for me. It costs more, but I have clients who are willing to pay the price for something unique."

She had never considered something like that. So many thoughts danced through Maggie's brain. So many options available to her, too. Would she be fearless enough to buck Mother's restrictions? Could she actually open a business like this? If only she knew.

"I want to show you one more thing." Agatha led her out and closed and locked the door. Then they went to the other door, which was locked as well. "This is my designing room." She opened it wide, allowing Maggie entrance.

With the windows on the front of the house like the ones in the handwork room and the parlor downstairs, light filled the room and spilled out into the hallway. Everything in the room was utilitarian. A comfortable chair, a table with sketch pads and charcoal sticks and pencils, and two kinds of furniture Maggie had never seen.

"What are these?" She laid her hand on a wooden cabinet with three rows of fairly small flat drawers. Two of these cabinets sat side by side against the back wall.

"Those are letter and drawer filing cabinets. I use them to store my designs. Without them, everything in this room would just be a jumble." Agatha opened one of the top drawers and let Maggie look inside.

She could see how helpful something like this would be, but she'd never seen one in Seattle. Of course, she didn't know what was in the offices at the many businesses.

Another type of wooden object flanked these filing cabinets, each set in a back corner of the room. "So what are these?"

Agatha turned the wheel on the outside of the one closest to them. She stopped it and turned it the other way, then reversed it once again. The thick door popped open and a large shallow metal box hung on the back of the door. Inside, several vertical dividers filled one side of the box. A shelf was a few inches down from the top and ran all the way across. Two shelves divided the other side section. Each of the areas created were filled with bundles of papers that fit the size of the space.

"It's a safe, where I keep the most important of my business files." Agatha shut the door and gave the wheel a twirl. "I couldn't get along without these either."

Maggie gestured to the room. "Thank you for showing all of this to me."

"Georgia tells me you like to design dresses, too." Agatha studied Maggie's face, making her feel almost uncomfortable.

Maggie didn't want her grandmother to realize the turmoil going on inside her, so she looked back at the room. "Yes, I design clothes. And I really want to do the same thing you do here...but maybe in Seattle."

"That's wonderful." Agatha clasped Maggie's arm. "But you wouldn't have to do it there. Wouldn't you like to stay with me awhile and work with me? I could help you learn everything you need to know about the business."

That idea hadn't even occurred to Maggie. What would her parents say if she suggested such a thing? *But it is something to consider.*

"You don't have to decide right now." Agatha put her arm around Maggie's shoulders. "If you decide you'd like to do that, I could contact your parents and extend the invitation."

All kinds of possibilities opened in Maggie's mind. But she knew she needed more time before she would dare to raise the issue with her parents.

"I will think about it," she promised. "It would be a wonderful opportunity. Thank you."

This idea went along with her previous thought about wanting to be the person who could buy her grandmother's business at a later time. Could she see herself staying here in Arkansas? Only time would tell.

Chapter 14

FLORENCE PICKED UP the fourteen-karat-gold, Elgin Monarch pocket watch with the train engraved on the cover. This would be the perfect gift for Joshua. Today was their twenty-sixth anniversary, and he hinted they would have a romantic dinner together tonight. These last two weeks had been wonderful, with him coming up with all kinds of interesting things for them to do. She almost felt like the young woman she had been when they married. If only she could forget that one night on the Oregon Trail when her heart was so dark and her thoughts so evil. But the memories wouldn't stay in the forgotten recesses of her mind. A lone tear made its way down her cheek.

The clerk behind the counter stared at her. "Are you all right, ma'am?"

She mustn't let him know what she was thinking about. "Yes." She pulled her hanky from her sleeve and dabbed it against that side of her face. "Today is my anniversary, and I was remembering the day we wed."

He nodded. "So will this be your gift for your husband?"

"Yes."

She quickly paid the man, and he wrapped the box in white paper and handed it to her.

"I hope he appreciates it."

"Oh, he will." She slipped the package into her handbag and hurried out to the coach.

Erik Jorgensen jumped down from his perch and opened the door. "Would you like me to take you anywhere else, ma'am?"

"No, I'm ready to go home." She wrapped her coat even tighter around her. The air today had a decided nip to it.

When they arrived at home, Erik opened the coach door and escorted her to the front door. "If you don't need me anymore, Mrs. Caine, I have an errand to run for your husband."

"That's fine. I'm not going anywhere else."

After she was in the house, she told Ingrid to bring hot water upstairs to the bathing room. A nice hot bath would warm her, and she'd be fresh for when Joshua came home. He hadn't said anything about going out anywhere, so she didn't know how to dress. Maybe Mrs. Jorgensen would know. Before she started upstairs, she went into the kitchen to ask her, which was unusual for her since they usually met in Florence's sitting room to discuss the week's meals and other things. Mrs. Jorgensen was busy spreading white, fluffy icing on a cake.

"I don't remember us talking about you making a cake today." It did look good though.

"No, ma'am, but Mr. Caine asked me to make one." Her movements were no longer smooth. They jerked as if she were nervous.

"So we are dining at home tonight?"

"Yes, ma'am."

Interesting. Well, she mustn't keep bothering their cook. Florence slowly ascended the curved staircase, trailing her fingers along the smooth, wooden banister, wondering what sort of surprise Joshua had cooked up.

After she had bathed with the rose-scented soap she kept for special occasions, she dried off and put on her wrapper. When she went into her bedchamber, Ingrid was just laying a gorgeous blue brocade dress across the bed.

"Where did that come from? I haven't seen it before." Florence ran her fingers across the soft fabric and realized it was made of silk.

"I believe Mr. Caine had Mrs. Murdock make this for you. Erik just brought it to the house." Ingrid headed out the door.

Florence sat on her dressing stool and looked at the lines of the new garment. They looked vaguely familiar. Where had she seen something like this? Then it hit her. The last drawing she saw Margaret making. But Florence distinctly remembered tearing up that drawing. A pain pierced her heart. What had she done? Had Margaret been drawing the dress for her? *How could I have treated her so shabbily?* So much of her life was filled with regrets.

By the time Joshua came home, Florence was dressed in the wonderful gift, and Ingrid had created a flowing hairstyle with a lacy snood. Joshua had always loved Florence's hair down instead of up, and it had been a very long time since she'd worn it that way. Since he had planned things to please her, she'd decided to make him happy too. With more than just a fancy pocket watch.

He led her downstairs to the parlor. A linen-draped table was set in front of the fireplace, where flames leaped and played, chasing the shadows away and warming the room. Lighted candles on several tables around the room joined the light from the candelabrum surrounded by flowers in the center of the table. Instead of having places set across from each other, they were on adjoining sides. Silver, crystal, and china sparkled in the ambient lighting. Just the way she liked it.

Joshua pulled out her chair and gently moved her the correct distance from the table. He even unfurled her napkin and placed it in her lap, his fingers lingering longer than necessary. She loved that feeling, and delicious tingles danced up her spine. Then he took his seat and clasped her hand in his. He bowed his head and praised God for the years they had been blessed to be together.

Florence had never imagined Joshua felt that way about their marriage after all these years. An ache started in her chest. Would he feel that way if he really knew what she was like deep inside? She blinked back tears before they could escape. Tonight was too perfect for her to mess it up.

Mrs. Jorgensen entered with the first course. She carried in a tureen and set it on the table. Then she ladled a creamy pumpkin soup into each of their bowls. The blended spices lent perfume to the air. In addition, the cook arranged hot *vols-au-vent* around the edge of the plate.

"I believe you like these." Joshua lifted one of the meat-filled pastries and fed it to Florence.

She couldn't say a word as she enjoyed the excellent seasoning. When she finished chewing it, she picked up one of his and fed it to him. "It's quite tasty, isn't it?"

His smile of agreement was quickly followed by him grasping her hand and licking the sauce that had seeped onto her fingers. The sensations of his tongue on her fingers while his eyes stared into hers with adoration would have buckled her knees if she had been standing. As it was, flutters in her midsection sent heat roaring through her veins.

Memories of the two newlyweds feeding each other the same way flooded her thoughts. When he pulled her closer and tasted her lips, she couldn't hold anything back when returning his caress. So easily, they soared into passion the way they had that first night when he'd introduced her to the delights of the relationship between a husband and wife.

Breathless, she finally leaned back in her chair. "Our soup is getting cold." She wondered if he could hear her, the words were so soft.

"But we aren't." The chuckle that followed his pronouncement was deep and intimate.

While they continued the meal of filet of beef, dilled carrots, and hot bread, Florence kept remembering why she'd married this man so many years ago. And she felt sure he remembered why he had chosen her. The meal took an inordinate amount of time. Time well spent in giving and receiving many kinds of caresses among the nibbles of food.

After they finished their slices of the wonderful spicy apple cake, Joshua pulled her up from her chair. Erik, Ingrid, and Mrs. Jorgensen quickly made the table and everything on it disappear, and the couple stood alone in front of the fireplace. As Joshua enfolded her in his arms, she leaned against his strong chest. With her ear pressed against him, she heard their hearts beating in identical rhythms. That's how their life should have been all these years. It would have except for that fateful night eighteen years ago.

A lifetime ago when she was too young and too selfish to think about anyone but herself. How she hated that woman who turned her own life topsy-turvy and never righted it. The foundation on which it was sitting had a large crack that could open at any moment and reveal all her foibles. She fought to keep from sobbing.

Joshua's arms tightened around her, and he leaned his head to kiss her hair. "I love you so much, Flory. You changed my whole life when you agreed to marry me."

She turned her face up and received his ardent kiss, hungry for more before the chance for them slipped away. Someday soon, she would have to tell him the truth, but she hadn't been able to work up the nerve to reveal the depth of her depravity to him.

When she was so breathless she could hardly think, Joshua put his hands on her shoulders. "Turn around, Flory. I have another surprise."

She obeyed, missing his touch when his hands left her. After only a moment, he slipped something around her neck. The metal felt cold against her heated skin. Her fingers touched the jewel-encrusted necklace. "What is this?"

He dropped another kiss against the back of her neck. "My anniversary gift to you. It reminded me of your eyes."

Florence went into the foyer and stood before the oval gilded mirror near the front door. She'd put it there when they moved into this house so she could check how she looked before she went out. Now she wanted to see her necklace. Staring at her own reflection, her eyes widened. The sapphire stones matched the color of the silk dress. She knew she had never looked this good before. Joshua was right. The stones and dress really played up her eyes.

She'd heard it said that the eyes were the windows to the soul. Florence was thankful that wasn't completely true, because the woman who looked back at her didn't reveal the ugliness hidden deep inside.

Florence awoke alone in their bed. Joshua had gone to work, leaving her asleep after their wonderful night filled with surprises, followed by the kind of intimacy they had missed for such a long time. The memory of the ecstasy sent a shiver of awareness up her spine. She picked up his pillow and hugged it tight, inhaling the familiar scent that meant Joshua, a mixture of St. Thomas Bay Rum shaving lotion and a musky male scent that was essentially his alone.

Her joy was too painful. Joshua was such a good man. He deserved a good woman, and Florence knew she was not good. Far too long, she'd been nothing but a bitter woman who was only concerned with herself and what she wanted. All that time Joshua had been building a business that provided her the things she thought she desired. But now she knew that material things weren't what she needed.

The time since Margaret left had been filled with Joshua trying to fulfill her deepest desires. Joshua loved her in spite of herself. He didn't hold her bitterness and quarrelsomeness against her...but she did. She was the reason God's greatest gift to them, their precious daughter, had wanted to go away for a while. What if Margaret never returned? It would be all Florence's fault if she decided to stay in Arkansas with her grandmother.

Why couldn't she have been the kind of mother her mother had been to her? Even if she didn't agree with something Florence did, her mother wouldn't have ever tried to make her daughter into someone she really didn't want to be.

That one night with her hateful thoughts had changed Florence forever. Everything that happened after that was colored by her choices. She insisted Joshua not tell Agatha or Georgia that Margaret was adopted. She nagged Joshua until he agreed to leave Oregon City where people knew about the adoption. Establishing a life in Seattle that was built partly on a lie had been her idea, but Joshua hadn't been very insistent that they be completely truthful.

Florence wished he had been, but she wouldn't put the blame on him. It rested squarely on her shoulders, and it had become a burden too great for her to bear. Tears clogged her throat, but she'd held them back for so many years, they didn't fall now.

Why had she been so hard on Margaret when she had that silly green dress altered to fit her? Of course, she looked better in it than Florence ever had. Even though she had been jealous, that wasn't the real reason.

A sudden thought grabbed her heart and squeezed like a vise. What if Margaret looked at other things in the attic? She probably didn't, but if she did, could she have found the white chest Florence had buried under so many other castoffs?

Florence jumped out of bed and dressed faster than she had in a long time. As she left the room, she caught herself just before she crashed into Ingrid bringing a tray with a pot of tea to her.

"Are you ready for some..."

"Not right now." She quickly interrupted the girl. "Just take it down to the kitchen. I'll come there to get it. I have something else to do first."

Florence watched confusion cloud Ingrid's eyes. She shouldn't have been so brusque with the girl.

"Yes, ma'am." Ingrid turned away and started down the backstairs.

Florence hurried to the door to the attic. She thrust it open and climbed the steep stairs. Morning light streamed in through the dormer windows. Even though dust motes twirled in the streaks of light, she noticed that the attic had recently been cleaned. No trails in the dust to tell if Margaret had moved anything else.

She glanced around and tried to remember exactly where she'd hidden it. So many wooden boxes and trunks were stored in the vast open space, she might have a hard time finding it. A long rope stretched across a section of the attic. The clothes hanging there were covered by dingy sheets, looking like dirty ghosts from her past. She pulled back the edge of the end sheet. Nothing was stacked behind them.

Trying to remember what was stored in each container, she eliminated some of them. Then she spied the haphazard stack in a dark corner. Older blankets lay across them. She pulled them off. As she dug deeper and deeper, she found things they had worn on the wagon train. Each garment carried a load of memories. Memories that weighted her down even more. Even the dress she'd been wearing that fateful night when Angus McKenna gave Margaret to them. She remembered the feel of the infant cradled against her shoulder. The way the tiny girl nestled close, trusting her.

Florence shook her head. She didn't have time to think about that now. She had to find out. Finally, she came to the familiar trunk.

With each belonging she brought out into the light more and more unpleasant thoughts assailed her. As she dug back into the past, she feared that all her lies would be revealed as well. When she reached the bottom without finding the white chest, she knew. Margaret had to have found it... and opened the Pandora's box of secrets Florence had kept hidden for so many years. Now there would be no way to get them all back out of the light into the darkness where no one could see them.

She left the mess scattered on the floor and hurried down the stairs, tripping more than once on the steep steps. When she reached Margaret's room, she searched high and low—everywhere a chest that size could be hidden. She opened the wardrobe, and the green dress hanging there mocked her. Behind it was an empty space where something could have been stored. Did her daughter hide the chest in there? Did Margaret take the chest to Arkansas with her? Should she ask Ingrid?

Immediately she knew that wasn't a good idea. If Margaret hadn't told Ingrid, Florence didn't want the servant to know. She went back to the bedroom she shared with her husband and sat in the chair beside the window. The memories that had been chasing her landed in the center of her mind. Every detail of that time eighteen years ago played through her mind. Her blaming God for her childlessness. Railing at Him because He gave three children to Mrs. McKenna. Wishing she could have one of the woman's babies.

And then the woman's death, which hung heavy on her heart, closely followed by God's indescribable gift. Finally, the tears she'd held in through all the intervening years gushed forth like the waves battering the shores of Puget Sound during a storm. She wept alone, wishing she could go back and do things differently this time. Would she ever regain her daughter's trust, or was it too late?

Chapter 15

THE DAY FOLLOWING their anniversary celebration Joshua had a hard time keeping his mind on business. Still, it was essential that they finish the construction in the building as soon as possible without causing the customers undue stress. Today three or four things went wrong, keeping him at work longer than he'd planned to stay. All he really wanted to do was get home to Florence.

Last night had turned out even better than he'd hoped it would. The special meal was delicious. The servants pulled it off flawlessly. Flory had bought him a very thoughtful gift for their anniversary. He'd cherish the gold watch until his dying day. She'd loved the sapphire necklace. It was the last thing she took off before she went to bed with him. He dared not think about what followed, or he would be out the door and on the way home for more of the same.

The Flory he'd known and loved as a young woman had returned last night with all the passion they'd shared. He was sure her heart was softening so much that when Maggie came home, she'd even treat their daughter in a totally different way. Everything he'd wanted to happen while Maggie was gone was finally coming to pass.

And Flory wasn't the only person changing. So was he. His focus, which had been completely on work for so long, had returned to the place where it belonged. Yes, business was important. Yes, he wanted to take care of his family financially. But more importantly, now he wanted all the facets of his life to be in the proper relationship with everything else.

God first. His wife and family second. The business and everything else following behind those two things.

Finally, all the problems at work had been taken care of, and he was on the way home. He pushed all the business details into the compartment in his mind where they belonged. While Erik drove the buggy, Joshua let his mind dwell on his still-beautiful wife waiting for him there.

166

When Erik stopped the carriage, Joshua jumped out and hurried toward the front door. He let himself in, expecting to find Flory waiting downstairs for him, but she was nowhere to be found. He took the steps two at a time and hurried down the hallway, thrusting the door open with a bang.

Florence stood beside the bed. She turned her face toward the door when the knob hit the wall. When she flinched, he grabbed the door and stabilized it, wishing he'd been more careful.

Then he noticed her face. Not the smile he'd been expecting. Instead, her tear-ravished expression tore at his soul. He rushed toward her and pulled her into his arms. "Flory, what's wrong?"

She leaned her head against his chest a moment. "Joshua, I must tell you something." Her voice trembled as did her body.

The cold, flat tone of her words told him that something was terribly wrong. What could have happened since he left her asleep this morning, her face still rosy from their lovemaking? Dread fell like a heavy cloak on his shoulders. *Lord, make me the husband she needs right now, whatever the problem is.*

"What is wrong?" He tried to keep his tone loving and hide the fear that clawed at him.

A sob shattered the stillness. "I don't know where to start."

This wasn't sounding promising. What could have happened while he was gone? "Maybe at the beginning would be good."

Her trembling increased, and he pulled her even tighter against him. A man of action, he found it hard to wait for her to speak.

"Margaret..." Her voice broke on that one word, and she didn't continue.

The question that had been burning in his mind for a long time came to the forefront.

"There's one thing I don't understand, Flory." He hesitated to ask, because he didn't want to make her feel bad again. But he wanted to know, needed to know. For Maggie. "Why did you start being hard on our daughter?"

He wondered if she was going to answer, because she didn't say a word for so long.

"I'm not proud of this either. But..." She let her voice trail away. "Remember how you told me for so long...it didn't matter to you that we didn't have any children? That our love was enough?"

"Right."

Where was she going with this? If he lived a million years, he'd never learn to understand the way a woman's mind worked. Men were decisive. A woman's mind took the long way around a subject. That must be what was happening here.

"When you doted on Margaret so much, I thought you'd only said that to make me feel better." The words came out in a rush this time. "So I decided I really was only half a woman. That idea festered like a splinter in my soul, making me into a bitter woman. I was trying to balance your spoiling by being harder on her, maybe harder than I should have been. Now you know, and I'm not proud of it."

Now they were getting somewhere with this discussion. "You do know that after the enemy of your soul fed you one lie and you believed it, he kept on telling you others."

She nodded. "Of course, I realize that now. Thanks to you." She stared up into his eyes.

He was glad he had his arm around her. "And we'll have no more of those kinds of secrets between us, will we?"

Pain and fear entered her eyes, and she dropped her gaze. He could tell something else still bothered her. For a moment all was quiet as he waited silently, praying for this woman he loved with all his heart. He couldn't imagine what had caused her so much distress, but he was ready and able to fight the battle for her. Be her protector. Supernatural strength from God flowed through him, preparing him to face whatever was to come.

Finally, she raised her head and turned her anguished gaze toward his. "Margaret found the chest of things I kept from the wagon train."

He didn't understand why that would upset Florence so much. She must have read his hesitancy, because she pulled away and paced across their bedchamber. She jerked back the heavy draperies and stared out into the waning sunlight. Her profile didn't reveal what was amiss.

"The adoption paper was in the bottom of that chest, along with the daguerreotype of her mother that Angus McKenna gave us." Florence turned back toward him. "I'm sure she'll recognize the resemblance."

He went to her and pulled her back against him, nestling her head under his chin. "Why is this so distressing to you?"

"Remember, I talked you into keeping the truth from her." Her words were ragged around the edges. "I'm afraid that was a mistake. What if she hates us for lying to her?"

For the life of him, he couldn't understand why that would happen. "But we've been good parents to her. Why would she hate us?"

She pulled away and stood before him, wringing her hands. "You've been good to her, but I have been too hard on her, at least the last few years."

How could he not agree with that? Hadn't he been hoping their time together would mellow Florence toward their daughter? "All right, let's discuss all the repercussions of this discovery, see what we can do about it."

"She changed toward me after she found the chest."

His analytical mind couldn't find a root cause for all this information. "How do you know when she found it?"

She started pacing again, back and forth across the expanse of the room, still wringing her hands. "It had to be before her birthday party, when she found the dress. That was when her attitude toward me changed. I wondered what was causing it, or if she had been this way and I hadn't noticed before."

Florence stopped and clasped her hands in front of her. "I haven't been the kind of mother I should have been for Margaret."

He didn't know what direction she was going with this, but he really wanted to get to the root cause of their family problems. "And why is that, Flory?"

She turned away, going to her dresser and nervously straightening the things on top. She kept her back to him, but he caught her glancing at him in the mirror. So he forced a smile on his face, even though he was confused.

"I've been afraid to tell you."

He started to move toward her, but she sidestepped, so he held his place. "Why would you fear me? Have I ever done anything to hurt you?"

She shook her head. "No. It's all my fault."

"I'm not trying to place blame here." He fisted his hands in frustration, then stuffed them in the pockets of his trousers. "I just want to know what's bothering you so much."

"It's not pretty, and I'm not proud of what I did." She thrust her head up and her chin tightened with determination. "But I'm tired of feeling like a fraud. You've been treating me like a queen, and I don't deserve it...or your love."

That was all he could take. He went to her and cradled her against his chest. "My love for you isn't conditional, Flory. You don't have to earn my love. It's a gift. Just as God's love doesn't come with strings attached."

Tears streamed down her face and made splotches on his shirt, the heat from them searing all the way to his heart.

"I really need to get this off my chest. The weight of it is too heavy." She hiccuped and lifted her eyes toward his. "I haven't wanted you to see the darkness in my own heart and soul."

Her words really began to scare him. *Lord, I need You now more than I have ever before. Help me be what I need to be for Flory.*

He led her to the two chairs sitting beside the window, with a lamp table between. After settling her into one, he pulled the other around to face her and dropped into it. Then he took her hands into his, drawing lazy circles on the backs with his thumbs. "Look at me, Flory. Nothing, and I mean absolutely nothing, can make me not love you. Do you understand?" He emphasized each word, giving it all the authority he could muster.

For a moment, she just stared at him, then nodded. "I didn't understand that for a long time, but I believe it now...after the last couple of weeks."

"I apologize for seeming to put business ahead of you." He squeezed her hands. "It was never my intention."

She heaved a sigh that sounded as if it came all the way from her toes. "Remember that time on the wagon train when we stopped because of Mrs. McKenna?"

"How could I forget? That's when God gave us our daughter." His voice broke on the last word, and he cleared his throat.

Florence tried to pull her hands from his, but he held on with a firm, but not painful grip.

"I had a hard heart toward God."

He shook his head, and she noticed. "Let me finish while I still have the nerve. I was railing against God for not giving me a child. I felt like half a woman. Like Rachel when she cried out to God. I should have been able to give you a child, but God didn't let me." She took a deep breath. "I even asked Him why He would give her three and not give me any. I told Him one of those babies should be mine, because I didn't have one."

A sob punctuated her words and her shoulders shook. "When...she...died..."

He stood and gathered her to him again, rubbing her back while she cried out the agony in her soul. When she finally quieted, he whispered, "Your words or thoughts did not cause Lenora McKenna to die. She wasn't strong enough to deliver three babies and live. The doctor had warned them that she was growing very weak."

"But I believed it was my fault." A sobbing sound shook her. "My dark thoughts have haunted me for a long time, turning my heart bitter."

He wished she'd shared this with him years ago. His heart ached for all the time she'd believed a lie. "You know, Flory, Satan told you that lie, and he kept you believing it."

She nodded.

Joshua cradled her against his chest. "Flory, I want to pray for you."

"I'd like that, Joshua." Her words were muffled against his damp shirt, but he heard each one.

He led her back to the chairs they had vacated earlier. After they were seated, facing each other with their knees touching, he grasped her hands in his. For a long moment, he remained silent.

"Father God, I know how much You love me and how much You love my beloved wife, but Lord, she doesn't understand how much You love her. Please wrap Your arms of love around her just the same way my arms have encircled her. Make Yourself real to her in her soul and her inner being. Show her how much You've watched over her and cared for her all of her life."

He opened his eyes and glanced up at Florence. Tears streamed down her cheeks, but her expression was one of peace instead of pain.

"Oh, Lord..." Her voice trembled. "I'm so sorry for the anger I had in my heart toward You." Now the words poured out in strength, almost tumbling over each other. "I do realize that Maggie was a special gift from You, and I should have cherished her. I should have turned to You with my dark thoughts instead of thrusting them deep in my heart and hiding them. I haven't been the woman You desired me to be, but I want that to change. And I will surrender my thoughts and desires to You."

When the outpouring stopped, a few tears leaked from Joshua's eyes. He'd never cried with his wife before, but it felt right. "And Lord, I've not always been the husband You wanted me to be for Florence. Nor the father I should have been for Maggie. I want that to change. Lord, help us make today the beginning of a new life according to Your will. In Jesus's name. Amen."

A comfortable silence filled the room around them, and he kept his head down and held on to his wife's hands. When he finally raised his head, his beautiful wife stared at him with a smile gleaming through her tears.

"I feel as though a heavy weight has been lifted from my soul." Flory stopped and took a deep breath, letting it out is a long whoosh. "I don't know if I've ever felt so free."

He stood and pulled her up into his arms. "I know what you mean. From now on, we'll face everything together." He used one hand to tip her chin up. "And no more secrets between us, right?"

When her lips met his they sealed the new promise.

Chapter 16

BECAUSE AGATHA WAS busy at work, the first few days in Arkansas were filled with Maggie spending a lot of time with Georgia, and Charles tagging along with them. The two women made several forays to shop for things she was sure Charles wasn't interested in. That didn't keep him from accompanying them like some kind of bodyguard. Maggie didn't understand why he felt they needed the retinue.

Maggie had been careful to pack each of the items she bought in the trunk so it wouldn't be damaged on the way home, especially the lovely forest green hat she found at *Les Chapeaux*. She took a long time choosing just the right one from the vast array displayed.

She had eagerly shopped for items for her father and herself, but she had a hard time buying something for Florence. But she knew she couldn't go home without a gift for her. She finally chose a lovely Persian patterned fringed shawl with predominant shades of blue.

Finally one morning Agatha arrived at breakfast and announced, "I'm going to take the day off and spend it with my granddaughter, daughter, and their friend." Her grandmother went to the stove and poured herself a cup of coffee. "I'm embarrassed that I haven't shown you around Little Rock yet, but several important orders came up just before you arrived. Now that those designs are done, I can take some time off."

Spend the day with me? The idea that Agatha would take the day off just for her was a surprise to Maggie. She felt special and wistful at the same time. If only they really were kin. This might be the last time she would have the opportunity to pretend they were family. She wanted to make the most of it before the truth destroyed the relationship.

"Now you just sit down, Miz Agatha. I be bringin' your breakfast." Shirley flipped two pancakes from her skillet onto a plate, smeared them with butter, then poured warm maple syrup over them. "You want one fried egg or two this mornin'?"

176

"One will be plenty." Agatha pulled out the chair closest to Maggie and set her coffee cup down before sitting. "I thought we could see some sights."

"That sounds delightful to me." Maggie put her fork on her plate and added a little more syrup to her pancakes.

Shirley placed the filled plate in front of Agatha. "Don' remember the last time you took off work."

Agatha had lifted her cup to her lips, but she took only a sip before putting it down. "I know, but with Maggie here, I want to spend all the time I can with her." She took a bite of the buckwheat pancakes. "Delicious, Shirley. Just the way I like them." Agatha glanced toward her then at Shirley. "So where are Georgia and Charles?"

Maggie didn't like the way the words sounded when Agatha said *Georgia and Charles* as if they belonged together. Yes, they had spent a lot of time flirting on the train, but the two of them really together didn't feel good to her. She didn't have any right to be jealous in this situation, but she couldn't stop the feeling. There was a real possibility Georgia and Charles would really become an item. If that happened, how would she feel whenever they visited in her home in Seattle? She didn't even want to imagine.

"Miz Georgia done ate. Went upstairs to change her clothes. She spilled syrup on her dress." Shirley stood with her hands on her hips. "And that Mr. Charles done gone out to the stable with Tucker. Said he'd prob'ly be back soon."

Maggie didn't question why she felt relieved at that information. She just knew she was glad they were in different places. How long would that last?

"Maggie, dear, where would you like to go today?" Agatha continued to enjoy her breakfast between their spurts of conversation.

"We've already visited most of the shops. So what I'd like to see is…everything! The whole town of Little Rock."

Agatha smiled at her. "We can take care of that today. I love Little

Rock, and I want to show you why I do." She took Maggie's hand and gave it a squeeze. "Perhaps I can persuade you that Little Rock would be a wonderful place to live and call home."

Maggie returned her smile, but quickly ducked her head to hide her tears. Where was home? Until now, she had thought it was in Seattle with her parents. Now she didn't know where—or to whom—she belonged.

Charles stood beside the surrey awaiting Maggie, Agatha, and Georgia. "Do they always take this long just to get ready for a drive, Tucker?"

The older man was perched on his seat, holding the reins. "Mos' times, they do." A deep chuckle followed his words.

"I guess I'd better get used to it." Charles placed one foot on the step at the side of the carriage and leaned his arm on his knee. "You know, after my grandma passed away, we didn't have any women in the house, so I'm learning things about them all the time."

This time Tucker's laugh bounced around in the cool, crisp autumn air. "Won' never be done with that."

"What's so funny, Tucker?" At the first sound of the feminine voice, Charles quickly turned to stand on both feet.

"Agatha, you sneaked up on me." Charles gave her his most beguiling smile.

She tapped him with her folded fan. "Don't go wasting all that charm on me, young man."

He chuckled. "Do you always have such nice weather in October?"

"It's not unusual, but remember, it can quickly turn cold."

His gaze went past her to Maggie standing close behind, but he didn't see Georgia. Today, maybe he would sit beside Georgia and let Agatha and her granddaughter be together. The scowl on Maggie's face reminded him that he really was worried about her.

He had thought that after they arrived in Little Rock, she would be her old self. But it didn't happen. Whatever was wrong with her had to be serious, because otherwise she wouldn't have hung on to it for so long. Even though he was interested in Georgia, it didn't mean that he had forgotten his desire to protect Maggie. But he needed to know what he should be protecting her from.

He offered his hand to Agatha as she stepped into the surrey. She scooted across to the other side of the front seat. When he helped Maggie up, she sat beside her grandmother. That left Georgia and him in the back seat. Just what he wanted. He was going to enjoy this outing.

"Miz Agatha, where we goin' first?" Tucker awaited her directions.

"Let's take Maggie and Charles by the Baring Cross railroad bridge, so they can see how we're connected to the other side of the Arkansas River."

Tucker started the team down the street at a comfortable trot. They would make good time, but they weren't going so fast they couldn't enjoy the scenery. Even though the air was cool, the sun shone bright.

As they went along, Agatha called everyone's attention to many points of interest—the mayor's house, the place the governor lived, churches, even the Little Rock Police Department. When they drove by a small building with wires running from it to poles along the street, Maggie asked what was in the building.

"That's the Little Rock Telephone Exchange. When it first came to town six years ago, they only had about ten subscribers. The number is much higher now." Agatha opened her handbag and put the fan inside. She realized she probably wouldn't need it for a while.

"Do you have a telephone, Grandmother? I didn't notice one on the wall at home or at The House of Agatha Carter." Maggie pronounced the name of her grandmother's business with pride.

"Not yet. I've been thinking about getting one in my office at work, but I'm not sure I want one at home. That ringing could be annoying if people called very often. I haven't decided for sure."

Georgia leaned forward. "I think you should, Mother. When Scott first heard about Mr. Bell's invention, he said it would really change the way people communicated with each other. But we weren't sure if we'd see it in our lifetimes."

Charles watched the way Maggie hung on to Georgia's words. She'd had to scoot sideways and turn most of the way around to see her aunt. He loved seeing her interested in something that brought her out of herself and made her forget for a while whatever it was that bothered her so much.

"Oh, I believe we'll see more and more people use that wonderful invention." Maggie's eyes sparkled. "Just look what the telegraph has done for the country. Instead of having to wait for the information to come through the mail, we knew right away that Grover Cleveland had been elected president."

Tucker stopped the carriage and glanced toward Agatha. "Cain't get no closer to the railroad bridge in this buggy, Miz Agatha."

"We can see it just fine from here."

Maggie's attention turned toward the front of the surrey. "I'm sure it took a while to build that bridge. It's long."

"Yes." Agatha stared across the fast-moving water. "That's our only real connection to the other side of the river."

"So how do people get over there if they don't take the train?" Maggie stood up and held onto the back of the seat. "There are buildings on that side of the river too."

"Steamboats go from this side to the other and back." Georgia put her hand on top of her hat when a gust of wind raised the brim. "That's the city of Argenta, although it's a small settlement. Many people in Little Rock want to annex it, but some people on

180

the other side of the river oppose the idea. You know how politics is."

"I've heard Daddy discuss it some." Maggie sat back down, holding her own hat to her head.

Georgia turned toward Agatha. "Can we take Maggie to see *La Petite Roche*?"

"If she wants to see it." When Maggie nodded, Agatha told Tucker to take them there.

Along the way, they passed the United States Weather Bureau. Charles studied Maggie. She looked as if she were taking mental notes. Her brow would pucker and she'd squint her eyes when she concentrated. For a while at least, she seemed to have forgotten whatever was bothering her.

When Tucker stopped the surrey at the side of the street close to the riverbank, Charles got down to help the women. After both Georgia and her mother were standing on the ground, he offered his hand to Maggie to assist her as well.

The women started walking down a well-worn path. Agatha stopped near the edge of the riverbank. "I don't really want to go any closer. I'm going to stay right here. What about you, Georgia?"

"I know Maggie wants to see the actual rock." Georgia smiled at her niece. "Let's go."

"I'd like to see that famous stone too." Charles fell into step behind her.

Georgia took a couple more steps forward, watching where she placed each foot. "See those bushes?"

Charles stopped beside her. "The ones with branches dragging against the bank?"

"Yes. The path leads around them, then turns back to the right. It's safe, but you have to be careful in some places." She grinned up at him.

He gave her a slow nod.

Until they reached the edges of the bushes, the path was wide enough for them to walk together, and the slope wasn't too steep. After they passed the bushes and turned to the right, he had to lead the way, being careful that the women had a safe place to step. Soon they came to a wider space where they could once again easily walk.

And there it was. A flat outcropping of whitish rock sunk deep into the side of the riverbank.

"It's beautiful." Maggie stood transfixed. "In a natural sort of way."

"I've always loved it here with the rock and the swift flowing water." Georgia shielded her eyes with one hand.

Charles stared at the formation, then glanced at the wide river. "I wonder if God knew when He created this that people would need the rock as a marker."

Maggie looked up at him and the golden flecks in her green eyes glimmered in the sunlight. "What a strange thing to say."

At first, her words didn't register in his mind, then their echo crept through his thoughts. "Why do you think it's strange? God cares about the people He created, and He places things in our paths to lead us closer to Him."

She cocked her head to the side and stared across the water. "I'm not so sure He does."

Her words fell like heavy stones between them, and Georgia gave a small gasp.

Charles had been so sure Maggie loved the Lord as much as he did, but those words didn't make sense if she did. He remembered her scolding him for not attending church that day in her father's office. What if she only went to church because her family did? Maybe she hadn't met Jesus on a personal level as he had. He thought she had when she was younger. He remembered how she had always been an active participant in worship. Something had definitely changed in her life, and it had to be a recent change.

"I'm going to try to get closer to the rock." Maggie moved away from him and Georgia.

"Do be careful. If you were to fall in the river, I'm not sure we could rescue you." Georgia frowned.

Maggie turned back toward them. "I won't do anything dangerous."

When she started making her way across the uneven ground, Georgia took a step to follow.

"Please stay with me." Charles gently took her arm. "I've been wanting to ask you a question about Maggie."

Interest flared in Georgia's eyes. "What about Maggie?"

How should he put this without giving her the wrong idea about his friend? "Have you noticed anything different about Maggie lately?"

Georgia pulled away from him and turned so she could see both her niece and him. "In what way?"

"I'm not sure how to put it." He ran his hand across the back of his neck and whooshed out a breath. "Something is bothering her, but I can't imagine what it is."

"I haven't noticed anything." Concern puckered Georgia's brow. "When did it start?" She glanced at Maggie then back toward him.

"The first time I noticed was at her birthday party, and she's been different ever since." When he looked at Maggie, she stood near the rock and stared across the water. "Something deep in her eyes is always there like she has a secret that has hurt her somehow. It's hard to explain."

Georgia watched Maggie for a moment. "I haven't really spent that much time with her so that I could tell if anything is wrong. She always seems the same to me."

That didn't gain him any information. He'd just have to look for a chance to talk to Maggie when no one else was around. He stared at a root beside his shoe while he pondered this. Nothing could be done today. So he shoved his concern into its compartment in his brain.

He glanced up at Georgia. The wind whipped her skirts around her, outlining her figure, and pulling strands of hair from under her hat. Such a beautiful woman.

Sidling up beside her, he tried to sound casual. "Georgia, I'd like to ask you a personal question."

Her attention flashed back toward him. "What kind of question?" Her tone was tentative and her gaze wary.

"I've come to admire you greatly on our journey. We've had a lot of fun together."

She smiled and nodded at his statement.

"When we get back to Seattle, I'd like to call on you." He glanced down, almost afraid to watch her reaction. "Perhaps even court you."

At her gasp, he whipped his gaze toward her.

"Is this a joke, Charles?"

A joke? She thought it was a joke? He stared at her. He couldn't keep the chagrin from his expression.

Her face fell. "You weren't joking, were you?"

"I thought…something was developing between us." He stuffed his hands into the pockets of his slacks.

"Yes, a friendship." She gazed toward the river. "I never realized you would think it was anything else. I'm old enough to be…well, I'm a lot older than you are."

He studied her, for the first time noticing almost invisible lines fanning from the corners of her eyes. Just how much older was she? Even if she were twenty-five or six, they could make a go of it.

"I'm thirty-one, Charles." Her tone had softened. "And besides that, I'm not interested in a romantic relationship with any man." She cleared her throat. "I think it would be best if we just forget this conversation ever took place. Agreed?"

Finally she looked at him. He had feared he would read pity

in her gaze, but it wasn't there, just steady regard and respect. "Agreed."

He had never been rebuffed by a woman before, but at once, he knew he deserved it. *What was I thinking?*

Chapter 17

MAGGIE STOOD AT the river's edge, watching willow branches sway in the soft breeze as they trailed in the water. Was Charles right? Did God place things in people's lives because He knew they needed them? Like that slab of rock hidden in the riverbank for centuries until flooding water washed away the extra soil at just the right time the Indians needed it as a landmark. The idea brought a strange kind of peace to her soul. But did it really fit with her past?

She wanted to believe it was true for her too. Perhaps God *had* hidden the secret of her adoption until the right time came to reveal it. Staring across the swirling water, Maggie recognized the enormity of such a discovery to the people who first noticed the white rock. Was her discovery of the adoption paper just as momentous? And did it happen at just the right time?

A steamboat whistle drew her attention. She turned to look upstream. Quite a ways up the riverbank, the boat pulled close to a dock she hadn't noticed until that moment.

"Have you ever ridden in a steamboat?" Charles stood close beside her, and she hadn't even noticed him approaching.

She took one step away from him to put some space between them, giving her a better chance to control her emotions. "No, have you?" Her soft words floated away on the breeze.

His wide smile revealed he'd heard them anyway, and the twinkle in his eyes made her think he had read her other thoughts. But did she really want him to? Probably not right now.

"Would you like to go?"

She considered his question for a moment. "I think Agatha has today all planned out."

"Then I'll have to take you sometime after we get back home. Steamboats come into Puget Sound all the time."

As they started back up the trail toward where Georgia stood, his hand lightly touching her back comforted her. She could count on his friendship now just as she had as a girl. At least she had one really good friend. Hopefully the truth, when he finally heard it, wouldn't drive him away from her.

When it was time to climb single file, Charles took her hand and led the way. She wondered how he knew where to step, because he kept looking behind to make sure she and Georgia were safe instead of watching the path.

Safe? She hadn't realized that all the turmoil she'd been going through since she found the white chest actually made her feel *unsafe*. But she did. What would Daddy and Florence do when they found out she knew the truth? Would her parentage change everyone's perception and acceptance of her?

She felt as if the ground shifted under her feet, shaking her very foundation. Thank goodness, the riverbank was solid and sturdy. The turmoil was all inside her.

Even though Georgia had been gracious as she rejected his presumptuous request, Charles still felt the sting of realizing he'd made a fool of himself. He'd never been in a situation like this before. His grandpa would have been ashamed of him for such a breach of conduct.

Actually, he was ashamed of himself. For putting her on the spot that way. For not being more careful about understanding the dynamics of their relationship. For actually failing to protect Georgia the way he had assured Joshua he would. If any other man would have made a move on her that way, Charles would have had to put him in his place.

He was just thankful no one else knew about his *faux pas*. For the rest of the journey, he would keep his mind where it belonged and truly fulfill his responsibility both to Georgia and Maggie...and to Joshua.

After Charles helped the ladies into the surrey, they continued their tour. He'd enjoyed the ride, but he watched Maggie and the scenery and didn't even glance at Georgia. Before he made his mistake with Georgia, he had asked her about Maggie. Maybe he should concentrate on trying to find out how he could help his good friend. He kept looking for some indication of what was bothering her.

Along the way, they met more than one horse-drawn streetcar. Other people rode in open buggies and closed coaches, and several men rode horses, looking like citified cowboys. Not too many cowboys in Seattle these days. Loggers and Indians, but not cowboys.

When they started down the street where the Anthony House— Little Rock's most popular hotel—stood, Agatha tapped Tucker on the shoulder. "Let's stop here for lunch."

"Yes, ma'am, Miz Agatha." The black man deftly maneuvered the surrey close enough to the boardwalk in front of the building, so the passengers could actually move from the step of the buggy to the edge of the wooden platform.

Charles exited the surrey first, then assisted the women as he always did. He followed the women through the doorway of the hotel into a large lobby area, with carpeting, brass fittings, and polished wooden banisters on the staircase. Light fixtures fastened to the walls were lit, even though sunlight poured between the pulled-back draperies on the windows.

In the dining room many of the linen-draped tables were in use, but Agatha headed toward an empty one near the front windows. "Let's sit here. I like to watch the people coming and going in the street."

After they ordered their food, Agatha looked at Maggie. "So, Margaret, tell me more about your dear mother. How does she spend her days?"

Maggie glanced up as if startled. Charles wondered why the question would bother her.

She hesitated a moment, then cleared her throat. "She stays busy most of the time. She's involved in many things at church and around town."

"What kind of things?" Agatha leaned toward her with interest written all over her face.

Charles wondered how long it had been since she had seen her older daughter. And he was thankful she didn't know about his blunder with her younger one.

"She and her friends often have tea parties."

"Sounds like fun. Do you go with her?"

"Not often. I have my own interests." A slight frown marred Maggie's face. "She enjoys all the balls and going out to eat with Father. Seattle has a couple of theaters, and Mother and Daddy often attend galas there. And she loves to shop."

"Yes." Georgia smiled toward her mother. "Florence took me shopping several times after I arrived for Maggie's party. We had a really good time, Mother. Seattle is not a small town. It's a city filled with an amazing assortment of things and interesting people to watch."

Even though he still felt uncomfortable, he forced himself to glance at Georgia as the conversation continued.

"I'm glad to hear that my daughter has a good, full life." Agatha's brow puckered when she looked at Maggie. "I wasn't sure how it would turn out when Joshua wanted to go west."

Maggie stared out the window, but Charles didn't think she paid attention to what was out there. At least *she* didn't know about what he'd done out there on the riverbank. They could continue their comfortable friendship.

"Of course, when she had Maggie, her letters were filled with anecdotes about my adorable granddaughter." Agatha patted

Maggie's hand, and Maggie gave her a tight smile. "A mother never stops worrying about her children, especially when they don't live close to her. So Maggie, would you say your mother is happy?"

Maggie thrust her hands out of sight in her lap. "I'm sure she is most of the time." Her answer sounded tentative to Charles. He stared at her, trying to pierce the façade she hid behind.

Georgia leaned toward her mother. "You should have seen the lavish party Flo planned for Maggie's eighteenth birthday. I'm sure most of the elite in Seattle were in attendance. And there was a ball. Maggie wore that green dress you made for Florence. It brought out her loveliness. Just the right shade for her unique coloring."

For a moment, Maggie winced as if in pain. At least her grandmother wasn't looking at her when she did. But Charles noticed.

He watched this conversation unfold with interest. Georgia was really involved in the discussion, but when her aunt added information, Maggie leaned back as if withdrawing from them.

When she had been talking, Charles saw her countenance change. All Agatha did was mention her mother, and the laughing Maggie disintegrated into a girl fighting to hide her tears. He recognized all the signs. He'd seen them before, he just hadn't put it all together until now. He wanted to offer her his handkerchief, but he somehow understood she hoped no one else would notice. Just as he hoped no one else would discover his mistake, he wouldn't betray her.

I have to find out what's going on with her. It must be something with her mother. Or is she just homesick? He and his grandfather had known the Caines at church, and they often attended the same functions around town. He'd never seen anything to indicate there was a problem within the family. He believed he would've noticed if anything were amiss between her and her parents, especially her mother.

Something momentous must have happened. As he watched her

blink away a fine sheen of tears, he vowed to find out what event brought her to this display of deep hurt. Then he'd plan how he could help her through the situation as any good friend would.

Chapter 18

AFTER ATTENDING CHURCH with Agatha on Sunday, the second week in Arkansas was filled with Maggie spending as much time as possible at The House of Agatha Carter. Before this, she hadn't realized how much was involved in running a business. Her grandmother taught her about ordering products, dealing with customers, accounting, and taking care of payroll. All of this would help if she ever started a design business of her own.

Now she had only one more day until they would start the homeward journey. Their two weeks in Arkansas had sped on eagles' wings, and Maggie found herself dreading her return to Seattle. She understood she had to know the truth, but she knew the confrontation with her parents could be unbearably painful.

After breakfast, Maggie quickly donned a forest green, jean wool skirt. She loved the soft texture and the strength of this woven fabric. The color matched the tatted edges of the ruffles cascading down the front of her favorite pinstriped blouse. When she looked in the cheval glass, the woman staring back at her gave a very professional appearance, if she could only tame those curls that insisted on escaping every chance they could. She shoved several kinky strands back into the bun on her nape and added more hairpins. Hopefully these would hold them in place.

Today she was going to do design work with Agatha. After looking at a few of Maggie's designs, her grandmother said she had a rare talent. And today she wanted her opinion on ideas for some new patterns she was working on. This was far more than she had dreamed would happen while she was here. She skipped down the stairs and found Agatha waiting in the foyer.

Agatha indicated Maggie's empty hands. "Where is your sketch pad?"

She stopped before she reached the bottom step. "Do I need to bring it?"

"Yes. I'll want to study all your drawings today. Perhaps they will give me ideas for our new fashions as well." A smile curled the ends of her grandmother's lips.

Maggie whirled around and took the stairs at a fast clip. Excitement throbbed through her, shadowed by intimidation. How could she possibly contribute to the wonderful designs her grandmother produced? After grabbing up her sketches, she also stuck the pencils in her handbag and ran back downstairs to join her grandmother, arriving out of breath.

When they reached The House of Agatha Carter, Grandmother told her to put her things in the office. "If you don't have a pad to takes notes, I'll give you one of mine."

"Thank you. Actually, I always carry one. I never know when I'll see something I want to remember." Maggie grabbed a stubby, flat wooden pencil and a small pad and thrust them into the pocket cleverly hidden in the side of her skirt.

As Agatha talked with each of her employees, Maggie took copious notes, along with creating tiny illustrations. She had no idea how long it would be before she could even consider trying to start a business of her own, and she wanted to remember every detail. After they had talked to each of the employees about their assignments for the day, Agatha led her into the office. "Now let me see your sketches."

Maggie pulled her drawings out of the handbag and handed the sketchpad to her grandmother. Agatha dropped into the wing-back chair behind the desk and studied the first drawing. Maggie tried not to fidget too much while she waited. Although Agatha had said they were good when she looked at them earlier, what if she changed her mind in the meantime?

"I like this design. Come here and I'll show you what is really good and what I would change and why." She gestured for Maggie to scoot one of the other chairs closer.

While Agatha pointed out the things she liked, Maggie couldn't keep pride at bay, no matter how hard she tried. When her grandmother suggested changes, every time Maggie recognized how much better the design became by just changing a line here or there.

She was so engrossed in what they were doing that the arrival of lunchtime surprised her. And she felt she had been given a priceless gift by her grandmother. After she put the sketch pad in her bag, she gave Agatha a hug.

"Thank you so much."

Her grandmother returned the embrace and sealed it with a kiss on the cheek. "My pleasure. You have a real gift. I hope you'll pursue your dreams relentlessly."

"I intend to." Maggie gathered up her things and followed her grandmother to the coach.

A cold wind blew from the direction of the river, and more and more leaves released their hold on the branches to dance in the capricious wind. The end of autumn was fast approaching.

"It's a good thing you're leaving tomorrow. You'll want to get across the mountains before the snows come. Sometimes the tracks are impassible for days at a time." Agatha patted Maggie's knee. "I don't want to worry about you. Be sure you have your father send a telegram, so I'll know you arrived home safely."

Maggie assured her that she would. The thought of being snowbound in any of the towns they'd come through in the mountains wasn't a pleasant prospect. She shivered at the thought.

Her grandmother took her back to the hotel for lunch, just the two of them. However, they quickly finished the delicious meal and returned to The House of Agatha Carter.

After spending most of the afternoon learning about keeping up with appointments and finances, Maggie and her grandmother headed to the house, which appeared to be deserted. Agatha went through the kitchen and out the back. Maggie followed her.

"Tucker, where is everyone?"

"Shirley needed to go to the store, and Mr. Stanton and Miz Long decided to go 'long. I be pickin' 'em up later."

As the two women walked back into the house, Agatha put her arm around Maggie's shoulders. "I've been wanting to talk to you privately anyway." She led the way into the parlor.

Maggie couldn't imagine what her grandmother wanted to talk about, but she'd treasure this time, just in case anything changed after she got back to Seattle. She sat in the chair that faced the sofa, and Agatha took her place at the end of the couch.

"Margaret, dear, your time here is drawing to a close. I've seen your interest in my business and witnessed your designing skills. I would still love to have you stay here and learn the business, perhaps even take it over someday. What do you say?" Agatha dropped her hands into her lap and quietly waited.

Maggie stared at the pattern in the Persian carpet, so like the shawl she had bought for Florence. She sat there stunned. She had considered staying to learn the business. But staying permanently? Her mind whirled at the thought.

"If you think your parents would object, I would be happy to pose the question to them myself," Agatha continued.

Maggie shook her head, then to her dismay, tears filled her eyes.

"My dear, what is it?" Agatha asked. "I thought you would welcome the idea, but certainly if you'd rather return home..."

"That's not it," Maggie choked out. "I would love to stay. It's just..." She found herself unable to continue.

"I believe I've come to know you very well in the short time you've been here." Agatha paused, and her brow wrinkled in concentration. "I know something is bothering you. I've prayed for you and whatever the problem is, but I've not gotten any peace about it. I believe the Lord wants me to ask you. Do you feel you can tell me about the problem?"

Maggie tried to clear the knot in her chest. Pain radiated from it, almost as if she was having a heart problem. "I don't know where to start." She blew out a breath.

Agatha chuckled. "I've always found the beginning to be a good place."

"I'm not even sure when it began." Maggie's thoughts jumbled together, and she took a moment to let them settle. "I'll tell you about what I found not long before my birthday."

"Whatever you want to do, child." Agatha's soothing tone calmed Maggie.

She explained why she went into the attic and how she found the green dress. "And then I noticed several trunks."

"And you explored them?"

Maggie recognized that Agatha had strong discernment, especially in this instance. "Yes."

"What did you find that disturbed you so much?"

Maggie recounted the clothing that had to be what her father and mother wore on the wagon train, and then the little white trunk buried deep inside a larger one. By now, tears streamed down her cheeks. She swiped at them with the palms of her hands. Agatha extracted a hanky from under the edge of her sleeve and handed it to Maggie. "What was in that little white trunk?"

Wiping her eyes, Maggie rose from her chair then handed the handkerchief back. "I want to show you."

She hurried from the parlor and up the stairs to her bedchamber. When she came back, she carried the small trunk. She sat on the other end of the sofa from her grandmother and placed the trunk between them.

After lifting out the blanket, she handed it to Agatha. "Did you knit this?"

Her grandmother inspected the piece, unfolding it and turning it over and over. "This is pretty, but no, I never learned to knit."

"Does Georgia?" Maggie handed her the sweater and cap. "I've never seen Mother knit anything either."

Agatha laid the things in her lap. "None of us has ever knitted, that I know of. Maybe a friend of Florence's did this."

Maggie moved all the other baby garments from the trunk, revealing the framed photograph and a piece of faded paper. She handed the picture to her grandmother. "Do you know this woman?"

Agatha studied it then turned her attention to Maggie. "If I didn't know this is too old, I'd think it was a picture of you. Where did you get it?"

"I found it in this trunk along with this." She carefully picked up the brittle, yellowed paper and handed it to her grandmother.

Agatha scanned the words. Shock widened her eyes, and she quickly returned to the first line. Now she took her time reading every word. Then she dropped the hand holding the paper in her lap. "My dear Maggie! They never told me." Agatha sat there, her stunned expression a good match for what Maggie had been grappling with for the last few weeks.

"They never told me either. And I didn't have the nerve to tell my parents yet that I found it." Maggie picked up the photograph again. "This must be my mother, whoever she is."

Agatha gazed down at the photo, then glanced up at her. "It took months for the wagon train to reach Oregon. When we received word that Florence and Joshua had a daughter, we assumed she'd finally had a baby. They'd wanted one for such a long time. Florence has always loved children."

Her grandmother stared off into space as if seeing the past. "By the time she was seven years old, she would ask to hold the new babies at church. I worried that she would drop one, but she was so careful with them. My beloved Drake died while I was carrying Georgia. Florence had just turned thirteen when she was born. She helped me so much with her baby sister."

All this information about the family made Maggie long to be a part of it. And Agatha revealed a different side of her mother that she'd never considered.

"Why didn't they tell me you were adopted?" Agatha stared at Maggie. "I thought you inherited my designing ability and my curly hair."

The words stung Maggie. She winced.

Agatha reached across the open trunk and took Maggie's hand. "Oh, you poor child. I didn't mean to hurt you. I'm just so surprised. I'm thinking out loud. You are my grandchild in every way that counts. No one can take that away from us."

Her grandmother's words went straight to Maggie aching heart, pouring over it like a soothing balm. She *wanted* to belong to Agatha.

"Do these names mean anything to you?" Her grandmother held up the paper.

"I've never heard any of them before I found the trunk." Maggie took the adoption paper and placed it flat on the bottom of the container. Then she started folding the baby clothes and placing them on top. "One question I've had is, why didn't my mother sign the paper? If Angus McKenna is my father, and he must be since he's the one giving me away, who is my mother?"

"Does it really matter?" Agatha moved the trunk to the table and scooted closer to Maggie.

When her grandmother pulled her into an embrace, she leaned her head on Agatha's shoulder.

"Florence and Joshua have been good parents, haven't they?" The words were whispered against her hair.

Maggie straightened. "Well, I have memories of happy times in the past, but for the last few years, Flor…Mother has really tried to change me a lot. That makes me think there was something wrong with my real mother. Or why else would she not want me to be myself?"

Agatha patted her hand. "The last few years a child is at home are always difficult for a mother." She turned a distant stare toward the window. "She wants to hold on so tightly just at the time she needs to start letting go."

Maggie heard the conviction in her grandmother's words.

Agatha clasped her hands in her lap and gazed down at them. "When your mother and Joshua decided to move west, my heart was broken. Their last months here were not pleasant, because I could not give them my blessing before they left. And now your mother appears to be doing the same to you." She sighed. "Remember, Maggie, your mother is only human. She may have wanted you so badly to be her own baby that she never wanted to even think about your adoption. I'm not saying what she did was right, but I do know she must have a deep mother's love for you. And now that mother's love is trying to hold on so tight that it's in danger of smothering you."

Maggie nodded, trying to absorb her grandmother's words, trying to understand the hurts and secrets of a woman she'd always known as only "Mother."

Agatha took charge again. "Obviously you can't stay here with this issue unresolved between you. I do think you need to return home and talk to your parents face-to-face about what you've discovered. The discussion will help both of you to see each other as God's children, created by Him for a special purpose, and that will help your mother to loosen her grip a bit. My offer to you still stands, but first, go be reconciled with your mother."

"Yes, Grandmother."

Agatha opened her arms, and Maggie went to her, letting herself be enfolded. Her grandmother drew her closer and began to rock back and forth. She crooned a nameless tune and rubbed Maggie's back. How soothing it felt. She didn't even try to stop the tears that cascaded from her eyes. Tears of relief, that she had someone to share her burden. Tears of fear, of not knowing what would happen next. And tears of joy, feeling the unconditional love of this amazing woman...her grandmother.

Chapter 19

CHARLES CHUCKLED AS he descended from the coach and helped Georgia alight. He'd enjoyed this shopping excursion with Tucker and Shirley. They each had a quick wit. Shirley didn't let any of the merchants cheat her on anything she purchased. The coach held several wooden crates of foodstuffs along with more than one tow sack. She must plan on feeding an army. Charles knew he, Georgia, and Maggie wouldn't be there long enough to consume all this food. After he assisted Georgia, she headed into the house, but he stayed to help Tucker carry in the boxes.

"Now you go on, Mr. Stanton. I's gonna tote this stuff inside." Tucker hoisted a crate onto his shoulder and picked up one of the burlap bags bulging with vegetables.

"I know you will." Charles agreed but instead of following the man's suggestion, he also carried a crate and a burlap bag as he headed toward the back door.

When the two men reached the kitchen and set their burdens on the table, the driver headed back outside. Charles crossed his arms over his chest and leaned against the cabinet, watching Shirley make short work of emptying the wooden boxes.

Georgia was filling the teapot with hot water from the well in the stove. Then she dropped tea leaves inside and put the lid on so they would steep. Since the air had turned rather chilly while they were gone, tea sounded good to Charles, especially if it was accompanied by some of Shirley's delicious cookies.

Georgia turned toward him and arched her brows. "Would you like cookies with your tea?"

"Sure."

She went to the cabinet, took out an embossed tin, and placed a few cookies on a plate. He thrust his hands into the pockets of his slacks, glad that he and Georgia had found a way to interact without it being affected by his idiotic blunder. He couldn't believe how cocky he had been, thinking that no woman was immune to his charm. He spent extra time with God every day since then trying to tame his foolish pride.

He viewed Georgia with new eyes now. "Today was interesting, wasn't it?"

"I always enjoy being with Tucker and Shirley." After checking the tea, she filled the cups and set them on the table before she settled onto one of the kitchen chairs. "When I was young, I often spent more time with them than Mother, especially if she had lots of orders."

"Tucker said your mother and Maggie are here, but I don't hear a sound. Do you think they're taking naps?" He felt something wasn't quite right and wondered where that feeling was coming from.

"Not my mother." Georgia took a sip of the hot drink. "She has more energy than I do." She held the plate of treats toward him. "Cookie?"

Charles shook his head. "I think I'll see if I can find them. Maybe they would like to join us for tea."

As he searched through the lower floor of the house, everything was quiet until he approached the parlor. Muffled crying and someone softly humming stopped him in his tracks. He wasn't sure whether he should go farther or not. *Lord, what do I do now?* When he didn't feel compelled to leave, he approached the archway that opened into the formal room.

Agatha sat facing the archway, with her arms around Maggie. He wondered if her grandmother had uncovered Maggie's secret.

Just then, a board under his foot squeaked. Agatha opened her eyes, her gaze homing in on him. She sat on the sofa with Maggie cradled against her chest. Without saying a word, he lifted his hands from his sides, palms out, and shot her a questioning look. He hoped she understood that he didn't want to intrude where he wasn't wanted. But deep in his heart, he hoped she wouldn't turn him away. He clamped his teeth together and shoved his hands into his pockets before Agatha could notice how tense he was. When their hostess didn't motion him to go away, he held his ground.

Agatha kissed Maggie on the top of her head, then she whispered words he couldn't hear. After a moment, Maggie shook her head, eased away from her grandmother, and mopped the moisture from her face with a soggy hanky. He wanted to offer her his fresh handkerchief. Before he could reach for it, she turned watery eyes toward him.

"It's all right." Maggie slowly rose to her feet and swayed slightly. "Come on in, Charles. You're going to find out all this anyway, so it might as well be now." She only hoped he would be as understanding as her grandmother had been. The warm glow of Agatha's complete acceptance still lingered in her heart, and she felt as if she could face anything right now.

Charles went to the chair across the table from them and sat down. He crossed one leg over the other, but then let it fall, as if he was having a hard time getting comfortable. Then he breathed out a large whoosh of air. She had never seen him so hesitant before, and it was all because of her, she was sure. Maybe he had also noticed something was amiss with her.

She dropped back on the sofa and clasped her hands in her lap. Agatha glanced her way. "I'll leave you two alone to sort this out, and go find Georgia. Is that all right with you, Maggie?"

"Yes." Maggie gave a flat, dull answer.

"Charles, where is Georgia?" Agatha's question sounded brisk, businesslike.

"In the kitchen." Charles's words held no clue as to how he felt right now. Maggie wished they did.

As Agatha walked away, he leaned forward with his forearms on his thighs and his hands clasped between his knees. On this trip, she'd seen him sit that way before when he was deep in thought.

"What's going on, Maggie?" His gaze bore into hers.

His tender tone brought tears to her eyes, but she blinked them back. She needed to just tell him right out and get it over with. "A while before my birthday, I found out I'm not who I thought I was."

At the bewildered expression on his face, she tried again. "I found a picture of a woman who is probably my mother. There's also a paper from an Angus McKenna giving me to Joshua and Florence Caine." *Please, please, understand and don't make me go into all the details.* If she had to repeat everything, she'd melt into another puddle of tears.

"I see."

"Do you? I'm afraid I don't."

Sleek and agile as a cat, he rose from the chair and started toward her. Then he stopped. "May I sit by you?"

She scooted the white chest away from the edge of the oval coffee table centered on the rug in front of the sofa. Then she patted the cushion beside her. His smile looked like the sun breaking forth from behind storm clouds as he slid down beside her. She felt drawn to him, but still apprehensive.

"I found her." Agatha entered, followed by Georgia.

Her aunt pulled Maggie into an embrace. "Mother said something was wrong, but she didn't go into details. Let me help you, Maggie."

They all shifted so Georgia could sit on the other side of Maggie from Charles. With as few words as she could get by with, Maggie spread out the story and illustrated it with the paper and picture.

Georgia picked up the photograph and stared at it. "This looks just like you. She has to be your mother. But where is she?"

"That's what I want to know." Maggie's breath stuttered.

"No matter what the paper says, it won't change who you really are."

Georgia's strong words settled over her like a blanket, warming her to the very center of her being. Maggie wanted to wrap them around her like a cocoon and just stay protected there. But she knew everyone might not realize all the ramifications presented in the paper.

"I'm not sure why my parents never told me about this." How could she express her feelings without making the others withdraw from her? That was the last thing in the world she wanted to happen.

"Perhaps they planned to and just hadn't gotten around to it." Her grandmother's voice carried a note of hopefulness.

"They've had over eighteen years." Maggie wished she could just grasp the hope presented and hold on. "I'm not so sure." She took a deep breath and let it out slowly. *What to say?* "Actually, the picture and paper were hidden rather well. I don't think they expected anyone to find them. Especially not me."

Charles rubbed his hand across his jaw. She heard the faint rasp of the stubble barely shadowing his face. "It's hard to believe any parent would hide such information from their child."

She heard a hint of judgment in his tone of voice and rushed to defend her parents. "I'm sure they did what they thought was best. Of course I won't understand it entirely until I talk to them."

Charles shook his head. "I had always thought of your father as the most honest, honorable man I knew."

Just what she had feared was happening. The news had changed his view of her and her family—and even caused him to question the integrity of her father. She twisted her hands together until her knuckles hurt.

Georgia gently placed her hand over Maggie's. "But the adoption doesn't change who you really are."

Maggie shifted to face her more squarely. "Doesn't it? My mother's name isn't on the paper. What if she didn't want me?" Once she started she couldn't keep the words from tumbling out, no matter what damage they did. "What if she was a saloon girl, or worse? Wouldn't that make a difference?"

Georgia grasped on to her hand and stared at her as if she could see straight into her soul. "No, it doesn't. You are who God created you to be. The Bible says He knew each of us when we were in our mother's wombs. He knit us together there. You were special to Him when He created you, *and* you're special to Him right now."

Maggie clung to her like a lifeline while her mind grasped the truth pouring into her spirit. "Do you really think so?"

"I do." Conviction filled her aunt's tone.

Agatha stirred in her chair. "Maybe He provided Joshua and Florence to redeem you from a different kind of life. That's what God does. Redeem people."

"And if I were the daughter of a fallen woman, would you still want to be my . . . family?" She couldn't believe she had blurted those words at them.

Agatha stood before her. "I know who you really are. You are my beloved granddaughter. Nothing and no one can change that."

Agatha and Georgia helped Maggie stand. They pulled her into a big hug with all three women winding their arms around each other. For the first time since she made the discovery, Maggie knew total acceptance. She basked in the love emanating from her aunt and true grandmother.

But she could not help but notice Charles, eyes distant, as he weighed this news of her and her father—his business partner. And she knew he struggled with the same question she did.

Could they ever trust her parents again?

Chapter 20

ALL THE HUBBUB at the Little Rock railway station couldn't keep Maggie's mind off the dichotomy of emotions about their departure. She wanted to get home and settle things about the adoption and her parents, whoever they were, but she also didn't want to leave her newfound grandmother.

Because of all the conveyances trying to reach the depot, they'd been delayed and had to board the train quickly. Since Charles helped Tucker load the trunks and his portmanteau in the baggage car, he was the last one to jump onto their car as the conductor shouted out his boarding call. He carried a large, drawstring fabric bag in each hand. Maggie wondered what could be in those puffy sacks. She hadn't noticed them when they climbed into the coach.

Charles dropped into the seat across from her and put the packages he carried beside him. He glanced at her, and dimples bracketed his wide smile. "Are you all right?"

She nodded and took a quick glance at the bags, then returned all her attention to him. "Just a little sad to be leaving Agatha."

"She and I planned a surprise for you and Georgia." The twinkle in his eyes told her she'd like it whatever it was.

Georgia looked up from the book she was reading. "What were you saying about me?"

Charles picked up one of the plump bags. "This is for you. Agatha thought it might make the trip more comfortable."

She put her book into her handbag and held out her hands. He laid the sack across them.

"It's very light for something this size." She pulled the drawstring to spread the opening and revealed a square pillow with lots of stuffing. "What is this?"

"For you to sit on when you get tired of this hard seat." Charles handed the other bag to Maggie. "There's more in there, too."

Maggie made quick work of opening her gift and pulling out the square pillow. The fabric of her bag and Georgia's bag were different designs from each other, and the square pillows matched the designs. These had to have been created by Grandmother's workers.

"I'm sure I'll get a lot of use out of this." She then peeled the outside covering from a larger pillow. "And what is this one for?"

Charles grinned at her excitement. "I'm sure your Pullman pillows weren't very comfortable, so you can use that one when you sleep. I know my pillow isn't nearly as thick as mine back home."

Georgia's parcel contained a larger pillow, too. "Was this your idea or Mother's?"

He shrugged. "Maybe a little of both." He didn't even try to hide his grin.

Maggie stared at him. If she had her guess, she felt sure the original idea came from Charles. She'd never known a man who was this thoughtful. He had been even as a boy, looking out for her and protecting her in school. Yesterday he'd had a hard time with the information she shared. Today he was back to his own usual self, but she wondered if he still harbored cautions about her parentage...or her parents. He didn't talk about it at supper or breakfast, so she had no way of knowing. And she didn't want to bring up the subject.

She couldn't really get rid of her feelings about him. Somehow she still hoped someday he would see her for the woman she had become, not just his adopted little sister. Maybe that was the problem. He still treated her like a younger sister. Or maybe the adoption was a problem to him.

After the first few days in Arkansas, Charles had stopped flirting with Georgia. Maggie didn't know what happened between them, if anything. But his change in demeanor allowed her feelings for him to return in full force. She really liked...loved him. *Liked* was such an insipid word. What she felt went far beyond that. She couldn't deny it. But she might not ever have a chance to explore these emotions.

Maggie knew her eyes were still red from crying at the station as she bid her grandmother good-bye about two hours ago. *My grandmother*. Only a few days before, she had wondered if Agatha would accept her after she learned the truth.

She couldn't have been more wrong. Not just about her grandmother, but also about Georgia. Her aunt had not shown any qualms in accepting her completely into the family, even though they still knew nothing about her biological parents.

She glanced at the seat across from her where Charles leaned against the window and snored softly. Not at all like the loud racket that erupted from her father when he fell asleep in a chair in his study. Maybe her gallant protector on this journey hadn't gotten as much sleep as he needed last night. Maggie surely hadn't, thinking about what would happen when she returned home. Both the wonderful and the uncertain.

As soon as she returned she would have to tell Daddy and Mother what she'd found and try to learn the truth about her first parents. But she didn't really want to think about that right now. She would work up the courage by the time they reached Seattle.

Maggie glanced out the window at the passing scenery. Most of the leaves had fallen from the trees. Dark naked branches thrust their way toward the sky. Intermingled were patches of evergreens that soon would be covered with snow. She hoped none of the white flakes fell before they were all the way across the Rocky Mountains. Just thinking about what would happen if a snowstorm came before they were on the other side made her shiver. She glanced from one end of the car to the other, where the stoves were stoked, providing a touch of warmth to the long railcar. If a blizzard overtook them, the feeble heat they provided wouldn't do much good.

A little louder snore caught her attention. She glanced at Charles, but he still hadn't awakened. She was glad he was napping. It allowed her plenty of time to study him. With his hat in the seat beside him, his hair had a mind of its own. The curls he usually tamed now sprang up, surrounding his face in haphazard manner. Dark hair, the color of rich coffee. She could imagine how it must feel, like fine silk thread. She'd like to touch the curls, at least once, but if she tried right now, she would probably disturb his rest.

Georgia sat beside her, reading a book again. Would her aunt be scandalized if Maggie followed through with what she wanted to do? *Of course she would.* And probably everyone else in the railcar.

Charles's strong brow and straight nose above full lips created a handsome picture, like a classical painting or marble statue. She'd try to sketch him from memory after they got home. Not here on the train. If she wasn't able to capture his likeness, she didn't want anyone else to see the mess she'd made.

During this trip, she'd had several opportunities to enjoy the strength of his arms and the gentleness of his hands. With him having fingers so long, Maggie wondered if he played the piano. She knew other men who did. Not her father, but a few of their friends entertained their guests at parties with their prowess on the instrument.

Her attention traveled down the length of his body, and she felt heat stain her cheeks. Charles was a fine specimen of a man, if she'd ever seen one. And she never had, or taken, the opportunity to actually study a man's body so intently. When her gaze slowly returned to his face, his warm brown eyes were open staring at her. A rush of heat exploded into her neck and face, probably turning her as red as Georgia's dress. She wanted to pull her attention away from him and hide her flaming cheeks, but she could do neither.

Charles had a hard time remaining still while he watched Maggie's eyes sweep him from his head to his feet and back again. He'd awakened just before her gaze left his face, but he only opened his eyes a tiny slit to peek at her. For some unknown reason, he didn't want to interrupt her perusal. He loved watching the emotions flit across her face. Was his pride raising its ugly head again? He thought he'd vanquished it back in Arkansas. This might be an ongoing battle in his life. Why couldn't it be easy?

Since they'd just left Little Rock today, Maggie's hair was styled with the curls bunched on the top of her head, instead of just being held back with a ribbon as it was most of the train trip to Arkansas. Those red curls had golden highlights when the sun shone on them. He would love to see them down around her shoulders and run his fingers through them. Why was he having these kind of thoughts about her?

Maggie's eyes connected with his, and he sat up straighter, crossing one leg over the other. He needed to rein in his thoughts. Maybe they both needed a little breathing room.

"Excuse me, ladies. I'm going to stretch my legs." He quickly made his way down the aisle toward the platform at the front of the car.

Maggie wondered why Charles left so quickly after awakening. She hoped nothing was wrong with him. Could he be sick? Should she go after him and see? She stared at the door that had closed behind him.

Georgia glanced up from the pages of her book. "He'll be back soon."

How did her aunt always know what she was thinking?

"When we were at Mother's and you shared your story, I noticed a difference in the way you looked at Charles." Georgia placed a slip of paper in the book and closed it. "Are you interested in him?"

Maggie couldn't contain her grin. "Perhaps."

Her aunt slipped the book into her carpetbag and turned all her attention toward Maggie. "So tell me about it."

How much should I tell her? Of course, the truth was always best. Because keeping secrets had led to the dilemma Maggie was in, she chose to start being truthful about everything. "He sees me as the little sister he has always protected. The adopted little sister. I think he has a problem with my background."

A twinkle lit Georgia's eyes. "He is trying to figure out his life right now too." She shifted in her seat and took Maggie's hands. "I really like Charles as a friend. Give him time to sort out his thoughts and feelings."

"Why do you say that?"

Her gaze sharpened. "On the way to Arkansas you may have seen him pay particular attention to me. I didn't notice because I thought of him in only friendly terms. But in Little Rock I had to...set him straight." She grimaced. "Apparently he didn't realize my advanced age."

They shared a laugh. Then Georgia continued, "Sometimes people get together for reasons that have nothing to do with love, the real love God intends between a husband and wife. There might be a reason to enter into a marriage of convenience, and often those turn into a love match, but sometimes they don't." She gave Maggie's hands a quick squeeze before letting them go. "From the very beginning, Scott loved me the way God intended." She stared out the window, but her gaze didn't rest on anything in particular. "That's what I want for you, Maggie. I'm not sure if Charles is the man for you, but God knows. Just listen to Him."

"I hope you're right." Maggie couldn't keep the wistful tone out of her voice.

"Right about what?" Charles slid into the seat across from the two women.

Maggie's head snapped around. "I didn't hear you come back."

"That's because you and Georgia were deep into your conversation." He glanced from one woman to the other. "Are you going to tell me what you were talking about?" Devilment danced in his eyes.

"No." She gave a smug smile and almost giggled. She wouldn't tell a lie, but she didn't have to tell him everything. Some things were better left unsaid.

He placed his hand over his heart and tried to look hurt. It didn't work. "I'm devastated."

"You are not," Georgia broke in. "Now behave yourself."

Their banter helped her relax. Perhaps now would be a good time to have a serious conversation. Now that Georgia was involved, she could keep them from getting into dangerous territory.

"Actually," Maggie looked straight at Charles. "I've wanted to ask you an important question."

"Fire away." He crossed one ankle over the other knee and propped his hand on it. "Whatever is on your mind."

Maggie wasn't sure he really meant what he said, but she had to chance it. "As a man who runs his own business, if you were interested in a woman, would you have a problem if she owned her own business?" She held her breath, waiting for his response.

His answer would be very important to her. She waited while he took his time to mull over what she asked.

"I'm not sure where this is coming from, but I don't mind women owning businesses. I admire your grandmother." He stared straight at her, conviction hanging heavy on every word. "She's using her God-given talents to make the world a better place. Is that what you're talking about?"

Maggie picked up on his last two sentences. "Yes. Something like that."

She shifted, trying to get more comfortable in a train seat that was becoming increasingly harder the farther they traveled. What had she done with that small pillow? She leaned over and dug it from her carpetbag as she gathered her thoughts.

After placing the puff under her, she turned her attention back toward him. "But even more than that, would you tell your wife she couldn't own and run a business?"

Charles dropped his foot back on the floor and leaned toward Maggie. "Are you talking about your designing ability? Agatha was very proud of your talents."

"Sort of." Maggie hedged, then decided she should lay it all out on the table. "I learned a lot from her, and I really want to start a designing and dressmaking business in Seattle sometime. Do you think that would keep a man from courting me?"

The words hung between them much longer than Maggie wanted them to before he answered. For a moment fear of completely losing her chance with him gained a foothold. If her parentage didn't stand in their way, maybe her wanting to own a business would.

"I don't want to give you some glib, easy answer." The silence stretched between them while Charles pondered what to say. Finally, he answered. "I'd need to pray with my wife as we seek what the Lord wants, but for myself, I would be proud of her talents and encourage her all I could."

Although she had been anxious because he took so long to answer, she accepted his words with her whole heart. Maggie hugged his words to her heart. Another reason to love this man.

Georgia cleared her throat. Maggie glanced toward her.

"I hope I'm not being presumptuous, but of course, I heard everything both of you said." Her aunt laughed. "How could I miss it sitting so near both of you?"

Charles laughed. "For a few moments, I forgot we had an audience. I guess I'm just so used to having you around."

"So you just take me for granted." Georgia joined in his laughter.

Maggie felt her cheeks heat. Why did she always do that? Was it just part of being a redhead with fair skin? Charles used to tease her that everything showed on her face.

"Maggie, I know there will be lots to discuss with your parents when we get home, but I wanted to tell you what I've decided about my own life." Georgia shot her a hopeful look.

She wasn't sure what her aunt meant, but Maggie welcomed the interruption. "Go ahead."

"I've been living in Portland since Scott died. With no relatives nearby." Georgia started pleating the edges of the ruffle running down the bodice of her dress. "He put it in his will that his partner could buy his half of the business if he offered a fair price. My attorney handled the sale, and I have more than enough money to live on the rest of my life, even if I live to a ripe old age." She dropped her hands in her lap. "And I'm not going to stay in Oregon. Now would be a good time to sell my house and move to Seattle to live near family."

Maggie threw her arms around her aunt. "I'm so glad. I'd love to have you in the same town."

After returning the hug, Georgia leaned against the back of the seat. "I'm not finished. I want to do something with my life too. So when the time comes that you're able to start your design business, I want to be your partner. I helped Mother with the business part before Scott and I married, and I could take care of those details while you design and oversee the sewing. We would have enough capital to invest in anything you think we need—sewing machines, a building, employees, whatever."

Stunned, Maggie sank back. Could this be the answer to her prayers?

She looked at Charles. His warm smile encouraged her.

"Actually, that sounds like a very good idea." His eyes held none of the censure she'd seen in her mother's face whenever Maggie mentioned being a dress designer.

Was God really planning to give her the desires of her heart? She hoped so, but there were still roadblocks ahead.

When they arrived at home, would she be able to face and accept whatever truth she heard from her parents?

Chapter 21

MAGGIE HAD HOPED she could do some sketching while they were on the train, but she couldn't. Some of the ride was fairly smooth, but when they reached the Rockies, the train swayed and bumped far too much. So whenever they stopped, she got off the train with her pad and drawing supplies and found a place to sit outside the depot and sketch. Often she sat by a shack. Other times, the station had a platform and other buildings surrounding it. She wanted to remember all the varying vistas the mountains presented. Charles procured food for them, and she would eat on the train after they were underway again.

At first, she drew only mountains and the valleys where they stopped, including whatever buildings the towns might have. On shorter stops, she had to work quickly to get the basic outlines down, hoping her memory would help her fill them in after she arrived in Seattle. But on the longer stops, she was able to almost complete a picture, even adding a few of the interesting characters they met along the way.

In one whistle-stop town, a saloon was right across the dirt road from the tracks. A forlorn saloon girl stood in the doorway, leaning her arms on the top of the swinging door. She looked lost, wistful. Loneliness leaked from her pores.

Compassion flooded Maggie's heart. She wondered what had brought this woman, who looked far too young to be working in a saloon, to this place in her life. She wanted to document her pathos in the picture. As she made quick strokes, Maggie's heart took over, and she poured her mercy into each line. Soon the drawing contained a very good portrayal of the woman, her blonde curls clustering around her shoulders and far too much of her skin revealed above the top of her dress, which slid off one shoulder. For some unknown reason, Maggie wanted to retain a clear picture of this downtrodden woman, so she could pray for God to send someone to help her leave the life she was living. Could her own mother have been a woman such as this? She prayed that if she were, someone rescued her from the situation.

In another town, their stop was longer, so Maggie had time to eat with Charles and Georgia and still get in sketching time. A scraggly miner leading a donkey with a large pack tied to its back soon filled a page of her sketchbook. She was getting pretty good at this. For years, she'd thought all her drawing abilities were confined to designing clothing. If she ever opened a design business, she might frame some of these sketches to hang on the walls in among the dress designs.

Finally, Maggie succumbed to the desire to try her hand at sketching Charles. *What could it hurt?* On the next leg of the journey, she often studied him as unobtrusively as possible, making note of the shape of his face, the way his hair lay across his forehead and curled above his collar in the back, his eyes, his ears, even his hands. Every detail she etched into her mind so she could get them down on paper. She figured the hardest would be getting his sculptured brows and lips. Over and over, her eyes traveled over these features until she could see them in her mind. An unfortunate effect of all this study was his entrance into her dreams every night. At least she wasn't anxious to awaken in the morning.

At the very next stop, she started her experiment. With each line she made, his handsome face took shape. She even captured the slight quirk of his right brow, and the hint of a cleft in his chin. She'd never studied a man as closely as she had Charles. She hadn't realized how strong his chin looked or how high the cheekbones were that gave a foundation to his wonderful dark eyes. To her amazement, the drawing emerged lightning quick. When she finished adding every shadow she wanted and smudged them so they blended into the whole, she quickly closed the sketch pad. She didn't want anyone else to see this drawing until she went back to it later to check how accurate it was. Even with the dress designs, she liked to lay aside a drawing and go back to it later. After the passage of time, she could look at it with a critical eye and see what needed to be changed to improve it.

Charles noticed Maggie when she closed her sketch pad so hard the sheets slapped together. He wondered if she had made a mess of whatever she drew. Maybe sometime he would be able to see for himself.

After a couple more stops, where the air grew increasingly colder, he wondered if they would get out of the mountains in time to beat the snows. By the next morning, the railcar was extremely cold when he awakened shortly before dawn. He made the trip to the necessary room with his whole body shaking against the freezing temperatures. The blanket on the bed didn't give enough warmth to keep him from shivering. So he got his carpetbag and went back to the privacy in the tiny cold room. The only way to protect from frostbite was to put on every garment he had in that bag. Two pairs of long underwear, three pairs of wool socks, three long-sleeved shirts, two pairs of wool trousers, and his jacket. If he didn't warm up soon, he'd see if he could get to his portmanteau in the baggage car. Now how could he keep the women warm?

Where is the conductor with wood for the stoves? He opened the door and stepped out on the small platform at the end of the car. In the early morning light, tiny snowflakes swirled between the two railcars. He didn't see anyone coming toward him in the next car. Without hesitation, he ducked back into their passenger car, rubbing his hands together. He grabbed his leather gloves from his bag and slipped them on icy fingers, then thrust them under his armpits.

He stared down into the stove, and only a few embers glowed in its belly. The passengers would be in real trouble if they didn't get wood soon. If he knew where it was, he'd get some himself. At least most of the passengers who had boarded the train in Little Rock had already reached their destinations, so a lot of the seats were empty, and only a few of the beds were pulled down from the wall.

When he arrived back beside his bed, he heard Maggie stirring in the bottom one.

"Maggie." He hoped she could hear his whisper. He didn't want to disturb the others who still slept.

"Charles? I'm so cold." Even through the curtains, he could hear her teeth chatter.

"I know." He took the blanket off his bed and thrust it through the slit between the curtains. "Use this to cover up too. I'm trying to find out what's going on. The fire in the stove at the back has almost gone out. I'm sure the front one has as well. I'm going to look for the conductor."

While he was talking, the brakes set up a squeal and the engine started slowing down.

"It feels as if we're stopping." Maggie's voice trembled as she thrust her head out, but held the curtains together under her chin. "Should I get up?"

"If you want to, but you need to put on all the clothing you have in your bag. I'm wearing all of mine, and I'm still not warm. Maybe we can pull down the empty beds and take the blankets. If we divide them among the few people left in this car, they should help us all warm up."

Maggie slipped behind her closed curtains. From the amount of movement he heard on the other side, he knew she was following his advice. *Good girl.*

He headed toward the front of the car. The door opened before he reached it, and the conductor quickly shut it behind himself. The man looked startled when he turned and saw Charles so close.

"Sorry to awaken you, sir."

"I'm just trying to find out what's going on." Charles clapped his gloved hands together, hoping to get his blood flowing through his fingertips.

"Well, we've almost run out of wood. I'm headin' to get the last of it. We have just enough to fill each of the six stoves one more time. I talked to the engineer. We were scheduled to stop for water and wood right up the rails, but that water tank froze. Thing sprung a leak. Some of the flow's on the track."

Didn't sound good to Charles. "Will this be a serious problem?"

The man slowly shook his head. "They's got fires goin' meltin' as much as they can, so we can get enough water. Some people that live nearby's helpin'. We'll have hot coffee and hot stew fer the passengers. Need to get through this next pass before we get snowed in." The man blew on his chapped fingers.

Charles pulled off his gloves. "Can I get into the baggage car?"

"Sure 'nough. Just come with me."

Before he could turn to go, Charles gave him the gloves. "Take these. I have another pair in my luggage."

They crossed the last passenger car, and only a few of the beds were pulled down here as well.

"Why don't we get everyone on the same car?" Wheels turned in Charles's mind. "Then we only have to heat one, and the wood will last three times as long."

"That's a good idea." The conductor unlocked the door to the baggage car.

The man headed toward the pile of wood in a fenced-off section while Charles looked for his portmanteau. At least the piece of luggage was on the top of the other trunks where he could easily reach it. After donning his other gloves, he closed the bag, then grabbed an armload of wood before he followed the conductor through the back passenger car to the middle one.

"You kin take that wood to the stove at the front of this car. I'll build up the fire in this 'un." The conductor wasn't even trying to be quiet. "Then I'll start movin' the others into this here car."

Charles followed his directions and soon had the fire crackling in the front stove. He headed back down the car toward the section where he, Maggie, and Georgia had been sitting.

Maggie pulled back the curtains on her Pullman and stood beside him. "What's going on? I thought we were going to eat at this stop."

"The water tank up ahead sprang a leak. The conductor said the ice flow froze partly on the tracks. Said it looked almost like an ice sculpture."

The train came to a complete stop.

"I want to go see it." Excitement tinged Maggie's tone, and her cheeks glowed.

Charles frowned. "I don't think that's a good idea." He didn't want her falling and hurting herself on the slick ground.

She pursed her lips in a little pout. "You could come with me, so you could see that I'm all right."

"I wasn't planning on going out into the cold weather again."

The conductor came through the car, heading toward the front passenger car. "You folks should get warmer pretty soon."

"Would it be all right if we take the blankets off the empty beds?" Charles followed the man toward the door.

"Sure as shootin'. Now why didn't I think of that? We can get the ones from all three cars." When the man opened the door, the wind whistled through until he quickly closed it.

"Did you feel that wind?" Charles stared down at Maggie.

Her still-braided hair hung over one shoulder. "I know it's cold, but when will we ever see anything like this again?"

How could he turn her down when she gazed at him like that? No wonder her father often gave her what she wanted. The woman had a strong power of persuasion.

"OK. Let's go." He grabbed a blanket and wrapped it around her as if she were a squaw. Maybe that would keep her warm.

Bundled up the way she was, Charles had to lift Maggie down from the train steps. They walked along the track until they could see the modest building up ahead.

Her shoe slipped on a slick cross tie. He put his arm around her waist to help her over a rough place on the ground. The snow was beginning to stick and cover the fallen leaves and brown grass. At least it wasn't so thick they couldn't see what was around them. When they reached the tiny platform beside the building, they finally saw the massive ice formation that reached from the ground and tapered a little near the bottom of the wooden water tank. One of the metal bands had popped off when the thing swelled.

"It's beautiful." Maggie huddled beside him against the wall. The wide overhang kept much of the snow from reaching them.

"I suppose it is." Charles wouldn't have noticed without the eyes of the artist beside him. Maggie never took her gaze from the massive block of ice that had been sculpted by God…and the cold wind. "What are you doing?"

"Memorizing how it looks. I'm going to sketch it when we get back on the train."

"Which we should do as soon as possible." He was getting really cold, even if she wasn't.

"I know." She pulled the blanket closer around her. "I'm so cold." Her teeth chattered so hard, she barely got the words out.

They hurried back toward their car. When they came through the door, they stomped the snow from their shoes. Charles looked up and found the seats were over half full. And everyone was huddled under blankets either alone or with their traveling companions. After coming in from the cold outside, the car felt almost warm to him.

"We should find Georgia." Maggie's eyes searched up and down the car. "She might be worried about us."

They arrived at the seats where they'd been sitting, and Georgia was nowhere to be found. He turned to the lady in the seat across the aisle.

"Have you seen the woman who was sitting here?" He hoped so. He didn't want to think about having to go back outside to look for her.

"She went back that way." The stranger pointed toward the tiny room at the back.

He glanced down at Maggie. "I think she'll return soon."

When Georgia came back from the necessary room, Maggie sat in their usual seat with her sketch pad and charcoal in her hands. She glanced up at her aunt. "I hope you didn't worry about Charles and me."

"The conductor told me you had gotten off the car to go see the ice flow." She sat down beside Maggie and glanced over at her drawing. "Is that what it looked like?"

"Sort of." Maggie continued to add details to the building, platform, and water tank with ice flowing from it.

"May I see it?" Charles leaned forward in the seat that faced them. Maggie handed him her pad.

"This is really good." He knew Maggie could design dresses, but he hadn't realized just how talented she was at sketching other things. "That's exactly how it looked. You even got the correct angles and shadows. I'm impressed."

His words brought a warm feeling to Maggie's heart. It felt good to impress someone, and not just anyone, but the man who had been important in much of her life.

Just then the door at the end of the car opened. Two men hurried inside carrying a large metal coffeepot and a number of mugs with a rope strung through their handles. They stopped beside the first people they came to and gave each of them a mug, then filled it with coffee. Slowly, the two men made their way down the car.

When they reached the seats where Charles, Georgia, and she sat, Maggie welcomed the warmth of the too-bitter brew. Grounds swam in the depth of her white ceramic mug, but nothing would keep her from taking in its comforting warmth.

The men continued on down the car. By the time they reached the end, two more men entered the front door. This time they carried a pot so large that it took both of them to haul it in. All the coffee was gone from the large mug when they stopped beside the seat Maggie shared with Georgia. The men used a metal dipper to fill the mugs with steaming stew.

"We're sorry this is all we got to feed you, but we might have enough to give everyone seconds." The men smiled and kidded each other about spilling some on the floor while they made their way on down the aisle.

Maggie felt very unladylike drinking stew from a large mug, but it not only warmed her insides even more than the coffee, the plain fare tasted wonderful for breakfast. She would have never considered eating something like this for her first meal of the day in Seattle. This journey was broadening her horizons and perceptions in so many unexpected ways.

The men came back up the aisle and made one more pass-through with stew. Not a single person turned down seconds of the delicious, nourishing soup. The railcar felt warmer, and the passengers happier, when they left. After everyone finished eating, the conductor came through with a burlap bag, gathering all the mugs. As he went out the door, Maggie was glad it was him and not her going into the winter weather. She had all the snow and cold she wanted today.

Georgia picked up Maggie's sketch pad. "May I look at the other drawings you made on the trip?"

"Of course." Maggie felt warm and full, which made her a little sleepy. She took out her large pillow and placed it between her and the window, so she wouldn't feel the cold. Her eyes drifted shut.

In her semi-sleep phase, Maggie was aware of Georgia turning the pages. She murmured phrases like *I like this* and *This is really good*, but Maggie didn't want to wake up completely.

Finally, Georgia exclaimed, "This is wonderful."

Since it was louder than anything else she'd said, it jarred Maggie into full awareness. She wondered which picture Georgia was looking at. As she opened her eyes, she heard a swiftly indrawn breath. Charles stood behind Georgia, gazing at the drawing as well.

Then his eyes sought hers. "Is that how you see me, Maggie?"

His question startled her, and she had a hard time pulling away from his gaze. *Oh, no.* She'd forgotten about the one sketch of Charles that she didn't want anyone else to see. She wanted to grab the sketch pad and slam it shut, but it was too late. What if he hated what he saw?

"Yes." She held out her hands, and Georgia placed the open pad there.

Maggie hadn't looked at it since she finished working on it. Charles's smiling face looked up at her almost as if it were alive. She half expected it to speak to her.

"I believe you've captured his real personality." Georgia stared at her. "I didn't know you were doing portraiture."

"I haven't been." Maggie felt a lump forming in her throat. "Only this one that is full face. I did incorporate people in some of the sketches of the towns we've traveled through."

Charles sat down across from Maggie. "Thank you. I've never seen anything quite so good. This is the face that gazes back at me from the mirror every morning. The depiction looks like it was drawn by someone who really knows me."

And loves you. But Maggie could never speak these words aloud. At least not unless she knew that he loved her...exactly as she was, unknown parents, adoptive parents, and all.

Chapter 22

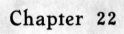

MAGGIE WATCHED SEATTLE slowly appear in the far distance, wishing she were a little girl again. She'd press her nose against the window and stare wide-eyed at each familiar landmark. She spotted the Territorial University— where Charles graduated—near the highest point in the city, then the tips of the gables on his home on Washington Street at Thirty-Second Avenue, and finally the roof of their mansion on Beacon Hill. Although the city had spread across a large area, it had a much less refined look to it than Little Rock had. But Seattle was home. And Maggie was glad to finally have all the travel behind her.

Before the train reached the station, it had to stop and wait for a log train to pass. Finally, they approached the platform. Up ahead, she noticed a small group clustered near the tracks. Soon she recognized her mother and father off to the side, watching as eagerly as the others. Her father had his arm around her mother's waist, and she leaned against him. Maggie hadn't seen them like this at home. And never out in public.

A memory flitted through her mind of a time before they moved to Seattle. Her parents cuddled her between them, and they stood as close as they were today. She had felt safe and loved in the protective cocoon they'd formed. But she couldn't recall anything like this in a long time. Daddy and Mother even looked younger somehow. Maybe they had enjoyed her being away from them. The new thought brought an ache to her throat. *Maybe I am the intruder who wrecked everything.*

The chugging of the powerful engine gradually slowed. Hissing steam joined the cacophony of metal against metal. She glanced at Charles and found him studying her.

"Are you all right?"

Maggie nodded. "Yes. I'm glad the journey is over."

As soon as the train came to a complete stop, Charles reached for their carpetbags. He tucked one under his arm and grabbed one in each hand. "I'll get these, ladies. You can take care of your handbags."

He led the way to the back door of the railcar. After exiting, he set the luggage on the platform and offered to help Maggie down.

"Thank you." She slipped her hand in his.

As with each time they'd touched in any way on the trip, heat radiated up her arm and sent sparks toward her heart. Too bad he only saw her as almost a younger sister. If only he'd notice that she was really a woman.

When her feet were firmly planted on the platform, he leaned toward her and whispered, "Just relax. We're with you."

He offered assistance to Georgia, and Maggie peered down the platform. Her mother hurried toward her, followed by her father. Both threw their arms around her at the same time. She ended up in one of those cocooned type of embraces she'd remembered earlier on the train. Despite her fears, she reveled in the warmth, the feeling of homecoming.

"Darling." Her mother's tone was soft and sweet. "I've missed you so much."

The hug tightened, and tears filled Maggie's eyes. "I missed you too."

When they stepped back, tears streamed down her mother's cheeks. Daddy took his white handkerchief, shook out the folds, and gently dabbed the moisture from her mother's face before turning to do the same for Maggie. His eyes appeared misty as well.

"How was—?"

"You're—"

"I'm so—"

They all started speaking, then stopped at the same time. Maggie took a deep breath.

With a flip of his hand, her father deferred to Mother. "You go ahead, Florence."

"How was the trip?" Her mother stayed beside her.

"Long…at least the train ride was." Maggie sensed that Charles had moved behind her. She glanced over her shoulder to see both him and Georgia. "But the two weeks in Arkansas seemed much shorter. We had such a good time with Grandmother."

How could she think straight with Charles so close to her that she felt the heat radiating from his body, even with the cold wind blowing over Puget Sound?

"How is my mother?" More tears leaked from Florence's eyes, but she caught them with the handkerchief. "Tell me everything. I've missed her so."

"She's a very busy and a lovely woman. I enjoyed getting to know her."

Daddy squinted in the bright sunlight as he turned his attention toward Charles. "Should I help with the trunks?"

Charles peered toward the baggage car. "I believe Morris and your man Erik have everything under control."

Maggie detected a note of coldness in his voice. Was the news of her adoption still coloring his view of her father? What if the two men weren't able to work together anymore? Maggie shook her head. Her father didn't need this added tension when she was planning to confront her parents about her past.

As the group headed toward the area where the coaches were parked, her mother walked beside Charles. "I know you're probably anxious to get home, Mr. Stanton, but maybe you could join us for dinner tonight. That way all three of you can share the details of your trip with Joshua and me."

Charles bowed stiffly. "Mrs. Caine, I would be honored to join you. What time will dinner be served?" He glanced at Joshua. "I would like to hear more about the business as well."

His tone was formal, almost businesslike. But her parents didn't seem to notice. Her mother picked up her brooch watch and squinted at it. "It's only three o'clock. Can you be there by six thirty or seven?"

"Six thirty will be fine." After assisting Florence up into the Caine's coach, Charles strode toward his own conveyance, his hands thrust deep into his pockets. Maggie watched him leave with sadness. For weeks she'd rarely been more than a few minutes from his presence. Already she missed him.

Daddy made sure Georgia was comfortable sitting beside her mother, then he helped Maggie into the coach and slid into the seat beside her.

Everything felt so familiar, ordinary, but the flutter in her stomach warned Maggie that everything was somehow different as well.

Maggie watched both her parents on the way home. Something had changed, but she couldn't decide what it was. Even the atmosphere in the coach was a far cry from anything she'd ever experienced in the vehicle. She tried to keep up with the conversations, but all the time she puzzled over this new situation. She hoped she would soon find out what was going on between them. Mother even had a glow about her that Maggie couldn't remember seeing before.

When Erik stopped the coach in front of the house, her mother walked to the door beside Maggie. "I've had Ingrid and Mrs. Jorgensen preparing a hot bath for you. I'm sure you'll feel better after you've had a nice long soak."

Florence was right. Nothing sounded better than to be truly clean again. She just hoped she wouldn't fall asleep in the bathtub.

After her bath and a bit of a nap, Maggie dressed carefully in a green wool shirtwaist with a froth of ecru lace forming a jabot and lining the cuffs. After five weeks wearing the same few outfits, it felt like a huge luxury to wear something different. She started downstairs, but stopped halfway when Charles came out of her father's study. His gaze caught hers, and he stopped, his eyes wide.

A look akin to appreciation filled his face. She took a deep breath, telling herself to remember that they were just friends.

When he held out his arm, she finished descending and slipped her hand through the crook he offered. She hoped he couldn't feel the trembling that had attacked her, and she was grateful to have something to cling to as they headed toward the dining room behind her father.

Charles helped Maggie into the chair beside him. She would face Georgia. The long banquet table was draped with a white linen tablecloth, but the only place settings clustered at the one end. Several tall, silver candelabra bathed the room with light that sparkled off the china, silverware, and crystal glassware.

Daddy cleared his throat. "I'll return thanks for our blessings and our food."

Everyone bowed their heads, and Maggie peeked up through her eyelashes. She followed her father's words by repeating them in her head, adding her own *Amen* to his prayer.

Conversation through the five-course meal danced around the table with Charles, Maggie, and Georgia giving all the highlights of the trip. Maggie watched both her parents as they hung on to every word—all the descriptions, the places they visited, the vast amount of country they traveled through on the train, even how Grandmother helped her learn about the designing business.

Both her parents listened and inserted questions and comments, but not one note of censure. Her mother looked carefree and . . . happy. Maggie couldn't remember the last time she'd seen her that way. She wondered what miracle had brought about this change.

Charles turned to her father. "Enough about us. I would love you to fill me in on what's been happening with the business while I've been gone." His eyes seemed to narrow somewhat as he gazed at her father.

"Everything's fine." Joshua waved a hand. "I have a lot to show you tomorrow. Those weeks gave us plenty of time to complete the remodeling. I think you're going to like it. The store, and the offices, look amazing."

"I look forward to seeing it." He smiled, but the smile didn't quite reach his eyes.

Joshua leaned forward, his eyes sparkling. "I think we should have some sort of grand opening celebration to introduce people to the improved store. Actually, Florence came up with the idea. Women like that sort of thing." A broad smile spread across Joshua's face. "And she likes to plan events, so we probably can leave it mostly up to her, which will suit me just fine."

"If you don't mind, I would like to view the renovations first before making any decisions."

This time the note of seriousness in his voice didn't escape her father. Joshua shot a glance of concern at Charles, but recovered smoothly. "Of course, of course. You have a lot to catch up on before we move ahead with future plans."

Charles gave a nod and turned the conversation to other topics.

After dinner Charles excused himself, begging fatigue from the journey, and left for his home. Maggie and her family retired to the parlor for coffee.

Other than the moment of unpleasantness between Charles and her father, the dinner had been so pleasant, the atmosphere so congenial, that Maggie almost decided not to bring up what was weighing on her mind. But as they settled into their seats, with Maggie beside her mother on the divan, she stiffened her spine and plunged ahead.

"Mother, Daddy, I really need to ask you some questions." She clasped her hands so tightly in her lap that her knuckles ached.

A hint of fear crossed Florence's face, but she quickly smoothed it away. Her face serious, she took Maggie's hand. "I think I know what this is about."

She knows? Her mind raced. Florence must have discovered that the white chest was missing. But if she knew Maggie had uncovered the secret of the adoption, why had she appeared so happy and at peace?

With the time for the confrontation arriving, Maggie wasn't sure she was ready. She took a deep breath and found herself unable to talk.

Florence squeezed her hand gently. "Maggie, I know what you want to say. I know you found the white chest, so you don't have to tell me about that."

Maggie studied her mother's face. She could discern nothing in her expression except concern for her. And she didn't miss the fact that for the first time, her mother had called her Maggie. Something really had changed her.

"All right. My questions are about my being adopted." Maggie stared at her parents to see their reaction, but they still looked calm. "I had no idea. Why did you keep the information from me?" She tried to keep her tone from sounding accusatory but didn't think she was successful.

She had already dealt with the pain. Now she just had to be strong to face whatever was coming.

Her father started to say something, but her mother patted his knee. "It's fine, Joshua. I can tell her."

As the story of the night of her birth poured from her mother's lips and heart, tears streamed down her mother's face. Soon Maggie's tears joined hers. What a relief to know that the woman who gave birth to her hadn't just abandoned her, hadn't simply given her away.

Georgia left the room and returned with several hankies, passing one to each of the women.

When her mother described the way she'd felt at the time, how she had questioned God and wished for one of the babies, she didn't make any excuse. She admitted her sinful thoughts and how they had become deeply rooted in her heart, keeping her from being the kind of mother Maggie needed. As Florence continued to call her *Maggie*, instead of her usual *Margaret*, she felt a bonding that she hadn't remembered ever feeling. Her mother even admitted to pushing Daddy to move away from the place where everyone knew Maggie was adopted, because she didn't want any reminders that she was barren.

Maggie was stunned. All these years when she'd resented her mother, the woman had been hurting in a far deeper way than Maggie could ever imagine. It was time for Maggie to stop thinking of her as Florence.

"So you weren't trying to change me so I wouldn't be like the woman who gave birth to me? I thought something was wrong with her. Maybe she wasn't married or was a saloon girl or something like that. You didn't want me to be like her." The words stumbled over themselves to get out.

A different kind of pain fell like a veil across Mother's face. "I'm so sorry. I never dreamed you'd think anything like that." She hurried to Maggie and pulled her up into her arms. "Your mother was a wonderful woman, who gave me one of the best gifts of my life."

Maggie's tears soaked her mother's shoulder. "My mother died. Why did Angus McKenna give me away?"

Her father came and enclosed both the women in his loving embrace. "I can probably explain that the best. He loved your mother so deeply that the man was completely devastated by her death. His grief was a tangible thing. Everyone on the wagon train felt it with him and grieved for him and you girls. At the same time, he had three daughters to care for, and he didn't even know how to take care of one baby. He did what he thought was best for his infant daughters."

One word stood out in Maggie's mind. *Daughters.*

"Daughters? You mean there was more than one baby? Where are my sisters? Did they survive?" She wanted to shout the questions, but she didn't. "I've often felt as if part of me were missing. Maybe I was just sensing the loss of my sisters."

Georgia handed more hankies around and took the soaked ones away.

"Angus kept one of the girls, and he gave the other one to another family on the wagon train." Daddy's words sounded sad and so final.

Maggie moved from the embrace and approached the fireplace. She stared at the flames, trying to let all this information soak into her heart. Her mother died. Her father gave her away. She was a triplet. This was a lot to take in all at once. But most important of all, Florence, this woman God had entrusted with her care, really loved her all the time. She truly was a mother to her in all the ways that counted. Maggie crossed her arms over her chest and gripped her upper arms so tightly she'd probably be bruised tomorrow, but she couldn't let go.

Time stood still. The other people in the room faded from her mind. Where did she go from here? What could she do about her sisters?

When she finally turned around, Mother, Daddy, and Georgia sat in the same places where they had been before. "I want to find my sisters." Spoken aloud, the words sounded stark and lonely. She shifted to face her parents. "Do you know where they are?"

Daddy's head drooped for a moment, then he looked back up at her. "The family that adopted Mary Lenora was named Murray. When we reached Oregon City, we stayed for a few years. They didn't, and we have no idea where they went."

That was not what she wanted to hear. She wanted something easy, to be able to rush right out and find them. But it wasn't going to happen that way. *Why, God?*

Georgia came toward her. "Remember me telling you that I thought I saw you in Portland one day? How the woman had the same color hair, the same walk. Maybe she's somewhere there, but it probably would be impossible to find her. Portland is a large city, and she might live in another place altogether and was only visiting there."

Maggie realized what she said was true, but someday, somehow, she *was* going to find her sisters. "What about the other one?"

Daddy stood and clasped his hands behind him. "The last time I saw Catherine Lenora, Angus had her cradled against his chest as they left Oregon City. He had been headed toward the gold fields in California, but that was long ago. It would be like searching for a needle in a haystack trying to find them. I'm sorry, Maggie."

"Mary Lenora, Catherine Lenora, Margaret Lenora. Did our father name us before he gave us away?" *And all our middle names are Lenora?* That felt like even more of a connection.

Mother gripped the hanky in one fist. "He insisted on the names. Your grandparents couldn't agree on a name for their daughter, so they gave her all the ones they considered— Catherine, Margaret, Mary, Lenora. Angus wanted the names to tie you to your mother. And we agreed. I would have agreed to anything to keep you. I'd been cradling you to my chest and talking to you when Angus and Joshua came to give me the good news. I already knew I didn't want to let you go."

Her mother had already loved her before she adopted her. This new insight was a balm to Maggie's spirit.

"So Angus kept one of my sisters. I saw on the adoption paper where he promised he wouldn't ever try to contact me again. Why would he do that?" She couldn't keep the hurt out of her voice.

Daddy came and gathered her into his arms. "He was so overwhelmed. I think he didn't want us to be afraid that he would come take you back from us. That would be a really hard thing to do, and I admire his strength in thinking about your good above his own wishes. He knew we would take care of you and love you with all our hearts." His kiss landed on the top of her head.

After a few minutes of silence, Mother got up. "This has been an emotionally draining evening. Maybe it should draw to a close."

Daddy gave Maggie a squeeze, then went to accompany Mother upstairs. Mother stopped on the first step and smiled back at Maggie. "I've always loved you and considered you a gift straight from God's heart." Then they continued up the steps.

Maggie looked at Georgia. "I can't believe I have two sisters."

"I know." Georgia took her arm. "We should retire as well. You've had a long day."

Halfway up the staircase, Maggie stopped. "Right now, my thoughts are muddled, but I meant what I said about finding my sisters."

Georgia nodded. "I know you did. Maybe when the time comes, I'll help you."

"I know you would, and I appreciate that." She continued up the stairs. She might be heading to bed, but she knew she wouldn't sleep. Plans and dreams of finding her sisters would keep her awake—all night.

Chapter 23

CHARLES EASILY SLIPPED back into the work at the new Caine Stanton Emporium and Fine Furniture store. Despite his worries, Joshua had done an excellent job of finishing the remodeling. Already everything in the store was in place, with areas that transitioned between the different departments. Tomorrow, Florence Caine would come to the store to help them plan their grand opening.

Since returning from the train trip three days ago, Charles had chosen to walk from the store all the way home. After having spent so much time in the railway cars, he enjoyed the physical exercise. And it gave him time to think about things. For several days he had tried to concentrate on the store. Of course, two things kept intruding on his other thoughts. On this Friday walk, he allowed them to flood his mind.

First was Joshua. The news that the man had not only adopted Maggie but also withheld that information from his own daughter had shaken his view of his new business partner. If he could lie to and deceive his own daughter, how could Charles be sure that he could trust him? His father and grandfather had always prided themselves on their honesty and integrity. Would Charles have entered into this partnership if he had known of Joshua's deceit? He doubted it. But the papers were signed, and for now he had no recourse. And he had to admit that the success of the renovations scored a point in Joshua's favor.

Second was Maggie herself. He recalled that sketch Maggie had made of him. When he first laid eyes on it, he almost gasped. The details were so exact but drawn with emotion wrapped around each pencil stroke. If he didn't know better, he would guess the artist loved him...deeply. But how could that be? Maggie was still a girl. Or was she?

Over the last six weeks Charles had grown to know Maggie in a new and deeper way. He had witnessed her patient endurance with the long train journey and the often uncomfortable conditions. He had seen her joy at meeting her grandmother and her blossoming interest in not only the business but also in the wide world around her. He had seen her strength and courage as she faced the stunning news of her adoption. And finally, he had benefited from her silent admonishing and forbearance as he flirted with Georgia.

He sighed. He had made such a fool of himself on the trip, thinking that Georgia would be interested in him. He had become prideful, arrogant, full of himself. He didn't want to make another mistake like that one. But on the return journey, Maggie had crept into his heart and taken up residence there in a way he hadn't experienced before.

Charles didn't want his heart trampled on again. It was his own fault, but it hurt nevertheless. Maybe not as much as it would have if he had become more invested in a relationship with Georgia.

How could he know if Maggie was also interested in him? Was the drawing all the proof he needed?

Today he had tired soon after noon, the rigors of the trip catching up with him, so Joshua told him to go home. The street led uphill from downtown toward his home, and he slowed the farther he went. So the last few blocks, he started whistling one of the new songs this year, "While Strolling Through the Park One Day." The fairly peppy rhythm helped him walk up the final blocks. He pretended he was strolling through that park with Maggie. A Maggie who was in love with him.

Evidently, Morris heard his whistle, because when he stepped up on the porch, the front door opened. "Welcome home, sir." The tall Indian closed the door behind him and held out his hand to take Charles's coat.

Charles slid it off his shoulders and handed it over before also removing his gloves. "I've told you that you don't have to be so formal with me, Morris."

"I know you have, but now that you're the master of the house, you deserve the respect." The houseman took the coat and hung it on the hall tree, then stuffed the leather gloves into one of the pockets.

Charles laughed. "Thank you." He started down the hallway, but turned back. "Haven't you and White Dove been wanting to visit your married daughter?"

Although his servant kept a straight face, he couldn't keep the smile from his eyes. "That we have."

"I suggest you leave as soon as you can get ready. You don't have to be back until Monday."

"But, sir, who—?"

"I'm not helpless. I can scrounge for food, or even go over to one of the hotels to eat. And the maid will be here during the day. I'll be fine. I'd just as soon have some peace and quiet anyway. The long journey has caught up with me, and I desire nothing more than a long nap."

Morris nodded. "Have you forgotten that Little Deer will be off for the next two days?"

Charles turned. "That had slipped my mind, but you go anyway. I'm not a child. I can take care of myself."

"All right. We'll get ready, but I do want to draw a warm bath for you before we leave."

"If it'll make you happy, go ahead."

Morris had been right. Charles enjoyed sinking into the steamy water. The warmth chased away the lingering chill, and he soaked longer than usual. When he finished scrubbing and drying off, he crawled under the covers of his bed and was asleep in seconds.

When he awakened, he noticed that the light had dimmed, and it was close to dinnertime. Hunting through his armoire for something comfortable and warm, he pulled out a flannel shirt and wool trousers. He dressed, then added a velvet smoking jacket he'd bought because sometimes the rooms in the large house felt drafty. Then he thrust his feet into well-worn, velvet house slippers.

Taken by hunger, he decided to raid the kitchen. Surely White Dove had left something he could fix himself to eat. He knew about the cookies in the pantry, but he really should eat something more substantial. Then he would spend the evening in the library reading one of the books he'd purchased from the latest shipment at the store—*Vicar of Wakefield*, *Kangaroo Hunters*, or *Wild Man of the West*. That is, if he could get Joshua and Maggie out of his mind long enough to concentrate.

Charles hurried down the hallway, nearing the stairs. Just then, his slick-soled house shoes slid off the top step, and his hip hit the edge. Suddenly he found himself tumbling down. He grasped for the railing, for something, anything, to slow his momentum. *Too late!* His head cracked against the marble floor. And everything went black.

Joshua worked for a few hours after Charles left, drawing up plans for the grand opening. As he worked, he had another idea for the event. The thoughts bounced around in his head, intruding on every other thought. He really wanted to discuss the idea with Charles before he raised it with Florence. Maybe he should get his driver to take him by the Stanton mansion on the way home.

After Erik arrived with the brougham, Joshua climbed into the coach, laying the satchel containing his notes on the seat. "Take me to the Stanton mansion up on Washington."

"Sure thing, Mr. Caine." Erik closed the door and climbed into the driver's box.

A cold wind swept across the water this afternoon and seeped into the enclosed space. Joshua rubbed his hands together. Although

Seattle rarely saw freezing temperatures in November, it did have bone-chilling rains and gloomy, cloud-filled days.

On the journey, Joshua studied the changes in this section of Seattle since he had last been there. Between downtown and the area where Charles Stanton lived, clusters of smaller homes were crammed together on many of the streets, some just hovels, but most adequate for a family. Joshua wouldn't want to live that close to his neighbors, and Florence surely wouldn't. But the occupants of these newer homes were also potential customers. Perhaps they should include some stock in the store that would fit a lower income while still maintaining high standards of quality.

When Erik pulled up the drive in front of the Stanton mansion, Joshua couldn't see any lights, even though the day was overcast and dreary. "I hope that boy is home, and this trip wasn't in vain."

The driver climbed down and opened the door a crack. "You want me to go see if he's here, Mr. Caine? You wouldn't have to get out in the cold again."

Joshua pushed the door open wider. "No, I'll go."

He stepped down and hurried to the double doors surrounded by sidelight windows covered with some kind of lightweight draperies. He lifted the brass knocker and let it fall with a loud bang. When no one answered the door, he lifted his hand toward the knocker again. Just then, he heard a strange noise coming from inside the house. A kind of groaning. He put his face up to the sidelight window and cupped his hands around his eyes, trying to block the outside light. He thought he saw a large, strange lump on the floor at the bottom of the stairs. That was a marble floor. If someone fell, he or she was hurt. Shouldn't one of the servants be around?

Joshua turned around. "Erik, I need your help."

The driver loped up to the porch. "What is it, Mr. Caine?"

"I'm not sure." Joshua turned back to the windows just as a longer and louder groan issued from the house. "Do you hear that?"

"Yes, sir. Sounds like someone's hurt." Erik peeked through the other sidelight window.

"Looks like maybe someone fell down the stairs."

Joshua tried the front door, but it didn't open. "Find a way into the house, wherever you can. We really need to get in."

"Sometimes the back doors are left unlocked for deliveries." Erik started around the house while he talked back over his shoulder. "I'll find a way in. You can bank on that, Mr. Caine." The younger man loped around the back corner of the large home.

The groans grew louder.

"Just hold on a little longer." Joshua shouted through the closed doors. "Help is on the way."

Chapter 24

PAIN SLICED THROUGH Charles's head like red-hot daggers. Darkness engulfed him. Even though he could hear and feel people nearby, his eyelids were so heavy he couldn't lift them. And trying increased the agony beyond the threshold he could stand. So he sank once again into the depths of nothingness, trying to get away from the earthquake of pain.

Loud groans aroused him from his hiding place. He wondered where they were coming from. Then he felt the rumbles deep in his own throat. Four hands lifted him from the cold, hard surface, but every movement added to his anguish. He tried to get away from the strong arms holding him. Fighting didn't work, because his strength had fled. So he quit bucking against them. Where was he? How did he get here? His memory was like a blank page in a book where the story had been erased. As he tried to delve deeper into his mind, a wall of pain stopped him.

The jostling as he was carried into the cold wind intensified his torment. His whole body shook, and the hands gripped him tighter. Quick bursts of conversation were over before his befuddled mind could make out the words. At least two men manhandled him, and he could do nothing about it. Was he a prisoner somewhere? If so, why?

Then he was in a closed vehicle traveling at a higher speed than the street should allow. Each bump and pothole jerked him, even though someone held him down. *Would this torture never end?* With a final muscle spasm, he fell into an abyss as dark as midnight, with even his surroundings slipping away.

Joshua was thankful when Erik stopped the coach as close to the front door of the mansion as he could. The younger man quickly jumped down and jerked the door open. Joshua really didn't want to hurt Charles any more than he already was, because his anguished moans had filled the inside of the coach as they traveled toward Joshua's home. After they slid Charles from the coach, each of them pulled one of his arms across his own shoulder. With the man between them, they made their way up the rock walkway toward the front door.

Joshua grasped the knob with the hand not supporting his young partner and gave it a quick twist. After pushing the heavy wooden door open with his other arm, Erik helped him move the unconscious man into the foyer. Charles's dead weight really dragged against them.

"Joshua." Florence stood at the bottom of the stairs, concern filling her eyes and tone. "What happened?"

He gritted his teeth trying to keep a good hold on the young man whose head lolled against his own chest. "Charles evidently took at tumble down the stairs in his house." While he talked, he and Erik eased their way toward the parlor with their burden. "No servants were about, so we brought him here."

By the time they got Charles inside the doorway, Florence joined them. "He won't be comfortable on the settee. Bring him down the hallway to the guest room."

She hurried ahead of the men, her heels tapping a loud staccato.

Joshua gave Erik a quick glance before turning his full attention to the man between them. No signs of Charles awakening yet. Worry bit at his mind. What if his young partner were seriously injured?

By the time they made it into the large bedroom, Florence had pulled the fancy spread off the bed and turned back the covers. "Is he bleeding anywhere?"

The men eased the young man down onto the feather mattress and lifted his legs. Joshua took off the slippers before tucking Charles's feet under the quilts. "We didn't find any."

He turned to his driver. "Erik, go find Dr. Wharton as quickly as you can."

"Yes, sir." Erik strode into the hall, and the front door slammed almost immediately.

Joshua turned back to the bed. He didn't like how pale Charles looked, almost lifeless. He felt against the side of his neck and noticed with relief that the young man's pulse beat steadily.

Florence touched his shoulder. "I'll get warm water for the washstand. The doctor may need it. And maybe I should get some cloths ready in case he needs bandages." She bustled from the room.

As Joshua studied the young man, he noticed that Charles's eyelids quivered occasionally, but they didn't open. And the man's fingers sometimes twitched. Joshua hoped those were good signs. If the doctor didn't get here soon, Joshua decided he might need to do a more thorough examination of his partner.

"Daddy, who is that?" Maggie's soft-spoken words drew his attention to her standing in the doorway.

He looked up. "It's Charles. He fell, and Jorgensen and I found him at the bottom of the stairs in his foyer. We're not sure how badly he's injured."

"Charles!" Her face went white.

She rushed across the carpet and took his limp hand. The look on her face told Joshua everything, and grief and joy struck his heart simultaneously. His little girl had fallen in love—with his business partner and friend.

"What happened?" She turned toward him, anguish covering her face.

He explained how he had found Charles in his home. While he talked, Florence came in with the basin of water and bandages, but Maggie barely looked up. Joshua's eyes met hers, and a look of knowing passed between them.

Florence crossed to Maggie and put her arm around her. "I'm sure Charles will be fine. He's just had a bad bump to his head, but we've sent Erik for the doctor just in case. Now come, Maggie, and let him rest." She guided Maggie from the room, murmuring all the way.

Not too much later the doctor arrived. Joshua shook his hand, then indicated the basin. The doctor rolled up his sleeves and washed his hands. "What can you tell me about what happened?"

"We're not sure. I think he tripped and fell down his stairs. I found him lying on the marble floor."

After drying his hands, Dr. Wharton pulled the chair close to the bed and perched on the seat. "How long has he been unconscious?"

"Don't know that either." Joshua shook his head. "About half an hour since we first found him. He couldn't have been there too long before we arrived."

The doctor pulled out his stethoscope. He pressed the wooden, bell-shaped chest piece over Charles's heart. "His heartbeat is steady and strong." He removed the stethoscope from his ears. "Did you examine him closely?"

"No. We hurried to get him here and send for you."

The doctor lifted one of Charles's eyelids and peered into his eyes. "His pupils are reacting to light. That's good."

Joshua let out the breath he'd been holding.

With practiced fingers, the doctor gently explored his patient's scalp. When he reached one side of the head, a loud moan escaped from Charles.

"There's a large lump up high on this side...hmmmm."

Joshua wondered what that meant. Was it a good thing, or was Charles more seriously injured than he'd thought? *Dear Lord, please let it be a good thing.*

The doctor glanced up at him. "Actually, that's a good sign. If I couldn't find a knot, I'd have to try trepanation to release the pressure on the brain. A very delicate and dangerous procedure. I don't like to use it if there's any other way to treat the patient."

Joshua hadn't heard that word before. "What is trepanation?"

"I'd have to drill holes in his skull." The doctor grimaced. "I only use it as a last resort. Not at all a pleasant thing to do."

Joshua nodded, relief filling him.

The medical man continued his examination until he'd studied every limb and the patient's torso, front and back. "I think we can wait awhile and see if he'll awaken on his own. I don't see any sign of broken bones or other trauma. He's young, and with tender care, he should recover quickly."

"We brought him to our home so we could take care of him, since his family's all gone."

The doctor went to wash his hands again. "I'm surprised none of his servants were in the house. You checked, right?"

"Yes, no one was there." All of this was perplexing. Joshua felt almost helpless, and he didn't like it one bit. "Is there anything we can do to help him get better?"

"Watch him closely. If he awakens and is lucid, give him sips of water and maybe some broth, but administer it slowly. Later he can have noodles, maybe some bread." Dr. Wharton picked up his jacket and thrust his arms into it. "I feel sure our patient has sustained a concussion. When he awakens, he needs to take care and not do too much too quickly." Dr. Wharton donned his bowler. "I'll be back tomorrow to check on the patient. In the meantime, if there is any change for the worse, send word. I'll come right away."

Joshua nodded and saw the doctor to the door. Then he went into his study and shut the door behind him. Kneeling beside the rosewood desk, he bowed his head and prayed for his partner, gratitude filling him that the prognosis looked good. And wonder filling him at the thought of his daughter loving Charles.

Charles *had* to recover!

Chapter 25

WRINGING HER HANDS, Maggie sat in the parlor with her mother. She had tried to hide her anguish from her father, but she knew she had done a poor job of it. Her heart ached. *Lord, please let Charles be all right.* Even if she and Charles would never have a future together, she couldn't deny her love for him. She wanted him to live and become the man she knew God wanted him to be.

When her father finally came into the room, she looked up eagerly. "What did the doctor say?"

"He says Charles likely has a concussion and that when he awakes, he needs to take it easy for a while."

"Do you need my help?" Maggie gave a relieved sigh. Charles wasn't going to die. "Could I sit with him?"

Daddy glanced at Mother, and a look passed between them that Maggie couldn't interpret.

Mother hesitated. "I'm not sure it's appropriate for you to be in there since you're a young lady and he's a single man."

Daddy stepped closer. "It's not going to hurt anything for her to be with him until he awakes. Maybe she could read to him. It'll help Charles to hear her voice, since they spent so much time together on her journey. Maybe he'll awaken sooner."

Maggie jumped up, hope filling her heart. "Maybe I should read healing scriptures over him."

Daddy put his arm around her. "That sounds like a very good idea."

Maggie retrieved her Bible, then hurried to Charles's room, where she pulled a chair close to his bedside. While she read to him, she glanced up often to study him. Reading a psalm she had previously memorized helped. She didn't have to look at the text in the Bible. She spoke the words with feeling that came straight from her heart.

His dark hair looked as if he had raked it with his fingers before he fell. His usually tanned complexion appeared pasty, and she could almost count the whiskers that barely peeked out of his waxen cheeks and chin. Tears streamed down her cheeks. She couldn't see his warm brown eyes, one of his best features. Worry for her dear, dear friend clawed at her. *Lord, please don't let anything serious be wrong with him.*

Charles heard the familiar voice calling to him. With words from Scripture. Words he'd heard and read so many times in his life.

"'Oh that men would praise the Lord for his goodness, and for his wonderful works to the children of men. For he satisfieth the longing soul, and filleth the hungry soul with goodness.'"

Words spoken by a familiar angel with curly red hair. Now how did he know that? Words from the Psalms. A voice that enticed him up from the darkness.

But he couldn't reach the light, so he let the words pour over him like a healing balm.

"'Then they cried unto the Lord in their trouble, and he saved them out of their distresses.'" The voice paused, and the angel took a deep breath. "'He sent his word, and healed them, and delivered them from their destructions. Oh that men would praise the Lord for his goodness, and for his wonderful works to the children of men.'" This time the breath sounded like a soft sob.

He tried once more to open his eyes and look at his angel, but his eyelids wouldn't obey.

"'And let them sacrifice the sacrifices of thanksgiving, and declare his works with rejoicing. They that go down to the sea in ships, that do business in great waters. These see the works of the Lord, and his wonders in the deep.'"

He drifted back into oblivion accompanied by the wonderful voice.

The comforting words of the psalm soothed Maggie. She just hoped they also reached Charles, wherever his mind was. Surely it wasn't a good thing for him to stay unconscious so long. She had to swallow several times between the words to keep from breaking into sobs. Even if she couldn't have Charles, she wanted to be able to see him sometimes. Her world would be a dreary place without his presence.

She read until her voice almost gave out, then she stopped before she completely lost it. Leaning back in the chair, she sighed and squeezed the tears from her eyes. As they made trails down her cheeks, she dabbed at them with her hanky.

"Please..." The word was spoken so softly, she thought she'd only imagined it. "Don't...stop."

Her gaze cut toward the man in the bed. Although he hadn't changed position, his eyes were open, staring straight at her. Pleading filled his expression as much as it had his words.

Afraid he might close his eyelids and slip away again if she didn't comply, she picked up the Bible and continued. Every few seconds she gave him a quick glance. He still had his gaze on her but hadn't moved another muscle. She continued reading for a few pages, then dropped the open book into her lap.

"Are you completely awake?" Her words were almost as soft as his had been. She was afraid anything louder would scare him back into unconsciousness.

He blinked a couple of times before slowly opening parched lips. "Yes," he rasped.

"Then I need to let someone know." She stood without taking her eyes off him, trying to communicate to him through her gaze how much he meant to her.

His eyes didn't waver from her either. "I know...but you'll...return?" Both his voice and his eyes begged her.

"Yes." She backed out of the room and hurried toward her father's study, thrusting open the door so fast it slammed against the wall. "He's awake!"

Daddy jumped up from behind the desk and ran out the door. "How is he?"

"He just woke up a few minutes ago when I stopped reading." She scurried behind him, skipping every few steps, trying to keep up with his long strides. "He wanted me to continue. I wasn't sure he was truly awake, so I kept reading a bit."

"Good job, Maggie." Daddy rushed into the room and dropped into the chair beside the bed. "Charles, I've been so worried about you. I've been in my study praying."

She noticed Charles's lips move slightly at the tip ends, probably trying to smile.

"Maggie." Her father glanced over his shoulder. "Go tell Mrs. Jorgensen that we need some water and broth for Charles."

Unable to contain her excitement, she went straight to the kitchen and burst through that doorway as well. "Our patient is awake!"

Mrs. Jorgensen smiled and started pumping water into a pitcher. "That is good, for sure. You take the water, and I'll dish up some nourishing broth for him."

When Maggie returned to the doorway of the guest room, both of her parents were leaning over the bed, talking to Charles.

"I brought some cool water for you." Maggie set the empty glass on the bedside table and filled it halfway.

Her father moved around the bed and helped ease Charles up against the pillows. Mother pushed behind his back. He winced and gasped a quick breath. He looked nearly as pale as the snow-white sheets, but his eyes held a spark of life now instead of looking so dull.

"Did we hurt you?" Mother's soft tone sounded soothing.

He opened his eyes and stared at Mother. "Not too much."

Maggie handed the glass to her mother and watched the way she gently tipped it to let only a small amount trickle down his throat. Then she pulled it back for a moment before offering him more.

By the time he had taken several sips, Mrs. Jorgensen entered carrying a mug with a tea towel folded around the bottom half. "Well, now, I've brought you some nice warm beef broth. It'll be good to settle your stomach and help you heal."

Mother and Daddy moved back and let the housekeeper sit in the chair beside the bed. She spooned the broth into his mouth, going slowly enough to keep from spilling any.

After several spoonfuls, Charles settled back into the pillows. "That tastes good, but I'm tired...want to lie...down."

Daddy helped him with Mother pulling the extra pillows out of the way. Maggie winced inside as she noticed pain flit across his features. Finally, he was nestled in the bed again.

She turned to go, but his voice called to her. "Don't go, Maggie....I like to hear you...read."

Soon after Maggie started reading, his eyes slid closed, and he slept. Mother must have been standing near the door, because she came into the room and leaned toward Maggie. "Mrs. Jorgensen has our dinner on the table. I don't think he'll miss you while he's asleep."

Maggie didn't really want to leave him, but she followed her mother from the room, her heart singing. Charles had awakened. And he was going to be all right.

Chapter 26

CHARLES REALIZED THAT his recovery was nothing short of miraculous. Without a doubt, when Maggie read healing scriptures over him, they accomplished what they were meant to do. He knew about the words in the Bible being alive and powerful. The speed of his return to health testified to that power, but he'd never before experienced the effects to this extent.

After only two days, here he was sitting up by the windows reading a book from Joshua's library. But he couldn't remember a word on any of the few pages he'd covered. His mind was so distracted. How had his life become so complicated?

He only had himself to blame. His own choices had carried him to this point. He had been so full of himself, claiming responsibility for the blessings God had given him. Even when they were in Arkansas, he had spouted Christian platitudes to Maggie at the same time that he had a firm grasp on the reins of his life, never giving a thought to what God's will was for him.

Certainly not to pursue Georgia Long as he did. *Vanity!* His actions had been dictated by his vanity. Well, no more. God had chosen to save his life when the fall should have killed him. *Thank You, God.*

The words Maggie read over him had reawakened his zeal to be a true servant of the sovereign God. To follow through on the commitment he made as a boy and all but ignored as a young man. When he was able to get out of the house, he'd be in the very next church service. He had made his true peace with God in the last two days, but he wanted to go to the Lord's house and submit to Him in that hallowed place as well. To give more to God than just lip service.

"Charles." Mrs. Caine's voice summoned him from his ponderings.

He shifted in the chair until he was facing her with a smile. "Yes, ma'am."

"Morris Tall Pine is here to see you." She ushered his tall servant into the room and turned away.

"I knew I shouldn't have left you alone." Morris never was one to beat around the bush.

Charles sat up straighter and closed the book in his lap. "How did you know where to find me?"

"Mr. Caine sent word. White Dove worried when we came home and you weren't there. Even cooked your favorite meal, but you never came home." The older man crossed his arms over his powerful chest and shook his head. "No neighbors even knew where you were."

"Pull that chair over here and sit down." Charles waited until his servant complied.

By the time he finished explaining things to Morris, the older man agreed to leave Charles with the Caines until the doctor told him he could go home.

After Morris left, Charles didn't even pretend to read. He had too many things bouncing around in his head. The chief of them was Maggie. What did she think of him since their journey together? After all, she'd witnessed him flirting shamelessly with Georgia. What a fool he must appear to her.

She had been a friend for so long, and he thought that was all he felt for her, friendship. Now he realized he wanted the two of them to have a different kind of relationship. So many things about her drew him. He loved the fact that she was interested in owning her own business. He would like to spend the rest of his life with a woman who thought about more than just what to wear and who was having the next party. Although with her interest in fashion design, she *would* take an interest in clothing. He smiled at the thought. She had so many dimensions to her. Dimensions he'd love to explore at his leisure over the coming years.

Not only that, but he was totally aware that Maggie was a desirable woman. Her childhood dusting of freckles had given way to a smooth creamy complexion with only a hint of the coppery dots he'd teased her about. Instead of girlish braids, she wore her hair in stunning updos that revealed the graceful slope of her neck. And her dresses enhanced every curve of her body.

His attraction to Maggie was so powerful it took his breath away, but it was much more than physical. His felt connected to her emotionally and spiritually as well. She too dealt with the loss of parents—even though she had never known them. She too looked to God for her strength. Why had it taken him so long to recognize what was right in front of him?

Lord, forgive me for my arrogance and self-centeredness. And for rushing ahead instead of waiting for You to show me the woman You planned. He quieted his mind and waited in silence—what he should have done months ago when he thought Georgia was the one for him. When he felt nothing but peace, he smiled.

He needed some way to find out if the portrait she drew was a true depiction of how Maggie felt about him. But how could that happen? He couldn't just come out and ask her. What if all of this was only in his mind? But would he feel this peace from God if it was?

And what of Joshua himself? Over the last few days, as he engaged in their business and now recovered in his home, Charles had found no reason to distrust his business partner. From what he could glean from his limited interactions with the family, Maggie had reconciled with her parents. But there was still much he did not know and could not guess about their relationship without asking directly.

At the knock on the doorpost, Charles cast a glance at his host standing in the entrance.

"Mind if I visit with you a bit?" Joshua waited for his answer.

Charles shifted in his chair. "Come in." He hadn't even noticed that daylight was waning outside the window. "I didn't realize it was time for you to come home." He started to get up.

"Keep your seat." Joshua slid into the chair where Morris had been sitting. "Has someone been visiting with you?"

"Morris came by to check on me. Thank you for letting him know I was here. He was worried when he didn't find me at home."

Some unexplained emotion flitted across Joshua's face but quickly vanished. "Think nothing about it. Have you been up all day?"

"I did take a nap earlier, but I'm much stronger than I was yesterday. I took a few turns around the room when no one was in here." Charles held up the book. "I even made it to the library to borrow this."

A smile split Joshua's face. "I'm glad. You don't seem to have any ill effects from your excursion."

"As soon as the doctor says I can, I'll be going home and back to work." He laid the book on the table under the window. "The sooner the better . . . not that I don't appreciate the hospitality."

He wondered what his partner would think about him having feelings for his daughter. *Having feelings* was a weak description of the love that was surging through him right now.

"You look as if you have something important on your mind." Joshua leaned back in the chair and laced his fingers across his stomach.

Charles cleared his throat. He'd never had a problem talking to Joshua, but now he felt as nervous as a college student in the dean's office. "Actually, I was thinking about discussing something personal with you."

Since it was cold, why were Charles's hands sweating? He wiped them down the sides of his trousers, hoping Joshua wouldn't notice.

"Would you like some coffee while we talk?"

"No. The women have plied me with plenty to drink today." Charles decided to plunge right in. "Actually, I want to ask you . . . if I can court Mag, uh . . . your daughter." He sounded like a bumbling idiot. *Why is this so hard?*

Joshua laughed. "Is that all?"

"Well, yes, sir. I'd like to court Margaret." Maybe this wouldn't be quite as hard as he'd feared.

"Why?"

"What did you say?" Charles glanced at the man to see if he was serious. From the look on his face, this *was* a serious question to him.

"I believe I asked a legitimate question. Why do you want to court my daughter?" No censure in Joshua's tone, at least.

Once more that lump clogged Charles's throat. He swallowed hard. "I believe we'd make a good match."

Joshua barked out a harsh laugh. "That is a weak answer."

"I love her, sir, with my whole heart." Those words tasted better than any dessert he'd ever eaten, and they forced the lump out of the way so they could emerge.

Joshua smiled broadly. "That's what I wanted to hear, my boy. A lot of people don't think love matters in a marriage. But it does. Soon after I met Florence, I knew I *had* to have her for my wife. Nothing and no one would stop me from winning her." Joshua stared at Charles. "Does Maggie know how you feel?"

Charles nodded, then shook his head. "No, sir. I didn't want to mention it until I had your blessing. And I needed to know more, sir, about you."

Joshua looked startled. "Me?"

"Yes, sir." His gaze raked the older man. "When we were in Arkansas, I was present when Maggie revealed how she found out about her adoption. News I can guess she has since shared with you?"

Joshua frowned and nodded slightly but remained quiet.

"I admired Maggie's courage in dealing with this unexpected news. Certainly she has the most concern in this matter. But I do as well."

"You don't like that she was adopted?"

"That is not it, sir. I dislike that she was deceived."

Joshua looked away, but not before Charles caught the deep hurt in his eyes.

Charles continued, "In both business and personal matters, I was taught to live with utter openness and honesty and integrity. And like Maggie, I found it hard to understand why you hid this knowledge from her all these years. If I am to be your business partner—or anything more—I need to feel an openness between us, and an understanding that you will never withhold anything from me that I must know. Do you agree?"

Joshua looked up. Their gazes held for a long moment, and as respect answered respect, Charles received his answer even before Joshua began to speak.

"I have deep regret that I allowed myself to be swayed in this instance. I never wanted to hide the information from her. But my wife was adamant, and I didn't take the time to discover why." His head bowed and he clasped his hands between his knees. "I just agreed to keep the peace, which was a coward's way out."

That had to have been a hard thing for Joshua to admit to him, and the respect Charles had been regaining for his partner rose even higher.

Maggie's father glanced up. "I'm pleased to let you know that we told our daughter the complete truth, and we've been wonderfully reconciled. It's more than we deserve, but God is merciful."

Charles respected Joshua's answer. "That He is."

"I suppose I should tell you the rest." Joshua straightened his shoulders. "Maggie was a triplet born on the wagon train, and her mother died. Angus McKenna was so broken up at losing the love of his life that he didn't think he had what it took to care for three baby girls. He gave two of them to different families."

Whoa! Maggie a triplet? Charles could hardly believe this new revelation. "Do you know where her sisters are?"

Joshua shook his head. "We don't. But I'm telling you right now, Maggie is going to want to find them one day, and the time could come soon. Are you prepared to face something like that?"

Charles took a long moment to ponder the question. "I believe I am."

Joshua studied him for an extended time as well. "Since we're being honest with each other, I have one other concern. I've known men to seek marriage for business reasons. I need to know if this has a bearing on your feelings for Maggie."

Charles met his gaze without wavering. "I'd love Maggie even if we had never gone into business with each other. I'm afraid that for too long, I was blind to what was right in front of me. Maggie is a blessing from God to me."

Joshua appeared pleased with his answer. "So tell me. Does Maggie love you?"

Charles shook his head, then nodded. "I believe she does, but we've been very circumspect."

Joshua threw his head back, and his laugh rang through the room. "Circumspect. I like that." He clapped Charles on the shoulder. "I didn't doubt you'd treat her in an honorable way, or I wouldn't have sent you on the journey. Now let me get this straight. Do you want to go through a long courtship, or do you want to marry her?"

"I want to marry her as soon as possible. Tomorrow, if I could." He couldn't believe he blurted those words to her father. But his heart felt merry, like in the Bible, the kind of merry that was a good medicine.

"Well, now, I have to tell you. With Maggie being our only child, you'll have to wait for the women to plan a wedding, and that'll take some time. How much, I'm not sure. So if you want to marry her fairly soon, you'd better get her asked right away. That way, you won't have to wait a year or two."

A year or two? He had no idea a wedding could take that long to plan. Charles knew he didn't want to wait so long. "So does this mean I have your blessing to ask her?"

"Wholeheartedly! I know you'll take good care of my little girl."

The way Joshua said *my little girl* went straight to Charles's heart. The man's love for his daughter was the same kind of love he would have for his own children. He winced a little. *What am I doing thinking about children when I haven't even told Maggie I love her, much less asked her to marry me?*

Since Charles was getting so much stronger, Maggie only got to see him when people were around. Her mother kept her busy with other things while she and Mrs. Jorgensen took care of his needs. But he came to the dinner table without anyone helping him the last two days, and the doctor left today just before dinner.

She dressed with care knowing she would be seeing Charles. Since winter was fast approaching, the temperatures had plummeted, making it harder to keep the house heated. She chose a navy wool skirt and jacket and wore them with a creamy silk blouse. Pin tucks lined with lace decorated the front. Since the neckline of the jacket dipped in a low scoop, it set off her figure to perfection. And Ingrid tried a new hairstyle that swept her hair high on her head and laced it with navy ribbon and white lace. Maggie felt regal in the ensemble.

As she swept down the staircase, Mother headed toward Daddy's study. "Would you tell Charles that dinner will be a few more minutes? Have him come by the fireplace in the parlor, and you can wait with him."

The smile on her mother's face held a note of triumph. Maggie couldn't imagine why.

Before she took more than two steps down the hallway toward the guest room, Charles emerged. Although he looked a little thinner than he did on their journey, dressed in a dark suit and white shirt with stiff collar and dark tie, he was extremely handsome. She stopped and took a deep breath before she relayed her mother's message.

A dazzling smile lit his eyes. "I'll follow you, Maggie."

The words sounded almost like a caress. She knew her love for Charles was making her crazy since she ascribed that thought to his words.

Charles waited for her to choose a place to sit. She settled onto a wing-back chair and sat erect with her hands clasped in her lap as any lady of good breeding would. Too bad her emotions had made her unable to relax around him. He sat on the end of the settee that was very close to the chair.

"You look lovely tonight." He hadn't taken his eyes off her since they arrived in the parlor, and his soft words carried added meaning to her heart.

Maggie was glad she and Ingrid took extra care with her toilette. She lowered her gaze to her lap while warmth suffused her cheeks. "Thank you."

The silence that followed rang with potentialities while Maggie tried to control her rampant emotions.

Finally, Maggie decided to break the silence. "So how are you doing?" She glanced up at his face.

"The doctor said I'm fine. I will return home tomorrow morning." He looked plenty relaxed. "I hate to think what would have happened if your father hadn't stopped by my house that day."

The idea widened her eyes, and she couldn't hold back a shudder. "I'm glad he did. No telling how long you would have lain there at the bottom of the stairs. You might not have recovered very quickly...if at all." She could barely force the last three words out on a whisper.

He rested one hand on hers. "But he did stop by and I did recover. I believe God was watching over me."

"Of course, He was." Maggie's ramrod stiff body relaxed a bit.

"I've been missing you, Maggie." His smile matched the tone of his words. "Your reading the Scriptures to me was also instrumental in my recovery."

"Since you've been up and around in the guest room, Mother didn't think it was a good idea for me to come back." She took a deep breath and averted her gaze from his. "You know the unmarried maiden and the single man thing."

"Yes, I do." She detected a smile in his voice. Then he leaned forward, even closer to her. "I want to ask you something."

Her eyes quickly returned to his face. "What?"

Now he removed his hand and glanced away. "Remember that drawing you did of me?"

Maggie wasn't sure what he was going to ask. She really didn't want to discuss that picture. The sketch had been private, just for her. She wished he had never found it.

"Why did you draw a portrait of me?"

The words hung heavy in the space between them while she tried to decide how to answer without revealing too much to him. She didn't want to destroy their friendship just because she wanted more from him.

She sighed. "I'm not really sure myself." She hoped he wouldn't want any more information from her. She tried to hold the gathering tears inside her eyes, but her lower lids weren't adequate dams.

"Maggie, please look at me."

She turned her eyes toward his face, hoping he wouldn't notice moisture glistening in them. "All right."

"I saw things in that portrait that indicated..." Now he hesitated, took time before he continued. "Perhaps the artist not only knows me well, but also has...deep affection for me."

Maggie's eyes widened and she averted her gaze, feeling a blush once more bleed into her cheeks, but she didn't say a word. How could she tell him what she felt for him when she had no idea if he returned the love? "Perhaps."

She knew the word was soft, and he might not have heard it above the crackling of the fire if he wasn't totally attuned to her. But she couldn't have said it any louder if she had wanted to.

He picked up one of her hands and held it in both of his. "Maggie, I asked your father if I can court you."

His words contrasted with hers in both strength and clarity. She welcomed every word and the emotions that fueled them.

Love rose like a tidal wave within her. Could he love her as she loved him? He wouldn't ask to court her if he didn't love her, would he?

"I'd like that very much." She could barely get the words out. Her heart felt as if it might take flight. "But Charles, when did you …" She stopped, not wanting to say the words.

"Start loving you?" He finished her sentence for her. His gaze made a leisurely journey across her face, leaving a path of warmth in its wake. "I think I always have loved you, since that first day you stepped into the schoolroom when you were six years old. I remember the way your curls wouldn't allow your pigtails to tame them."

That answer shocked her, and she raised her brows. "Really?"

He started to answer, but she noticed the very moment he realized to what she was referring. The smile drained from his face. "You were right there in front of me all the time, and I didn't realize how my love for you was growing." He gripped her hand even harder. "And I made a really stupid mistake on the train trip to Arkansas. I asked Georgia's forgiveness, and we made peace with each other."

Maggie nodded. His fingers relaxed, but he didn't let go of her hand. Instead, he wove his fingers with hers into a more intimate clasp. The kind of clasp she'd dreamed of having.

"Only after we returned to Seattle did I let God reveal to me that I should be looking at who He placed in my life so long ago."

She stared at their intertwined hands and knew she wanted her life to be intertwined with his forever.

The sunshine of his smile bathed her in the heat of his passion. "I hadn't planned on telling you quite this way, but I'm glad I did. I feel like jumping up and whooping and hollering, but I can't right now."

"I'm glad too." This time her words carried great conviction. "But Charles, there's something else about me you should know." She relayed the conversation she'd had with her parents the night they returned from Arkansas. The circumstances of her adoption. The struggles of her mother. And finally, the existence of her two sisters. Then she turned to him. "It's important to me that I know who I am. And that you know who I am too. When I first revealed my adoption, you appeared..."

"...shocked? I have to admit, I was." His eyes revealed the truth of that statement. "But not because you were adopted. I didn't like that your parents hadn't told you. Frankly, I worried that if your father had deceived you on this personal matter for so many years, he might also choose to deceive me in matters of business."

The words struck her heart, and she stiffened. "But he is not like..."

"I know," he interrupted. "He explained everything to me and apologized too. And I've already experienced firsthand not only his respect for the business, but also his concern for my personal well-being." He smiled. "I could almost be thankful for falling and hitting my head."

"Me too," Maggie blurted, then put her other fingers to her mouth for a moment. "I didn't mean that. But I am glad to have you near me again."

"Are you?" His voice softened. "Well, that really leaves me in a pickle." Charles gently placed her hand in her lap and got up. He went to stand with his back to the fireplace and stared at her as he spoke. "I want nothing more than to sweep you into my arms and kiss you senseless, but I don't have that right yet."

She returned his intense look. As she imagined a kiss from his sculptured lips, a longing rose deep inside her. Her stomach began to flutter, and she placed her hand over it to calm it.

Maggie loved this man. When she was young, she'd often dreamed about marrying him, but that kind of infatuation was in vain. Now she'd come to know him deeply and had learned to respect his finer qualities. A man who truly trusted God. A man of honor who was willing to admit his faults and to correct them. A protector.

His hypnotic gaze held hers, and a communication so private it couldn't be voiced passed between them, opening her heart to him in a greater way than ever before. This wonderful man could turn her insides out, and the results were exhilarating...and scary at the same time.

"Maggie, there's more." He held out his hand toward her.

Without hesitation, she arose and went to stand in front of him. He clasped her hands and held them against his chest. Her fingertips detected his heartbeat in perfect harmony with the strong pulsing of her own.

"What?" Now her words could be quieter, and her tears had disappeared.

He leaned his face so close to her that she felt his soft breath against her forehead. "He gave me permission to ask you to marry me. We have his blessing."

Her eyes widened again, in joy and wonder this time. Everything was happening so fast. Faster than she'd ever imagined.

"So, will you marry me, Maggie?"

She turned her face even closer to his and stared into his eyes. "Yes."

His lips touched hers as softly as a butterfly hovering over a flower, but his didn't flit away. Instead they settled more firmly, connecting their hearts in a way she had never imagined was possible. Everything faded away except this moment with her beloved. Their kiss sealed their promise, and all the fears, all the worries, all the struggles of the past few months melted away.

Finally, Maggie knew who she was. Margaret Lenora Caine, adopted daughter of Joshua and Florence Caine. Natural daughter of Angus and Lenora McKenna. And beloved fiancé of Charles Stanton.

Her journey was complete. She was home.

Coming in *May* 2012

Mary's Blessing

Chapter 1
Outside Oregon City

April 1885

P A?" Mary Lenora Murray shouted back over her shoulder as she picked up the heavy picnic basket. "You ready to go?"

Why does he always drag his feet when we're going to church?

Her father came into the kitchen from outside, letting the screen door slam shut behind him. He smelled of heat, hay, and sunshine, with the strong tang of muck from the barn mingled in. By the looks of his clothes, attending church was the farthest thing from his mind. His ratty trousers held smudges of several dark colors. She didn't even want to guess what they were. And the long sleeves of his undershirt, the only thing covering his torso, were shoved above his elbows. Grayed and dingy, the shirt would never be white again, no matter how hard she tried to get it clean.

Mary bit her tongue to keep from scolding him as she did her younger brothers and sister when they made so much racket entering the house. No doubt he would give her some excuse about having too much work to gadabout with them, even to church. Not a big surprise. She'd heard it all before too many times.

He set a bucket of fresh water beside the dry sink and gripped his fingers around the front straps of his suspenders. He always did that when he was going to tell her something she didn't want to hear.

"I'm not going today." His stubborn tone held finality, as if he didn't want her to talk back to him. But she was tempted to tell him what she thought about it.

This time he didn't really make any excuses. Just this bald-faced comment.

She took a deep breath and let it out slowly, trying to calm her anger. She'd give him a sweet answer even if the words tasted bitter in her mouth. "The new pastor is coming today. We're having dinner on the grounds after the service. Remember, I told you when we got home last Sunday." She flashed what she hoped was a warm smile at him and prayed he couldn't tell it was fake.

"What happened to the last one? He didn't stay very long, did he?" Pa started washing his hands with the bar of homemade soap she kept in a dish on the shelf. "Don't understand why that church can't keep a pastor for very long. Someone musta run him off."

Mary couldn't keep from huffing out a breath this time. "I told you about that too." She clamped her lips closed before she asked the question that often bounced around her mind. *Why don't you ever listen to me?* She was close enough to an adult to be treated like one, and she'd carried the load of a woman in this household for seven years.

She was beginning to sound like a shrew. She'd laughed at Kate in Shakespeare's play *The Taming of the Shrew*, but she didn't want to be like the woman, so she made an effort to soften her tone before she spoke again. "His wife died, and his father-in-law begged him to bring the grandchildren closer to where they live, so he headed back to Ohio. He'd have a lot of help with the younger ones, living in the same community as their grandparents."

Mary had never known her own grandparents, none of them. Not her mother's parents. Not her father's parents. Not the parents of whoever gave birth to her. She didn't wonder about any of them very often, but today, her heart longed for someone who could really get to know her and love her for her individuality.

With bright red, curly hair and fair skin that freckled more every time she stepped into the sunlight, she didn't resemble anyone in this family that adopted her. Since they were Black Irish, they all had dark hair and striking blue eyes, not like her murky green ones. And none of them had ever wanted to know what she thought about anything...except her mother. How long was it since her mother and older sisters died of diphtheria? She had to think back and count up.

Hundreds of people in and around Oregon City—including Dr. Forbes Barclay, their only physician at that time—died in an epidemic of the dreaded disease in 1873. However, her mother and sisters contracted the disease five years later when they went to help Aunt Miriam and Uncle Leland settle in their house on a farm about five miles from theirs. On the trip to Oregon, one of them had contracted the dread disease and didn't know it until after they arrived. The people on that farm were the only ones that year who were sick with the horrible scourge.

No one knew they were all dead until Pa went looking for Ma, Cheryl, and Annette a couple of days later. He saw the quarantine sign someone nailed to a fencepost and didn't go closer until he had help. When he came home, he told Mary she would have to take over the keeping of the house. *Seven long years ago.*

"Well, I've gotta lot to do today." Her father reached for the towel she'd made out of feed sacks. "You and the others go ahead. I might come over that way at dinner time."

No, you won't. Mary had heard that often enough to know he was trying to placate her so she would leave him alone. So she would.

"Frances, George, Bobby, come on. We don't want to be late." She shifted the handle of the loaded basket to her other arm. "Frances, you grab the jug of spring water. We might get thirsty."

Her father's icy blue eyes pierced her. "Might get pretty warm."

"We'll be picnicking in the field between the church and Willamette Falls. It's cooler there, especially under the trees with the breeze blowing across the water." She started toward the front door.

"Keep your eyes on the boys." His harsh command followed her. "Don't let either of them in the river. They could drown."

She nodded but didn't answer or look back at him. All he cared about were those boys and getting them raised old enough to really help with the farming. He already worked them harder than any of the neighbors did their sons who were the same ages.

When did my life become such a drudgery? Had it ever been anything else? At least not since Ma died, which seemed like an eternity ago.

Daniel Winthrop whistled while he dressed for church. He looked forward with anticipation to the moment when he would lay eyes on Mary Murray. Even her name sounded musical.

He'd been waiting and planning what to say when he approached her. Today he would start his subtle courting. With the situation at the Murray farm, he knew he would have his work cut out for him, to convince her she could start a life of her own with him. After he achieved that, he'd ask her father for her hand.

Visions of coming home to her each night and building a family together moved through his head like the slides of photographs in the Holmes Stereopticon they enjoyed at home. He loved her already, but more than that, he wanted to get her out of that house where she was loaded down with so much work and responsibility.

Daniel had often gone with his mother when she bought fresh produce from the Murrays. So he knew what her life had been since her mother died. Their families came to Oregon on the same wagon train, so he'd known her almost all his life. He was only a couple of years older than her.

Mary needed to be appreciated and cared for, and he was just the man to do it.

"Daniel, we're leaving soon." His father's voice prodded him from his dreams.

With a final peek into the cheval glass, he straightened his necktie before he headed out the door of his room. "I'm on my way."

He bounded down the stairs and took their picnic basket from his mother. "Something really smells good." He gave a loud sniff. "Do you need me to test and make sure it's all right?"

He welcomed her playful slap on his hand that crept toward the cover on the basket, and her laughter reminded him of the chimes he had heard in the larger church in Portland.

"Not a single bite until dinner." Like a queen, she swept out the door Father held open for her.

Their familiar ritual warmed his heart. He looked forward to creating family rituals with Mary. Once more he whistled as he headed toward the brougham. Nothing could cloud his day.

When they pulled up to the Methodist Church, his father guided the team toward the back where a large area paved with fine gravel gave plenty of space for those who arrived in horse-drawn vehicles. While Father helped Mother down from the open carriage, Daniel took the reins and tied them to one of the hitching rails that outlined the space. He chose the rail under a spreading black cottonwood tree, so the horses would be in the shade while the family worshiped.

He scanned the lot, looking for the Murray wagon. Not there. Disappointed, he stared at the ground. *Please, God, let Mary come today.*

Clopping hoofs and a jingling harness accompanied a wagon taking too fast of a turn into the parking area. Daniel cut his eyes toward the advancing disaster. Two of the wheels did indeed lift from the ground. Before he could get a shout out, he heard Mary's sweet voice.

"Lean to the right, boys!"

George and Bobby, Mary's brothers, scrambled across the seat, followed by Frances. The wagon wheels settled into the tiny rocks, and Mary pulled on the reins.

"Easy. Settle down." Even though she spoke to the horses, he heard every word.

His heart that had almost leaped from his chest also settled down when he realized she was no longer in danger. *Thank You, Lord.*

The wagon came to a standstill, and Mary put her dainty hand to her chest and released a deep breath. The dark green cotton fabric, sprigged with white flowers, looked good on her, setting off her red hair, pulled up into a bunch on the top of her head. Without a hat or bonnet covering it, the sun danced across the curls. He loved seeing the wisps around her face. That's how he pictured her when he dreamed about their future.

Mary sat a moment without moving. She was probably scared out of her wits. Where was her father? He should have been driving the wagon, not her. How long had it been since the man had attended services? He couldn't remember the last time. It was not a good thing for a man to neglect his spiritual nature. He'd just have to pray harder for Mr. Murray.

Daniel hurried toward them. "Hi, Mary."

She looked up, straight into his eyes, fear still flickering in the back of her gaze. "Daniel. Good morning." Her words came out riding on short breaths.

He took hold of the bridle of the horse nearest him. "I can hitch your team under the trees for you."

After releasing another deep breath, Mary nodded. "Thank you. I'd like that." She turned toward her siblings. "Frances, you get the picnic basket, and George, you carry the jug of water. Go find us a pew, perhaps near the back of the sanctuary, and put the things under the bench. I'll be right in."

The younger children climbed out of the wagon and followed their sister's instructions. Mary watched them until they'd gone around the side of the building toward the front. Then she stood up.

Before she could try to climb over the side, Daniel hurried to help. He held out his hand to her. She stared at it, then looked at his face.

"I'll help you down." He gave her his most beguiling smile.

For the first time since she arrived, she smiled back, and pink bled up her neck into her cheeks. Her blush went straight to his heart. *Oh, yes, he loved this woman.* The twinkle in her green eyes emphasized the golden flecks. He'd actually never noticed them before. He wished he could continue to stare deep into her eyes forever.

Mary slipped her slim fingers into his hand. Even through the white cotton gloves, he felt the connection as warmth sparked up his arm like fireworks on the Fourth of July. She glanced down so she could see the step. When she hesitated, he let go of her hand and both of his spanned her tiny waist. With a deft swing, he had her on the ground in seconds. He wished he had the right to pull her into an embrace. *Wouldn't that just set the tongues a-wagging?* He couldn't do that to her. Mary needed to be cherished for the treasure she was. And as far as Daniel could see, her father really didn't treat her that way.

He watched her walk toward the front of the building, enjoying the way her skirt swayed with each step, barely brushing the tops of her black patent shoes. *That is one beautiful woman.* He turned back to her team. Walking beside the horses, he led them toward the hitching rail where his family's brougham stood. Her team would enjoy the shade just as much as his would. As he crossed the lot, several other conveyances entered, and he waved and exchanged greetings with each family. His chest expanded with all the happiness he felt this wonderful day.

The church was the first one established in Oregon City. At that time it was the Methodist Mission, but it grew as the town did. Along the way, members of this body had a great influence on what happened in the burgeoning city. And that was still true today. His Winthrop ancestors, who settled nearby, had been instrumental in both the growth of the church and of the town. He felt a sense of pride at being a part of something that important, and he wanted to increase the town's assets, because he planned to raise his own family here. Maybe establish a dynasty of his own, watching his sons and daughters, then his grandchildren, prosper in the wonderful town.

His woolgathering slowed the progress of tying the horses to their spot. He needed to hurry so he wouldn't miss the beginning of the service. As he opened the front door, Mrs. Slidel struck the first chord on the new Mason and Hamlin reed organ. The church had ordered the instrument from the manufacturing plant in Buffalo, New York. When it arrived only a couple of weeks before, the music added a special feeling to the worship and helped most people stay on the right tune. He hummed along with the introduction to "What a Friend We Have in Jesus," his favorite hymn.

Glancing around the room, Daniel finally spied Mary and her siblings sitting on the second pew from the back on the right side of the aisle. He squared his shoulders and confidently approached the wooden bench. He asked if he could sit with them, and she scooted over to make room. Just what he wanted. He would be sitting right beside her.

Throughout the service Daniel had a hard time keeping his mind on the proceedings. Mary sat close enough for him to touch her if he leaned a little to his right. He was so tempted to bump against her arm, but he held back. He imagined clasping her hand in his and holding it for longer than just a few seconds while helping her down or through a doorway. Really wrapping his large fingers around hers and intertwining their fingers. Just thinking about it caught his breath.

He whooshed it out, and she turned toward him, her eyes widening with a question. After flashing a smile at her, he glanced up at Reverend Horton. The man's delivery was smooth, and his words made a lot of sense. He'd be a good pastor for them, but Daniel couldn't keep a single word of his message in his mind. Not while he could feel Mary's presence with every cell in his body.

Instead in his mind, he searched up and down the streets of Oregon City, seeking a place to turn into a home for him and his beloved. If the right house wasn't for sale, he could build her one. She could help him choose the design. That's what he'd do. Build her the home she'd always dreamed of. His heart squeezed with the knowledge of what he planned to do. He could hardly keep the idea to himself. He hoped it wouldn't take too long for him to convince her that they should marry.

He'd even hire servants to help her manage their home. Whatever her heart desired, he'd do everything he could to present her with everything she wanted. He only hoped it wouldn't take too long. At twenty years old, he was ready to move on to that other phase of his life…with Mary by his side.

"Now let us bow our heads in prayer." Reverend Horton raised his hands to bless the whole congregation.

Daniel lowered his head. How had the man finished his sermon without Daniel noticing? Next Sunday he'd have to listen more closely. He really did want to get to know the new pastor and his family.

"Amen." After the pastor pronounced the word, several other men echoed.

Daniel watched his father rise from the second pew near the front on the left side of the aisle and take his place beside the new preacher. He placed his arm across the man's shoulders. "Dear friends, on your behalf, I welcome our new pastor. Now let's all meet his lovely family." He waved toward a woman sitting on the front pew. "Mrs. Horton?"

The woman stood and turned toward the congregation. She was pretty, but not as young or as pretty as Mary.

"And," Father's voice boomed, "these are their children."

Four stair-step youngsters stood beside their mother. The tallest a boy, the next a girl, then another boy, and the shortest a cute little tyke of a girl. As if they had rehearsed it, they bowed toward the people in unison.

Several women all across the sanctuary *oooed* or *aahed* before a loud round of applause broke out. The three oldest children gave shy smiles, and the youngest tugged at her mother's skirts. When Mrs. Horton picked her up, the girl waved to the people, clearly enjoying all the attention.

"I hope you all brought your blankets and picnic baskets." Father beamed at the crowd.

When Daniel glanced around, he became aware there were several visitors. He felt sure they came out of curiosity about the new pastor. Maybe they would return to the services next week. He certainly hoped so.

"We're going to spread our food together. I believe there are plenty of sawhorse tables set up near the building. And you can pick a spot under the trees to settle for your meal. Just don't forget to take the time to greet our new ministerial family while you're here." Father led the Horton family down the aisle and out the front door.

Daniel turned back toward Mary. "Perhaps you and your brothers and sister could spread your blanket beside my family's."

A tiny smile raised the tips of Mary's sweet mouth. "If you're sure your mother wouldn't mind, I'd like that."

"Oh, yes. I'm sure." He stepped into the nearly empty aisle and moved back to let Mary and her family precede him, and he quickly followed behind.

His heartbeat accelerated just thinking about spending special time with the object of his affections. Without thinking, he started whistling a happy tune.

Mary glanced back at him. "I didn't know you whistled."

"Oh, yes. I'm a man of many talents." His heart leaped at the interest he read in her gaze. Things were well on their way to working out just the way he wanted them to.

FREE NEWSLETTERS
TO HELP EMPOWER YOUR LIFE

Why subscribe today?

❑ **DELIVERED DIRECTLY TO YOU.** All you have to do is open your inbox and read.

❑ **EXCLUSIVE CONTENT.** We cover the news overlooked by the mainstream press.

❑ **STAY CURRENT.** Find the latest court rulings, revivals, and cultural trends.

❑ **UPDATE OTHERS.** Easy to forward to friends and family with the click of your mouse.

CHOOSE THE E-NEWSLETTER THAT INTERESTS YOU MOST:

- Christian news
- Daily devotionals
- Spiritual empowerment
- And much, much more

SIGN UP AT: **http://freenewsletters.charismamag.com**